THE GREAT HEXPECTATIONS SERIES BOOK ONE

The Little Lies

MARIE F CROW

AUTHOR OF THE RISEN SERIES

Copyright

The Little Lies is a work of fiction. All names, characters, locations, and incidents are the products of the author's imagination or are used fictitiously. Any resemblance to actual events, locales, or persons, living or dead, is entirely coincidental.

Table of Contents

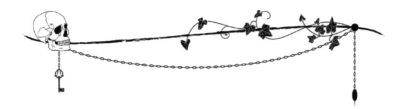

THE LITTLEST

OF LIES

CAN BE

THE DEADLIEST

OF WEAPONS

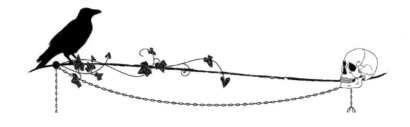

Your Grandmother mentioned it has been a while since you were on a date."

"Did she?" I ask the rather large man named Cass sitting across the table from me.

He's shoveling food into his mouth like it's a cavern. Starving children eat with more manners than this man is displaying. I'm fighting against every social grace I have to keep my face pleasant, but I already know it's a losing battle. I don't do pleasant. I do here and now and that's pleasant enough for me.

He makes a noise of agreement between chewing. "She said you're too busy with work to find a good man."

I try to keep my smile in place, but I'm sure it slipped. I know those words are code. Anytime a relative remarks on a female working too hard, it really means they think her priorities are misplaced. The whole 'can't find a good man' simply means, in their opinion, she's putting her job before her biological clock and time is running out. The fact this man thinks he has the potential of filling in the role of a 'good man' in my life only speaks to his misguided ego, or the desperation of GiGi Jo.

"Well, she's a charmer like that." I smile, swallowing down my angst to provide my own southern code, disguising my real opinion of this whole conversation.

"Yeah, Jo is a real sweet one. Not too many like her anymore."

He actually winks at me as he tells me this. With his brow beaded from sweat in what could be considered an ice box of an Italian restaurant, the action seals any debate of me finishing this meal.

"What did she tell you about me?" Cass grins, thinking I have nothing but cooing heading his way.

"Not much," I shrug, holding back the fact that if she had, I wouldn't have even faked enough interest over the blind date to provide my grandmother any hopes despite its obvious outcome.

It's not a problem for Cass. I can tell by how he is settling into his, thankfully, sturdy chair, he is about to fill me in on more than I want to know about his life. He's not about to broad stroke the reasons he's a 'good man'. He's going to fine-tooth comb it.

"I'm a funeral director over at Southern Respite," Cass says when I neglect to ask, as if it's a panty dropping fact in itself. "I prep the bodies, see to their families, and walk them through the service. It's really a humbling experience being there for people in their time of need. Very touching, if I am to be honest."

"Mmmhmm," I agree, pushing the red sauce laden noodles around on my plate. "I'm sure that's very rewarding."

"Oh, it's not about the money." Cass leans closer to me, smirking, "Don't get me wrong. The money is nice in a town considered a retirement destination, if you know what I mean."

I do and it does nothing to improve my mood, my opinion or remove my panties.

"It's completely about helping the families? That's so caring of you." My voice drops to a whisper of admiration tickling his obvious male ego.

Cass scoots in as close as his bloated belly will allow him, dangerously dripping his plaid tie into the sauce of his plate. "Of course," he assures me.

He thinks I'm swooning over his generosity; his kind soul pulling at more than just the strings of my heart. He's already picturing what I'm wearing under my little black dress I found at the bottom of my closet, freshly Febrezed, just in time to hear my doorbell ring. He's curious what my deep red hair will look like swaying around my body with his motions, hoping to hear his name falling from my lips. In his mind, he's already debating if I will take my heels off or leave them on, raising them high above our heads like a trophy.

"What do you do for work?" Cass asks when I don't offer to tell him, his eyes dipping lower than they should.

I'm still pushing the soaked noodles around with my fork while he stares at me like I'm what's being served for dessert. I debate for a moment telling a lie, some very people pleasing fib; some form of what would be considered a normal sounding version of what I've accepted as a job. I know my GiGi Jo would want me to, with her obvious concerns for my lack of contributing grandchildren. But what fun would that be?

With the same mock infatuated voice, and false flirting smile, I tell him the truth. Grandchildren be damned.

"People pay me to raise their dead to sort out issues like wills or to get that last goodbye. I walk them through the service, preparing them for the chanting I will do and how I will slice my arm to feed their long-lost somebody my blood so they may tell them which of the kids were their favorites. But you know, Cass," I tell him, leaning in with the same eagerness he had, "it's *really* about the families. It's so humbling to watch a half-decomposed shell that someone like you made turn into a loving, only somewhat deranged, family member again. It brings those left behind such peace of mind. Just touching, if I'm to be honest."

Cass blinks at me, trying to figure out if I'm sincere or not. Maybe he's just afraid I'm wondering what he's wearing under that ill-fitting white dress shirt. Perhaps he's worried if I'm in a mental debate over the possibilities of him leaving his black loafers on or maybe just those incredibly sexy black calf socks of his later tonight.

Cass makes a sound of chuckling caught throat-deep in fear. "Your Grandmother said you were a funny one."

"Did she?" My smile is still plaster pretty.

"Yup," he says, slowly. "She said you like to make jokes."

"Like the jokes you make when you slide the drainage tubes into women?"

Cass pales, stammering as he tries to figure out what a sweet little lady like myself could possibly be saying to him. So pretty. So demure. So correct.

"Now, who would tell you such a thing?" he asks, nervously looking around to see if any of the tables near to us overheard my question.

I sip the sweet red wine I ordered, knowing perfectly well what illusion it must present with the conversation we are having right now.

"Miss Henkins," I tell him calmly, as he appears to sweat even more.

Cass switches from half laughs, to shock, to a blend of emotions I can't quite name, amusing as they are.

"You're making one of those jokes right now, aren't you? Miss Henkins has been dead for years."

"I know. She's standing right behind you."

Cass turns in his chair, prepared to see the very person he's praying he won't. Of course, he doesn't, but he turns to me and then behind him a few more times just to be sure. I keep my smile and my red wine ready for my next round of humiliation.

"Tell me, Cass," I purr, twirling the wine in its glass until it forms a small twister of ruby and garnet, "what does one do with the perfect set of tits? You know, for the family's sake? So they don't go to waste?"

Cass doesn't answer me. He knows exactly what I'm talking about. He just doesn't know how I know his dirty secrets. To be fair, most don't. Miss Henkins still standing behind him, she does. Her smile tugs oddly on the skin of her face when she hears my question. A question she's been screaming to be heard, as he said, for several years.

"If you'll excuse me," Cass stands, patting the moisture on his forehead with the linen cloth he pulled from his pocket. "I'm suddenly not feeling very well. Must be the food…"

His words trail off with his backwards escape. He's afraid to turn his back to me. I wave with just my fingers before blowing him a kiss through the air.

"Does this mean you're not coming back to my place for dessert?" I shout across the restaurant with a mock of a pout and broken heart.

I watch as he almost runs from the restaurant, tripping over his feet with his sudden departure. I also watch Miss Henkins following his clumsy exit, her perfect tits still proudly displayed in the tight red dress she was wearing at the time of her death. Upon her shoulders, resembling the same shade as her dress, she wears a shawl of blood and gore, dripping deep into her cleavage before running the length of her body. Her perfect blonde updo is ruined from where her skull sits open and uneven from her quickly labeled 'accidental death' from the eighth floor of a hotel window. Luckily for the restaurant owners, no one but me can see the little pieces of her skull she leaves in her wake. Nor can they see various chunks of dark matter and the wet trail following her departure.

Henkins has a few reasons to still be touring the town - from her sudden death after going public with her divorce, to the bankruptcy, the blackmail, and all the many other rumors which still feed the town to this day. Cass is just the unfortunate one to have her clinging to him, for the moment.

At least she's smiling now. Between her screaming insults at him the whole ride here and his complete lack of table manners, I knew shortly after sitting down the wine would be the only redeeming thing about tonight. Maybe I should have lied. Maybe GiGi Jo is right about my misplaced priorities. After being around Cass for the short time it took to roll my stomach with his heavy cologne, I'm still pretty sure the dead man who will be licking my forearm from my self-inflicted wound in a few hours will be a better ending to a night than anything Cass would have offered.

"Sorry, GiGi Jo," I tell the woman I know whom, without a doubt, is sitting by her crystal ball listening to every moment provided her tonight. "Grandchildren be damned."

Signaling for the check, I can almost hear her long string of words no one would believe to be in her verbal dictionary.

"Are you Harper Buckland?" the young waitress asks me as she timidly hands me the white slip of paper.

I don't answer her. I let my eyebrow arch, asking her why she wants to know. It was my smile she mistook for an invitation of conversation.

"Is it true what they say about you?" she asks me after looking to see what name is on the blue plastic card I handed her to pay.

"What they say about me? That's a long list, kid," my mouth says. It's not what my brain wanted to say, but that option wasn't polite to a minor.

"They say you can talk to the dead." She didn't ask if it was true. She's just repeating some of the town's favorite gossip.

"Oh, that old tidbit?" I shrug, tapping fingernails the same shade as my smiling lips against the table.

"Can you really bring people back, too?"

I want to sigh, roll my eyes, get up and leave with more grace than my date had. I want to do anything other than wear this smile and pretend to care as someone barely old enough to be out past midnight recites one of the town's scandals – witches.

"Yes. It seems so."

"What if it's a child?"

I do sigh, now. I've done this enough times to know how this will end. The family will plead with me to help them. The child will then refuse to return to their grave after it's raised. Which I will then have to force them back as the family screams over the sight. Even as I'm doing only what they asked of me, doing the exact thing I explained to them would happen, it will be me who becomes the monster. Then, in time, when they recover from what they witnessed, the very thing they were once happy to hear could be done, becomes the same thing they use to validate their hate and the town's hate for me.

"Sorry. I have rules against children. Let's just call them.... age requirements," I explain, holding out my hand for the bill.

"What if it's a child who refuses to stay dead and not one to bring back?"

Her words chill me. The expression on her face is etched too deep for someone so young. This is the face of someone who has seen too much, too soon, and I have feeling she's about to show me everything she hasn't wanted to see.

"What's your name?" I cautiously ask her.

"Her name was Becky."

She didn't tell me *her* name. She just told me the name I know will come to haunt me in the coming days. As she watches me with pleading eyes, I know I'm about to break all of my self-made rules. This moment will become another cautionary tale for me, and I will recite it on my weakest nights.

"Write your address down. I have a few things to do tonight, but I'll try to make it by afterwards."

Her face lights up with hope. It makes me cringe. I try to look anywhere but at her as she scribbles down my future doom on her order slip. She hands it to me with a smile before skipping off to run my card.

Suddenly, I'm missing Miss Henkins' screaming insults and bone-littering skull. Revenge is something simple to understand. Grief is a whole different box of unwrapped regrets with a glitter of remorse that clings to anyone who touches the box. A box I'm about to pull the bow on, spilling its contents wide for all to see, and that glitter will stick to us all before it's over.

These final resting places are always the same. Even if the irony of calling them 'resting places' is lost on the many. Some may be better kept or surveyed, but the goal is always the same: to give the living a spot of denial of their very own. It provides a place they can come to with the lies that their loved ones are never truly far away. For some, they never really are.

As I walk among the rows of names with the old and new flowers spread across the stone bases, I understand why they ask me to do it, to bring back their departed. They crave that one more moment. They seek to fill the void from the 'goodbye' they never got. Unfortunately, as their loved one sucks the blood from my arm to heal what has been done to their bodies, they find neither. There's nothing peaceful about what I do. The Ripples are about to discover it for themselves.

I let the many voices call to me from where they rest, hopeful it's them my magic will touch tonight. Having been forgotten by the ones they cared for in life, some just want to chat, be remembered, and heard. Their whispers grow louder in the back of my mind as I begin to drop the shields I wear like a castle wall around my gifts. With invisible fingers, they tug on my hands, my arms and even my hair to gain my attention. I can almost hear their sighs of disappointment when I walk past them.

The Ripples are waiting for me a few rows ahead. Dressed as if for a funeral, they are covered in their most expensive mourning attire. The women appear to have stepped out of a salon with their humidity defying hair perfectly arranged. The men already have the southern proof of our early summer nights staining their ironed shirts. There is no conversation floating to me. Silence and envy – the perfect southern storm.

"Hello," I call, hating myself for accepting this job.

They acknowledge me only with their eyes. It's a rousing endorsement.

Clearing my throat to smother the wit of my tongue, "Do you have the items I requested?"

"What are you going to do with them, if we do?" a woman leaning on the black Lexus asks.

I know her only by name. She is Deon Ripple. Someone who has more rumors attached to her divorces than the local gossip papers are even willing to print. Which says a lot for a small town filled with bored people.

GiGi always jokes the Ripples are all vampires since none of them age, none of them gain weight and none of their spouses ever last. Staring at Deon, in her black dress only the rich could pull off as mourning attire, I don't argue with GiGi's logic.

"I use them to anchor the person to this location. They also serve as something of a 'remember when' token to pull their minds back from the void." I keep my voice neutral hiding my annoyance of repeating what was already explained when we signed the contracts.

"Yes," Deon exhales the smoke from her cigarette, "so you said. That's not what I asked. I asked, what are you going to do with them?"

I place my best retail working smile on my lips. "I arrange them around the grave. The person will only be able to move to the extent of the objects. They will literally anchor the person, pulling from the energy of the memories the items contain, as I already said."

Deon doesn't acknowledge my answer. She stares into the night sky. The only motion from the whole group is her hand pulling the cigarette to her lips and then back to a neutral position. The rest of their family is standing mutely, watching our exchange with worried expressions.

"If you don't want to do this, I can leave," I offer, growing bored with the standoff.

Deon drops her still smoldering therapy device to the ground and walks my way. Maybe someone who doesn't willingly slice her arm open for money would have been intimidated by the glare Deon is projecting. Perhaps someone who doesn't help run a shop hosting more of the dead than living would tremble with the unknown of what may happen next. Unfortunately for Deon, those people aren't me.

My smile never slips when she stops in front of me. Her perfume meets me like a taunt. The sharp scent jeers me with not so subtle hints of warnings over what she could do to me, if she so desired. Her brown eyes are measuring me, looking for a weak spot in my observed demeanor. I sigh, waiting for her to finish trying to dick check me.

"The items...?" My voice trails the question, no longer hiding my annoyance.

"My siblings tell me you're the best at this. I have my doubts. I have plenty of people I could have called for the information we need, but they picked you, not me." Her brown eyes almost spark with her anger.

"Cool. So, you don't like me and I'm not your biggest fan, either. Understood. Shall we begin?" Titling my head I give her my best smile. "Or I could leave, you could wait for one of your people to arrive, but seeing as it is ten thirty at night, my guess would be you would have to reschedule. I do remember being told this was of an urgent, time-sensitive matter. I suppose those words mean different things to different pay scales?"

"Deon," one of the brothers calls. It's a short clip of a warning.

Deon doesn't move. Her eyes return to their normal simmer, still threatening to return to their blaze with a mere mood swing. "Fine, but if this goes wrong, it's on you."

With how she's phrased it, I'm not sure if she's still trying to loom over me or regain her status in the family with her brother. Another perfect woman, this time brunette, hands me a large beige tote bag. She does her best to not brush the fabric against Deon as I take it. At least one member still fears her.

I shuffle through the contents, wondering what this person would have considered their favorite items before death. The smell of the cigar box welcomes my exploration. A tie, creased from the constant ironing, is still perfectly folded. The gold watch feels heavy in my hand. It's cold like the family before me. There are a few other very male items inside, but oddly not a single framed memory exists. These are all just things, possessions the man once boasted over. Starting to understand why the siblings are so vacant of emotions for what I am about to do.

"Isn't that what you asked for?" Deon asks.

My mask of neutral must have slipped some, letting her see my opinion over what they have brought. "I asked for his favorite things. If this is what you brought, then this must be what I asked for."

I don't wait for her verbal volley or her eyes to try to convince me of how scary she may become upon hearing my answer. I'm here to work. Not to play ego games with a rich heiress.

The even number of items spread easily around the flower-heavy earth. They have started to wilt from their days spent in the summer heat, but despite it all, in denial, they desperately cling to their vivid colors. Some of the smaller items disappear among the many fern branches used as filler. Luckily, retrieving these objects is not part of my contract.

Deon, having returned to the cluster of siblings, watches every move I make. With a new cigarette in hand, I can tell she's still silently debating if this is worth the price. Seeing as I'm one of the only people I know who can do this, I should charge more.

Normally I put on a bit of show. I mutter mashed together Latin, forming new words to match the raised pitch of my voice. Maybe I'll stand for a few moments, swaying to unheard music with my eyes closed and head hung low. Knowing what is waiting for me later tonight, I prefer to just get it over with and head to yet another bad decision of my life.

When I started, I used a large machete or some other impressive blade. Upon learning police officers get a little suspicious with town rumors, and blood coated blades sliding across my back seat, I switched to a simple pocketknife. The knife bites into my skin with its sharp point. Walking in a circle, I connect the items with the sprinkling of my blood, tying them to me and to each other. Where I go, the person will go. Where the possessions rest, is where he will stop, unable to leave the circle, keeping me safe and those around us safe from any sudden field trips the person may wish to take.

Turning to face the rather large, ornate headstone I call out to those waiting behind me, "Who am I calling?"

Of course, it's Deon who answers. I'm starting to think the rest of her family has a genetic defect resulting in no tongues.

"That's pretty bold font in front of you. I can read it from here."

"Yes, but that's not what I asked." I smile, turning Deon's earlier words around on her. "I asked who am I calling?"

The same brother from before answers, aware of where Deon's temper will take tonight. "Our father. He is our father." He pauses, quickly adding, "Was our father."

If I were facing him, I would offer a look of understanding, but I'm not and Deon has trampled all my 'customer service' politeness I had managed to store this week.

Before GiGi Jo taught me how to channel, I would pour forth words with rhymes and a tempo of commands. Now, I just focus. Like a rarely used muscle, I concentrate my will, mentally picturing the body underneath me waking, forcing life back into the shell from which it escaped. I pull the energy from beyond the veil, commanding it to obey me. With Richard Ripple only being dead a few weeks, his energy is easy to pull. It hasn't anchored itself to the other side yet. Richard seems to also have questions he wants answered.

I'm not shocked anymore when the ground bubbles up like a volcano. I don't gasp when the person frees themselves, being almost ejected from the toppled center, with a gravity defying motion. Those who pay me, they do. I can hear the collective inhale from behind me as the man they knew as their father stands before them in his discolored, dark suit.

My throat feels dry, overused, when I call out to the man. "Richard Ripple, Father to those who stand behind me, come and drink of life to be of life once more."

With his eyes upon me, there is no doubt Deon is one of his children. Even faded from death, his brown eyes hold a rage over trying to be commanded. In life, he was the one barking orders. Now, he's having to obey them. Everything from his posture to the scowl upon his face proves he is less than thrilled to find himself is this predicament.

I could make the dead drink from me, forcing them to comply with my demands. I don't. I leave that choice to those I summon; giving them a chance to choose if they wish to be risen. Some don't. There's been a few times the dead have seen why they are brought back, and walk back to the mound of dirt, refusing the magic only to be swallowed by the earth once more, settling it perfectly as if they were never disturbed. Watching him try to talk without the spell completed, I'm wondering if he too is about to defy the spell, to defy his children and to defy me.

His frustration is mounting. He's unable to talk and unable to move past the boundary. Richard is close to becoming the raging dead. The dead who have lost control and must be put down before the rage becomes uncontrollable, making them unable to be of any use to those who wish to speak with them.

"Richard Ripple, Father to those who stand behind me, come and drink of life to be of life once more." I harden my voice almost shouting my command.

I don't wait for his response. Using the same knife from before, I cut across the spider web of blue lines along my arm. When the first river of red slides down my arm, Richard, with all his determination to not listen to me, lets what's left of his ego slip away. His hatred for me still flashes in his brown eyes, but he doesn't deny his cravings.

He swallows the hot blood like it's one of his favorite whiskeys. As it coats his face, those hate filled eyes awaken to a deeper shade. His skin sheds some of the pallor of death. When he stands, dropping my arm hastily, he almost appears as if he would have in life.

"Why am I here?" Richard demands from me.

"You will reside within your given boundary. Bound by your treasures in life, you cannot step over them in death. You will answer those who have need of you until of the time they don't. Once released, you will return to rest, freed from this space and its obligations."

His eyes scan the items, spinning his body to examine his new confines when hearing my decree. "And if I step over them?" he asks more insulted than curious.

"The spell which grants you life will be broken. You will be nothing more than a husk left exposed and unburied." Answering him, I'm already wrapping my arm to stop the bleeding. It never bleeds long. Nor does it scar. When I was younger, I asked about such things, wanting to know the why of it. Now, I just accept it with gratitude that at least something in life is tilted to my favor.

"Very official." Richard draws these two words out making the short sentence seem like a paragraph. Looking to his children who have remained mute, he asks me, "Are these whom I am supposed to answer?"

Only Deon has the courage to not squirm under her dead father's gaze. "We are. We paid a lot of money for you to be here. I expect answers."

I'm not sure if the sound Richard makes is a laugh or shock, but by the way his children look away, I know it's a sound he made often. "Poor, Deon. Still trying to pretend you have any authority?"

Holding my hands in the air to place this round of family feud on pause, I walk away from the crazy brewing around me. "You have one hour before the spell wears off."

"You're just leaving?" Casting sideways glances to her father, a smaller female almost rushes towards me.

"Don't move the objects until after he returns to the ground," I explain, still making my exit.

"Shouldn't you stay?" she shouts again.

"Nope. You paid me to raise him. He's very raised," I explain with my best southern charm.

"What if –" she starts before I cut her off.

"He won't."

"But what if –"

"He can't," I repeat. I already know where her fears are taking her. "And if he does, Deon knows plenty of people she can call for information. She has it all under control."

I can hear Richard's short laugh following me out of the cemetery. It's not an amused laugh. It's a challenging laugh, and despite my better judgment, I turn to where they still stand gathered, unsure of the next step. For such a power-filled family, it's refreshing to see them floundering.

I motion to the watch upon my wrist. "Tick tock. He won't bite," I add, but the smile Richard flashes fills even me with doubt, "or he might. Either way, stay on the other side of the objects, ask your questions, step back when the earth starts to bubble. Super easy."

Deon makes a sign of dismissal with a wave of her hand as she steps up to the invisible circle. "Got it."

"I bet," I whisper under my breath.

As much as I enjoy leaving this family to their own demons, I know I'm about to wade into a different cesspool of denials. This family eagerly waits for their dead to return to where they belong. I have a feeling Becky's family is clinging to the lie the dead belong with them.

My mind swirls with the possibilities of what is ahead; the many lies, the many tears, the defeat of it all. I'm lost in a purgatory of mental chains. So lost, I never saw the shadow following me. I felt it. It tickles along my spine setting the hair of my arms to attention. Only one thing sets my nerves this alert: magic.

Exhaling, I let my well-built walls crumble again. I can feel it now. The owner follows me leaving a slight space between us. Their magic tastes like candy. It's sugar sweet with a lingering of tart upon my tongue. This is old magic. The kind of magic which has been passed down through deep roots of a family tree. Someone well versed in the craft is following me, watching me. Inhaling, I pull those thick bricks back into place around me. I seal them tight and keep my pace even.

From my purse I pull my little mirror pretending to check my makeup from the disaster of a dinner date. I tilt it, gaining a view from over my shoulder. In the small oval I can see her. She flashes me a smile with lips painted purple. Wearing jeans and an oversized tee shirt, she appears harmless. She's just another person visiting her beloved family.

Her reflection waves to me before coming to rest on a statue of a weeping angel. Her hair has been dyed a soft lavender. It hangs thick with slight waves framing her face. Nothing about her scream's danger. Nothing but the taste of her magic still clinging to the walls of my throat, that is. The smirk placed upon her too friendly lips to cause a warning feeling in the depths of my stomach, hints at what I already know. The way my body still vibrates, even behind my walls, I know this wasn't a chance meeting.

She doesn't follow me to my car. Her magic doesn't stalk me along the cobbled path. With a snap of closure, the mirror falls back into its space in my bag. Whatever she wants, whatever this means, will have to be discovered later. Like the red soaked noodles still fighting my stomach from dinner, my life is already drowned in drama. I have no need to play tag with a bored witch. As it stands, GiGi Jo plays enough games with my life.

The house wasn't hard to find. At this hour, most of the houses are blanketed in darkness with its occupants settling down to end the day. This house is the blaring opposite. Every light still burns, keeping the darkness of night safely beyond their property. Like a toddler scared of the monsters in the closet, Becky's family has all their night lights glowing.

I should have taken the time to change before coming here. With time being a cruel mistress, I went home only long enough to grab my car before heading to see the Ripples. My dress didn't bother me then. Standing here now in the middle of upper-class perfection, I look like a bad cosplay of Elvira in my tight black dress, but with red hair and a shorter hem.

The door opens before I can verbally prepare or force the large gap to shrink upon the displayed cleavage. Exactly how I think I look is displayed upon the face of the woman standing in the doorway. Her tanned features twist between confusion and disgust. Her blue eyes scan me from my half-curled red hair, to my too tight dress and all the way to my thin heeled black shoes. I could explain my appearance and put her creased forehead to rest, but it would require more words than I am feeling equipped with at this moment.

"Harper Buckland," I say, holding out my hand in greeting.

The woman doesn't hide her examination of my hand. She smiles her best smile of false hospitality, leaving my hand floating between us. "Miranda Torte," she says with a nod and still no effort to touch me. "She said you might be a little late. I guess we all have our own internal clock, don't we?"

Dropping my hand, I match her smile of charm. "I suppose we do."

"Well, do come in." Miranda is an easy read of discomfort. Her hands stay folded together, but they never stay still. Her eyes dart from me to her perfect, magazine interior of her house. Everything has a space, and everything is put in the perfect place. Except for me. She can't imagine me fitting anywhere in her self-made perfection.

"Don't worry," I tell her. "I won't stay long."

She has the decency of well upbringing to blush when I read her inner monologue. "Of course," she stammers before extending a hand to invite me inside, but we both notice her double checking to be sure none of the neighbors are watching when she closes the door.

The small entryway opens to a well-lit floor plan. Waiting to be further escorted, I can see most of the house from where I am standing. The fake scent of their air freshener encases the space. It's the type of thick fragrance you know will cling to you long after you've left the home. With how subtle the rest of the décor sits, it's a stark contrast to have such a bold choice for the air.

Miranda slides past me, tucking her body as far to the wall as she can to avoid touching me on passing. "This way."

Normally, I would make an off-colored comment about her behavior, but with her obvious effort to avoid me, it allows me to look around with more than just my eyes. I send the whisper of my magic ahead of me. The magic touches the walls, flows around the corners, searching for any hints of what the teen told me. It pulls from the surfaces it touches and returns with nothing but memories of loss.

In my mind I can hear the sobs and the shouting of misplaced rage over a recent death. I watch the slideshow of this family breaking. Miranda has put a lot of effort into maintaining the illusion of her well put together home as a way to escape from the failing family bonds.

Her anxiety isn't over just me being here. It's over what cracks I may turn into large fissures *from* being here.

Miranda steps to the side to allow me to enter their living room. The muted shades once again make me too vivid. I feel on display when the rest of the family stands upon hearing us enter.

The girl from earlier is still wearing her work uniform. She waves at me, and when her father clears his throat, she fights to hide her smile.

"I told them you would come." Gazing over my shoulder to her mother, her smile returns.

"That you did," her father says. "I'm Chad. You've met our daughter, Bella. Welcome to our home."

Taking that as the only invitation I was going to receive to have a seat, I pick the armchair furthest from the potential fallout. "Hello, Chad. Bella said you are in need of help."

Miranda is already squirming before she can join her family on the two small sofas. Interestingly enough, she doesn't sit on the sofa with her husband. She sits with a little boy who watches me with eyes too guarded for his age. Wearing his green striped pajamas, he looks frail hiding in his mother's embrace.

Chad and Bella are staring at the couch across from them as if daring either of the other two to speak first. Miranda is whispering into the little boy's hair, ignoring them. It's a cold stalemate with me awkwardly stuck in the middle of their passive war. On most nights, I enjoy watching a family self-destruct, but this is a bit much even for me.

"Want to tell me about the little girl?" I ask with hopes that attaching bells to the elephant in the room will make someone acknowledge it.

Miranda's whole-body tenses when hearing my question. "Ben, let's go ahead and get in bed."

Her attention is for the little boy she helps from the couch, but her eyes are all for me. It's not the first time tonight I've been gifted a glare of anger. With my choices tonight, it won't be the last time, either. I still have to face GiGi.

The room still wears its blanket of silence as the two leave. It's tucked securely around us leaving no edges but cradling their raw nerves with false comfort. Like the fake perfume from the air freshener, it sits heavy, smothering the ability to fully breathe. Only when Miranda and Ben are safely away does conversation begin again.

"Can't we just show her?" Bella whispers to her father.

Chad slips to his nervous habit of clearing his throat when words unsettle him. "We don't even know if it's true."

"Dad..." Bella lets the unsaid words trail off, but her eyes hold what she doesn't say. Reading her posture, it's easy to see she is tired of being stuck in the middle, too.

Chad temples his fingers to hold his suddenly heavy head. "Your mother," he starts, but stops to look where I am sitting in an overly stuffed chair. "What is it exactly you do? I've heard the rumors about your family my whole life, no insult intended, but what is it exactly you are going to do?"

"You mean if I find out your wife has the undead kept as a pet?" I don't mesh my words. It's late, making my filter thin. "I'll put it back to rest where it belongs."

His eyes do a quick dance around the room as he weighs his thoughts. He's trying to choose his words carefully, afraid of what ripples he'll make with the wrong choice. "I haven't seen her," he whispers to some far-off point in the room.

"But?" I ask, trying to force his conversation.

"But there are things I cannot explain."

"Like?"

"She redid a room downstairs in the basement. She kept it locked, but just recently when Bella started talking about you, she emptied the room while we were all out."

"Then there's Becky's room." Bella, too, is verbally encouraging her father but for Bella the dam is broke. "She yelled at me when I went in there after her death. I was going to clean it up, but she went irate when I moved the toys around on the shelves. Last week she just upped and boxed the whole room, but we don't know where the boxes are. Then there's the weird late night grocery shopping and the random trips with just her and Ben. Ben won't even talk about where they go. In fact, Ben doesn't talk much at all anymore."

Chad holds up a hand to slow the steady rushing of words from his daughter. "Things have been a bit off, to say the least."

So far all I've heard are examples of grief, mood swings, and someone trying to hide their outburst. "People do weird things when they lose someone. What makes you think any of this has to do with something I handle?"

"The call from the cemetery." Chad's eyes are still far away. "Someone dug up our child."

I've heard a lot of explanations for why someone calls me. Sometimes the long laundry list of people they have suspicion of, or even for, can run for hours with their demands for a curse or a hex before I stop them. There's the normal need due to greed and the constant one last conversation, but this is a first. My face must show it.

Chad does his throat clearing again before he explains. "The cemetery called one morning when I was driving to work. Asked me if I could swing by before heading into the office," he pauses shrugging. "I thought it was more paperwork or something of that nature. When I got there, they took me out to her grave."

Chad's eyes are everywhere but here in this room at this moment when his words fail him. He's seeing that day again. Whatever he saw there still haunts him.

Glancing quickly to Bella, he pulls himself back to the present to tell me, "The whole area was disturbed. The flowers we had just placed were covered with dirt. Someone had dug the grave the night before and then hastily recovered it."

"I don't remember hearing about this around town. How did this escape the local gossip?" I ask him, pretty confident such a scandal would have been plastered across every paper the town prints.

"We agreed to keep it quiet. The sheriff was afraid it would cause too much panic. He said he would look into it privately."

"How did I miss this round of investigation?" My tone isn't altogether friendly. When you live in a town this small, the police normally know who to ask questions to when certain things happen. The fact they never showed to knock on our door, shocking.

"You had an alibi." Chad at least has the decency to blush, confirming my thoughts.

"Now that you know it wasn't me, you think your wife dug up your child?" My tone still isn't friendly.

Chad stumbles over his words unsure of which way to answer.

"Yes!" Bella isn't unsure of hers.

"Yes, they do." Miranda's voice cuts through the living space. "The sheriff even pulled me in to question me. Me!"

"Well did you?" I ask the outraged woman.

"Of course not! Why would I?"

"Other than the constant fighting, the crying when you think no one is watching you cook dinner, the talking to a pink bunny-slash-bear looking stuffed animal?" I ask her, bringing forth all the images my magical snooping told me from earlier, but it's what I ask next which sets her off completely. "Or the fact you keep toting little girl's clothing to your car at three a.m.?"

Miranda looks to Chad and Bella before returning her shocked expression to me. Part of her is wondering how much they have told me about her. The other part of her is wondering about how much the town has told her about me. Both are fair. Neither are completely accurate.

"Or maybe it's how Ben, her twin, right, can't stop looking over his shoulder as if Becky will still be there?" I tilt my head with my question, trying to look supportive and less accusatory. "If Becky's ghost was here, I would see her, but since I don't, I imagine he's used to seeing her in a different way?"

"You're insane!" Miranda hisses.

"Actually, I'm not. Having been formally tested as a child by people with the same suspicions of me as you, I can assure you, I'm perfectly sane."

"I want her out of my house!" Miranda is no longer talking to me. Those hate-filled eyes are now all for her husband and the daughter who brought me here.

"Let's just hear her out?" Chad asks of his wife. "She's the only one who can help us."

Sitting like the unspoken stain on a perfect rug, I wait for tempers to return to a somewhat idea of normal before speaking. "Tell me where Becky is supposed to be, and I'll stop by there tomorrow."

"What's that going to do?" Miranda asks.

I can hear the guarded tone in her voice. It clashes with the hopeful look held in Bella's eyes.

"I can try to feel if it was magic or vandalism." I explain, "If it was magic, I can help. If it was vandalism, I can't help."

"It's a start." Chad is desperately trying to extend an olive branch to his wife. The branch may be splintered, but it's not completely broken. Not yet.

Miranda only acknowledges her husband with a slight twitch; a motion so fast with her eyebrow only years of marriage could decode it.

"It's settled then," I state, standing, eager to be free from this fragile, matrimonial bliss. "I'll let you know what I find."

I don't wait for the guided tour towards the front door. Besides, it isn't Miranda who is following me out. It's Bella.

"When will you know?" Bella asks me with a fake smile and a hushed voice so as to not be noticed as exchanging words.

"Tomorrow." I'm returning her smile in a game we have both learned in our years of working with the public.

"Not tonight?" Bella is making a lot of noise opening the door to cover our conversation.

"It's already late. Police tend to get antsy when they see cars at a cemetery this hour. Especially mine."

"She's at the Southern Respite location. The back garden area."

Of course she is, I think to myself, hating small town life. For Bella I smile and nod letting her know I understand.

The porch lights are off before I even step off the first step. Miranda obviously doesn't want the upper-class neighborhood to see me leaving from her home. I don't blame her. Most of those who call upon me meet me in secret, or at least in a less than raving reviews location. They don't want to be seen. Miranda is no different.

She's the type who comes to GiGi's store, Great Hexpecations, under the guise of shock and offense that such a place exists in their community. She's also the type who leaves with a rather large bag of bought items with hopes to keep her frenemies in check and her husband on a tighter leash. She may even pull the items out and look at them from time to time, but they would most likely stay stashed in the bag hidden under some piece of furniture in her bedroom. They would be her dirty little secret used to empower her on taxing days.

Pulling from the drive, I let my inner, insecure toddler emerge. Honking the horn three long times as I drive away in my farewell brings a smile to my face. I don't hide my amusement when curtains shuffle in windows around the homes near theirs. I'm almost sad I won't be around tomorrow morning when Miranda's neighbors find oh so innocent reasons to be walking by with a false smile and curious wave.

"Child," rebukes the female ghost who seems to always be lurking in my back seat, as if a Honda is the best place to linger for an afterlife. I don't mind so much. No one asks to borrow my car or even ride with me. They always complain how off it feels to ride in it.

I don't answer her. I normally don't. I smile wider and she rolls her eyes. Crossing her arms, she settles in for the ride back to where I share a home with the only woman whom I have now as family. At this hour GiGi would normally be in bed, but I know she is also finding oh so innocent reasons to be up still. Reasons I don't have the energy to deal with or answers to share, but I will because the woman literally will not rest until I do, and I owe her. I owe her everything.

GiGi Jo wasn't awake when I arrived home last night. My walk of shame wasn't any less traumatic. There's almost something a touch depressing about sneaking through the house and down the stairs to the converted basement I have claimed as my own since the age of eighteen. Doing it all squeezed into a tight dress didn't make the situation any better.

Now as we both sit, steaming our faces with our morning coffee in the too early morning hours. With my disheveled messy bun and thick robe, I'm staring into the depths of the dark liquid as if it holds all the secrets to my day. GiGi is staring at me like I have the answer to hers. Even the little kitchen nook in which we sit, with its many green hanging plants, seems to be watching me.

I can feel her heavy eyes reading everything I'm not saying, but she hasn't asked for one single crumb of detail about my date. The date I have a feeling even she knew would be a disaster.

"I have a new case," I speak into the room to break the standoff.

"Case?" She asks, dropping more sugar, into what very well may already be, a diabetic coma of a hot beverage. "I didn't think you were doing those anymore?"

"My bank account says I am, and the clients were a little demanding."

"Plural?' GiGi catches my slip up. "How many cases?"

"One case. One..." I stall, searching for the correct term. "Request."

"You raised the dead, again?"

I can hear the disappointment in her voice. I take a little longer on the next sip of coffee before answering her. "Well, one is a family who wants to figure out what happened to their dead and other was a family demanding to know something from their dead."

GiGi settles a little deeper into the wooden wingback chair. I'm not sure if the sounds of protest are a warning for her or to me.

"You took the job from the Ripples, didn't you?"

Obviously, the warning was for me. "You don't really say no to the Ripples," I offer with hopes of diffusing her building anger, but this bomb isn't a simple little snip of wires.

"You don't say yes, either!" GiGi shouts.

I wince as she storms from the nook and into the kitchen. Her small frame suddenly seems very terrifying. She's wearing her classic black outfit, but it's the matching shawl of a deep purple which now flows behind her like a villain's cape. I can hear the cabinets slamming as she searches through them. I can also hear her fluid Italian hinting at exactly why the slamming continues.

"GiGi," I call, coming into the battlefield like the sacrificial calvary. "It's not that big of a deal."

I can already smell the herbs being crushed under the stone pestle. The harsh smell of rosemary and rue mingle in the air. Her Italian hasn't even paused, much less dimmed in its creative pitches. It's as vibrant as the purple dried flowers she's tossing into the pestle of petal death.

"Evil eye? Really?" I ask her, folding my arms to cover my pink unicorn print pajamas. It's hard to lecture someone while wearing unicorns.

"Least you remember some of the things I've taught you," GiGi says. Her glare does not allow it to be confused with a compliment.

I sigh, bracing against the wooden doorway. When she's this angry, even with all the wit and bravado I own, I'm not brave enough to come much closer. I remember the feeling of the same pestle hurled from across this very room when I dared her one too many times as a teen.

"I have warned you about those people," she starts, mostly under her breath but just loud enough to allow me to hear what she thinks of my decisions. "Once they learn of what you are, they will never stop. They will have you casting, cursing, rising for their every evil plan. How could you be so stupid?"

At least she's speaking English. After twenty-five years, I still haven't picked up anything other than the most basic of Italian, and most of that is just creative words to tell people what I think of them and their actions.

"Asks the woman who owns a Pagan shop?" I ask her, tucking a little closer to the doorway. "It's not as if people don't already know about us."

"Knowing we own an eclectic shop of charms," she emphasizes her idea of the shop, "is not the same as coming out and saying look what I can do."

I roll my eyes. "It's like you think this town doesn't already think the worst of us."

"Why should we care what people think of us?" GiGi asks, spooning the crushed herbs into a small drawstring bag. She's adding various stones and words I cannot hear. "Most of these people can be found in the shop during the week and then clutching their little beads on Sundays. They all gather round gossiping about those who shop with us as if they weren't just in asking for something to make their husbands horny or their friends less successful."

"Then why do you keep the back room there?"

When she stills and looks up directly at me upon hearing my question, I instantly wish I had just kept silent. She's taught me the rules since I was a child when my abilities first started showing. When my parents came knocking five years after their death, she began enforcing the rules. I am well aware what the back room is for. I've spent many a night in there lost in the collection of books and scrolls to better train myself.

"Sorry," I offer when her eyes haven't yet returned to her work.

"We keep the back room for emergencies and Pinterest fails," she huffs. "Basic bitches who watch too many shows, read too many romance books, and then somehow stumbles upon something legit leaving us to have to clean up after their girl power moment."

"I know," I tell her slipping a little further from the room, certain the Italian will start again. "Just seems a little ironic we can out ourselves for that but have to remain broke for not using it for our own uses."

GiGi Jo sighs having heard my thoughts before on such matters. "People who come to us out of desperation aren't likely to tell others they came to us. Doing it for cash and favors means everyone will want to ask to be next. Don't you remember why you stopped?"

I do. It seemed a simple enough job until it wasn't. It destroyed so much more than just my faith in myself. I destroyed a whole family that night.

Hugging myself with the memory, I nod. "This was different. Is different. They just want answers."

"So did the Pickens. They had questions they couldn't handle the answers to."

I can still hear their screams in my darkest dreams. She doesn't have to remind me.

"Look," she tells my silence, "you're going to do whatever you want to do. We both know this. Just promise me you'll be careful. If you're really going to go back into this line of work, you must be careful. For many reasons."

She doesn't need to list the reasons. I know them all. From the risks to myself, to her, and even to the people who hire me, I know them all. Unfortunately, it's not just the money which has me shopping for cases. I just can't tell her that yet. One case and she's crushing herbs for protection. If I were to tell her the complete truth the neighbors would be calling the fire department with the amount of smoke her incense and candles would cause.

I nod. "I'll be careful. Promise."

"What's the second case?"

"Not sure, yet," I begin chewing on my lip with my thoughts. "The oldest daughter thinks her mother has somehow brought back the little girl who died not too long ago. The whole place tastes of fresh grief but I didn't feel the dead there. But it was odd..."

My words trail off with my thoughts floating upon what I saw last night. Hearing my pause, GiGi is just about coming undone with her own imaginary monsters, or at least the ones she imagines for me. She has become transfixed, not moving until I finish.

"She, the mom, has gone through a lot of effort to hide something. Okay, picture this," I say, settling myself on a bar stool across from the kitchen island from which she watches me. "Perfect Pinterest house. Matching. Subdued. Almost boring. I think the colors were Don't Judge Me grey and Everything Is Fine Here white. I have seen model homes with more life than this home held."

"Mmhhmmm," she answers, waiting to see where my mental ramblings will travel.

"With all this effort to not stand out, why put heavy fake air fresheners in every outlet all through the house?"

"How fake?" GiGi asks, as if the caliber or quality of the scent clarifies anything.

"Whore house fake. My dress still smells like their home fake. Going to take more than just dry shampoo today and not from my oily roots fake."

"Ah," GiGi answers.

"Ah?" I repeat. "Just 'ah'?"

GiGi shrugs. "I can't account for people's taste."

"You can't account for people's taste? Is that really where you're going to leave it?" I ask her with both of us knowing she's hiding her thoughts with bland words and clipped sentences. "What aren't you saying, Old Lady?"

"Nothing," she starts but her acid tipped tongue isn't ready to relinquish the fight, "because I would never have gone against my better judgment and taken on cases dealing with people's tacky taste or their complete lack of it."

"Mmhhmmm," I mimic, sipping from my cup of steamy salvation as I wait. I know her verbal train has just left the station and we have many miles of track ahead of us.

"If I had been asked to take a case with a child, which we aren't supposed to do to begin with, I would know better than to wonder about the scent profile of their house and wonder more about why a family would want to have such a scent profile. Sometimes the migraine isn't from what is in front of us but what is hidden around us," GiGi informs me with her abundant sarcasm.

I almost feel sorry for whatever herb she is sacrificing to her passive aggressive anger. The pestle sounds like nails on an old chalkboard, scratching more than just my nerves with her fit.

"Hidden like the real reason you're angry with me, or hidden like what's in the box, Somerset, hidden?" I ask her, fueled by the bravery of caffeine.

She wants to yell at me, rail about my life choices in the past few hours, but she won't. GiGi prefers to let me hang myself and swing in the noose for a bit before stepping in. She once said it was the only way to truly understand consequences. I think it's more of she enjoys the 'told you so' moments. So, she won't save me from my own descent into trouble, but she'll judge every minute of it. We stare at each other, neither willing to admit fault or fears out loud, but understand each other none the less.

"I'll be careful," I assure those hazel eyes swimming in the unsaid.

"I'll be at the store," she shares, but it's what she doesn't say which hangs in the air, forcing me to retreat from the kitchen faster than my ego would have preferred.

What she doesn't say is how she'll be waiting if I need her. What she doesn't admit is how worried she is about me. Mostly, what she doesn't say, what we never say, is 'I love you'.

Becky's grave wasn't hard to find. Where the Tortes may keep a simple home, down to their very practical cars, Becky's final resting place is anything but plain. In fact, it pretty much screams 'child buried here' with every available option offered to grieving parents. It also screams of Cass's dirty fingers all over it.

Even for a recent death, the ground shouldn't be this disturbed. The sod still holds its individual square shapes, at least where there is sod. The dirt itself is tumbled, not even packed down as it often is after a funeral. Flowers have been tossed to either side of the ornate, marble headstone. With as many funerals as I have attended, this is just a quick wrap-up to ease a grieving family. This is wrong.

The dirt is still damp in my hand from being removed from the depths of earth's belly. It still holds the smell of soil and danker things. What it doesn't hold is the scent of magic. It also doesn't have a single magical tingle or vibration.

"Dirt interesting to you?"

Sighing, I stand hearing the voice of Miranda behind me.

"I told Bella I would come have a look," I try to explain.

"At dirt?" Miranda asks.

She's wearing jeans which somehow hug every curve, but don't hold a hint of being provocative. Which means they aren't the cheap ones I buy with hopes my butt won't look as flat as my bank account. Her grey top is the perfect shade of neither being too dark nor too faded, which pulls the black of her little ankle boots perfectly together. Even her high ponytail looks polished, and not a rushed hair style to start the day.

"At everything." I tell the woman who is judging my outfit of torn jeans and burgundy top with the same mood as I have judged hers.

"You still don't honestly think I have dug up my own child, hauled her body from this place to," Miranda pauses, trying to pick the right words, "to hide somewhere when I'm lonely?"

I didn't. Not exactly, anyway.

"I can't imagine you getting your hands that dirty," is what my brain decides to say. My mouth has the sense to quickly close.

Miranda pivots to leave but adds a quick parting shot before she does. "If you're done with the dirt, please be sure to put it back. My daughter's death may be a joking matter to you, but to me, it's not. Although the rumors say you have no problem getting your hands dirty."

I watch her perfect swish of her heel and the matching sway of her hair when she leaves. I could respond, but honestly, I deserve that one, and dropping the clump of dirt in my hand, I don't say a thing.

"Making friends I see?" Cass's voice creeps up my spine.

Turning to face another of life's middle finger moments, I see Miss Henkins has been joined by a few more angry women in various scenes of death. "Likewise," I tell him knowing full well he won't understand the joke. Watching the weeping wrists of one of the ladies, I wish I didn't get it, either.

Seems I am not the only one still a little shaken by last night. He turns fully around still expecting to see someone. When he doesn't, he turns back to stare at me and my honey sweet smile.

"Anyway," Cass says clearing his throat and tugging on the suit jacket three sizes too small for his robust frame. "I was told you were here. Seems you showing up at these places tends to spook the families."

"I wonder why that is?" I ask, tilting my head with feigned innocence before jumping to the next conversation. "Can you tell me about this grave? The marker says it has been over a month, but the ground still looks unsettled. This can't be good for easily spooked families."

"This is a private matter," Cass almost whispers it, and his demeanor tells me everything I need to know to twist the information from him.

Leaning over to pretend to wipe the marker, I let my tee shirt hang open a little too wide. Just as I thought, his eyes don't shy from roaming at the hinted prize. "So sad for the family. It must be painful to see their child's grave like this. Especially from a man whose only concern is helping the family."

"Well, this isn't my fault!" he exclaims. "Look," he points to the base of the marker hoping I'll bend further down to examine his explanation. "See how the dirt is disturbed all the way to the base? If this was my fault, it would be marred by our machines."

I lean further over, letting his need to be a creep override his need to keep a 'private matter' private. His many lady friends roll their eyes over his antics.

"And here," he begins pointing to the well-maintained grass we are standing on, "there would be marks, or at least indentions if we were doing this every single night!"

Without robbing him of his view, I ask, "This happens every single night?"

Cass steps closer than I would like. He whispers, "Sometimes several times a day my crew will say it's disheveled worse than other times. They won't even touch the spot saying it's cursed."

"Huh?" I remark before rapidly standing. "Well thanks for letting me know."

"That's it?" Cass asks sounding almost disappointed.

For a moment I have a thought to be a better person than I am but then I remember who I am talking to. "I'm sorry. Did you want to do dinner tonight?"

It isn't just Miss Henkins' eyes which grow wide hearing my question. Cass looks like he's being choked and is making the sounds to match.

"Or did you have plans already?"

"Yes!" Cass quickly answers. "Plans. So many plans. All week in fact."

"Oh?" I fake pout hearing his answer, letting the pout fully reach my face and slump my shoulders. "All week?"

"Yup," he says already walking backwards. "All week." He stumbles over a few of the vases, attempting to stand them up without pausing in his escape. "All week."

"What about next week?" I call after his retreating form.

"Next week, too! I think all month. Pretty sure all month." He tells me this while waving, hoping I'll take the hint.

"But you'll check for me?" I shout across the yard like a lovesick teenager.

"Absolutely!" He shouts back with a nervous chuckle aware those around us have found reasons to head this way. "Absolutely!" He shouts again, waving and pleading with his face to not ask anything more.

I don't. I wave, a little more energetically than I need to though. Miss Henkins waves her goodbye as well. Which is fine. It's her new friend waving with her wrist wound that made me cringe before I could catch myself. The thin slit became wide gaps as what is left of the tendons twist her hand side to side. The blood which was slowly weeping now travels with a much more eager speed along the flesh of her arm. When it reaches her elbow, it baptizes the little headstone by her and the family standing near her is completely oblivious. They smear her blood as each member of the mourning family touches their lips to the marker, sealing their departure with a goodbye kiss. When they walk past me, nodding with the dead woman's gift upon their faces, sometimes I wish I couldn't see the things I see.

The brass bell over the shop door tinkles its little 'hello' as I enter the store. It didn't need to. GiGi is already leaning on the counter waiting for my entrance. I hate when she does that. I also hate her one arched eyebrow of a greeting.

"It's not magic," I tell her as I walk past her to where she keeps the mini fridge behind the counter.

"Not magic or magical? A little girl coming back from the grave has to be of one or the other."

I stall, still unsure of my answer as the cold soda tickles my mouth with its tiny, carbonated bubbles. I smile to the many ghosts who roam the wooden shelves of books when they wave, having learned long ago, conversation happens on my terms. Well, they all wave but Janice.

"What's with her today?" I ask, pointing with the half empty can where the dead teen is swinging the many hanging pendulums for sale. Her normal behavior isn't one I would call perky with her dark hair and eyes lined with enough black shadow to cause a nationwide shortage, but today her mood is definitely grumpier than normal.

GiGi is caring enough to glance in the direction I point, as if maybe this time she will be able to see them, before asking, "Her who?"

"Right," I remark, still watching Janice in her obvious funk of a mood. "Doesn't matter."

I should have picked my words more carefully. You never let a teen hear you say their mood swings don't matter. You never, ever, let a dead teen hear it.

When the whole display is shoved from the shelf, GiGi turns to me with a look of exasperation. "Janice?" She asks.

I make an expression of sorry before finishing off the can and while watching the teen answer GiGi's question with a middle finger. "Did something happen today?"

"Other than my granddaughter embarking on another possible road of self-destruction?"

"Yes, other than that."

GiGi tilts her head thinking over today's events while I was stumbling along my path of good intentions. Her teal butterfly hairpin holding her grey bun catches the overhead lights. I can't remember a time she hasn't had it, and when I've asked about it, her answer is always a wink and a mischievous smile.

"Now that you mention it, there was a gentleman here earlier. Didn't say much. Just walked through the store, touching random stuff, but didn't buy anything."

Her words from earlier slither with their warning, wrapping their coils around my mind. "The Ripples?"

GiGi scoffs, waving her hand to wave away my fear and my words. "This man felt different. Definitely wasn't a random visit. Back to your problem. Not magic but has to be magical?"

I shake my head over her easy dismissal of the event but travel down this line of logic. "The dirt was nothing more than grave filled energy. I could feel the mourning. I could sense the many people who have come and gone, but nothing of magic."

"Anyone stand out?" GiGi has started replacing the display. Even with her back to me I can sense her facial expressions with her thoughts.

"Nothing, but Mr. Creepy did show his face. Thanks for that, by the way."

GiGi shrugs, turning to glance over her shoulder. "At the rate you're going, cobwebs are most likely in more spots than just the corners of the store."

"Ew."

"As of late the only company I hear you having is battery operated."

"Okay, really. Back to the topic?"

GiGi shrugs again. "I think what you're looking for is a source."

"Are you still making sex jokes? What is a source?"

"I'm not, and it's a token or item used to store very specific types of magic to be used at one location and have the results upon another location."

GiGi strolls over to the deep purple bookshelves labeled 'Occult Reading'. Most of the books there are completely laughable, boasting of easy spells to make everything from your wallet and breasts bigger to making the one who got away beg for you back. GiGi doesn't reach for those. She pulls a rather plain covered book from one of the top shelves. Thumbing through it, she brings the book to me at the counter. Being this close to her, I can smell her oil made from the herbs she punished earlier.

"Can smell you're still worried about the name spoken earlier." I tease her and her new choice of perfume.

"Speaking of sources," she begins, blessing me with a glare which is more menacing than her small frame should allow, "they can be anything from lockets to full standing dressers. The magic is embedded in the object instead of casting a spell, which makes it useable to anyone. Very dangerous and literally any number of complications."

"Okay, so you're telling me you think the most perfect, upper class, Pinterest project home, Miranda somehow just stumbled across one of these things?"

"No," GiGi says. "I think someone stumbled across her."

"Here, crazy white lady, have a little box of sum'tin sum'tin to bring your dead daughter back. First hit is on the house." I mock, still unsure of GiGi Jo's idea.

"She most likely didn't pay with cash." GiGi completely skips over my sarcasm. "Things like this have a higher price tag."

"Black Card?" I ask, continuing with my bad jokes.

"What's a Black Card?" She asks.

"It's a very prestigious credit card." I try to explain, realizing my jokes are going down in flames.

"Never heard of it."

"Well, you wouldn't. We're poor." Pulling the book closer in hopes of completely escaping this dumpster fire of a conversation, I ask her, "Where would someone like me stumble across someone, to stumble across something like this?"

"If I tell you, are you going to go there?" GiGi sighs, already knowing fully well I will.

To avoid having to give her false hope, I just smile as my answer. I don't use words to be held against me later.

Her sigh deepens. "There's a few places, but for something this strong, you would have to go to a place where many gather. This isn't a one stop shop kind of trinket."

"What does that mean?" I ask with more questions waiting behind the one I asked. "Who gathers? Why would witches gather?"

"This isn't a witch spell. It's too strong. You're looking for something older, stronger. Something I wish you would have the common sense to walk away from right now."

I keep smiling, not trusting words to encourage her to share this new information with me, even though I have plenty of words obstructing my throat with their emotions. All this time she's convinced me we are the only ones like us around here. How would my childhood have been if I knew I wasn't alone in what I can do, what I can see? But these questions I won't ask her. Not yet.

"Go to Grimore's. Ask for Charlotte. If anyone would know about something this powerful floating around, it would be her."

There's a sadness in GiGi's eyes. I've seen this look before in the eyes of parents knowing they can't stop their children from exploring the world. It's the heavy look of knowing about the evils waiting in the darkened corners and also knowing they can't protect them from being discovered. It's the look of unsaid warnings, whispered prayers, and the curse of broken hearts.

"How do I get there?" I ask, not willing to step on the trip wire of the emotional bomb between us.

"It's not a where. It's a thing," she says, handing me one of her many beaded bracelets. "When you are ready, if you really must do this, stand in front of a black mirror."

I wait, listening for instructions, a hint, something to make sense of it all. She gives neither, walking away to leave me with nothing but my attitude and slim hopes.

"And?" I ask when she begins to walk away.

"And if you're supposed to be there, you'll be there."

"Is this more of the hocus pocus shit?"

"Darling," GiGi says with a smile so wide I can't help but worry, "everything we do is hocus pocus shit."

Rolling the brown glass beads between my fingers, I don't argue over the sound of her laughter. It would be stupid to do it. Standing in a store named Great Hexpectations with cursed items instead of security cameras, with ghosts who roam the aisles as if searching for some missing ingredient to their afterlife, and with a woman with more hidden talents than I can even begin to understand. She's right. Right down to the plants reaching their long tendrils out towards me to be petted; everything we do is hocus pocus shit.

This is stupid.

Or so I've said a thousand times to myself. Standing in front of the old scrying mirror in one of the upstairs rooms isn't nearly as stupid as the seven outfit changes, I've done since arriving home. Never mind the many different ways I have styled my hair with each look.

I have gone from simple pre-k teacher to biker chick and each one looked as ridiculous as the one before it. My face is still flushed from the many times I have washed off my makeup only to reapply it. Reverting to what I know, I finally settle on the basic browns and creams I use for just about every look. With hair this red, and skin this pale, you don't grow brave with bold colors. Especially not when walking into some magical gathering place you didn't know even existed until a few hours ago.

Running my hands through my high ponytail one more time, I plant my feet in front of the mirror, waiting for something to happen. Nothing does. I close my eyes, thinking perhaps it only happens when one isn't looking. Opening one eye at a time in a slow, hesitant wink of a style, I'm still standing in the upstairs room.

"This is stupid," I repeat to an empty room. It answers me with complete silence.

Marie F. Crow

The sound of my cell phone causes me to scream a very girl-like sound. I don't have to check the caller ID. I know who it is, the same way she knew to call.

"Yes, GiGi?" I answer.

"Put the bracelet on, stupid," her voice states before hanging up on me.

Pulling the brown beads from my jacket pocket, I roll my eyes, not just at the silent phone, but also at my own stupidity.

"Put the bracelet on, stupid," I mock, but no sooner than it slides over my hand to settle around my wrist, that room explodes with sounds.

Grasping onto the back of a bench seat, I try to swallow down the bubbling stomach acid sensation as I look around this new room. The walls are covered in various tapestries in every color of the rainbow. Lights are hung behind a few, casting their pastel glow through the room instead of harsh overhead bulbs. There is no matching décor or any obvious theme. From the random style of seating, to the completely random frame prints, everything seems to have been collected at various times, various moods, and various moments from the owner's life.

Just like the décor, all around me the room is packed with many different people and they are all watching me. The pretty preppy girls in one corner are glaring over their smoking mixed drinks. I've been on this end of a similar crowd enough times to know the whispered words are not a glowing review. I smile nervously to the couple who's bench I am clinging to before patting it like a long-lost friend and attempting to slowly walk away. After my third wobbly step, the room slowly returns to the claustrophobic level of noise it was at when I discovered it.

I nod to those who nod to me. Except I don't just nod, I do that silly wave thing to further betray my complete unease. Which earns me wider grins and more side glances as I weave my way to the bar area.

"What's your poison?" Asks a female bartender when she notices me wedging myself on a bar stool.

"My social anxiety," I mutter. "Water." Is what I say loud enough to carry over the crowd.

"Big spender," she teases in an almost friendly way.

Flashing another nervous smile, I use the mirror behind her to watch the room. I'm glad to see I'm no longer the topic of all their eyes, at least openly. The only group still whispering while watching me is the group clinging to their high school cheer days with matching pigtails and pleated skirts. When they catch my eyes watching theirs, they mock wave and smile before melting into loud laughter.

"Don't let them get to you," the bartender offers, placing the glass of water in front of me. "You would think after two hundred years they would find something else to occupy their time."

"Two hundred?" I don't even try to hide my shock.

The bartender lets her eyes slowly travel me with suspicion, much as everyone else already has. "First time?" she asks.

"What gave it away? The stomachache? The complete lost girl look? Or my complete lack of knowledge about everything around me?" I hadn't meant for it to sound so cranky. The words did that all on their own.

"Yes," she answers. "Don't worry about it. Everyone has to have a day one somewhere."

Her smile is warm. It settles my nerves. Even my stomach is calming itself being so near to her. As I feel myself start to lean upon the wooden counter, I ask her, "You're fucking with me right now, aren't you?"

She leans in close still wearing her soul soothing smile. "Yes," she says again, but her eyes are different. They were a soft brown when I sat down. Now they are black with sparks dancing inside of their coloring.

My fingers itch to touch her face. I want to explore her mouth with mine. I'm curious about her perfume, the heat of her skin against mine and the way her hair would feel wrapped around my fingers. Would it be heavy like velvet or smooth like satin?

"That's enough!" Comes a tense female voice. It shatters my feelings with as much force as a sledgehammer to glass.

Blinking, I turn to the woman standing behind the bartender. Her hands are placed upon her hips with a face of complete disapproval framed by frizzy waves of reddish blonde hair. She's older, with her age etched in her face, and she wears her frustration like a leather coat, dark, tight, and protective. Shaking her head, she pushes the younger woman to the side to come stand in front of me.

"You must be Jo's girl." She states, but my mind is fighting to comprehend her words.

"What?" I ask, as if my confusion is from the many voices and the not-so-subtle music playing around us.

Sighing, she tells me, "Drink your water."

It sounds like the best advice I've ever been given, and I drink the water like someone dying from thirst. My mind is still swimming. I can feel the blush coloring my face when I think of my reaction to the bartender and GiGi Jo's earlier jokes.

"Sorry. Not sure what came over me," I whisper to the remaining water.

"Happens a lot," the woman says, once again glaring to where the bartender has retreated to wait on another customer. "Like I said, you must be Jo's girl. Been wondering when you'd show up."

For not the first or even second time today, my face contorts with my confusion. "You know GiGi? Wait, you've been what?"

She makes a soft sound of amusement. "Wow. She really does have you on lock down."

I stare at this woman. She's younger than GiGi, but not by much. Unless she's like the ex-cheerleaders, which, honestly, I have no idea how that one is even possible. Her hair is long and untouched, with more frizz than curl. The strawberry blonde shade collects the many pastels around us casting her in a rainbow haze. She looks as harmless as the bartender did, as harmless as everyone around me does, and I'm starting to think that's all a lie.

"What brings you here?' She asks when I don't offer any more depth to the conversation.

"Right!" I almost shout with my brain still melted. "I'm supposed to talk to someone named Charlotte."

"Yeah. I figured." She extends her hand across the expanse of space between us. "I'm Charlotte."

"Oh!" I shout again, still sounding like someone of more pep than I normally hold. "Nice to meet you," I tell her, shaking her offered hand.

"You really are new to all this aren't you?" Charlotte asks, and when she senses my confusion again, she offers, "Never shake someone's hand if you don't know what they are. Easiest way to get overtaken in one of these places."

"I'm sorry," I shout over the music change. "And what does that mean?"

"You know what," Charlotte starts, "I'll let Jo fill you in. What did you need to talk to me about? Must be pretty important if she let you come here alone."

"Yeah, right," I tell her, shaking my head to try to clear the remaining cobwebs. Nothing she is saying is making any sense. I need to fully understand what is happening if I am to discover what is taking place with the Tortes. "Have you ever heard of a source of magic? Something to contain a spell?"

Charlotte's eyes briefly roam the room behind me. "Yeah. Who hasn't?"

"You mean other than me obviously?"

Charlotte shrugs while drying a glass. "Other than you, obviously. Although Jo wouldn't send you here to simply ask about them unless she thinks there is one out there. Is there one?"

I've messed up just about everything from the moment I arrived, but even me, in all my many moments of glory, can tell Charlotte isn't focused on the glass in her hands. Her constant glances behind me has nothing to do with random eye contact. Whatever a source is, I've danced along a tripwire asking about it and the room is just waiting for one more wrong step to witness the explosion.

"It was just a random conversation we had." It's my turn to mimic her bored posture. "Thanks for the water."

"Look, kid," Charlotte says as she watches me try to escape from the stool, "if there is a source out there in your part of the world, it's bad. It's not just bad for whoever has it, which I'm guessing is a mortal since Jo seems to feel some sense of duty, but also for whatever let it get away from them. Which makes it bad for our world, for all of us." She leans across the bar top to whisper, as much as one can whisper with all the noise around us, "Don't go asking too much about it. Just find it."

"When I do?"

"Jo will know what to do. I'm guessing it's best if you do nothing." Charlotte returns to drying the same glass she's been working on for the whole conversation. "Don't get me wrong. A Necro like you has your place and all. It's just not with things like this."

"A what?" I ask, once again feeling overwhelmed and lost.

Charlotte slams the glass onto the wooden bar, shouting. "She hasn't taught you a damn thing, has she? What is that woman thinking?"

I hold my hands up in a gesture of surrender, unsure of what to say. "I'm just going to," I stall, unwilling to admit I have no idea how to leave this place, "go to the bathroom. Where is it?" I ask thinking it's the safest question I can manage right now.

Charlotte points to a side area, still shaking her head. "Be careful, kid."

"Of a bathroom?"

"Of everything. You have no idea how deep you are in the proverbial shit storm."

"Anthem of my life," I tell her, waving goodbye.

I should take her warning glance with more caution and listen to her words a little deeper. I should put my ego aside, and right here and now, ask her how to leave. I won't. I won't do any of it. Turning, I wade my way deeper into the shit storm she warned me about.

The hallway to the bathroom is just like the many other dive bars and clubs I've had the misfortune of visiting. If it's decorated, I can't tell. For some reason, as always, hallways tend to become another staging area with their walls as support for the many standing people. There's no polite way to nudge a path through the lounging crowd, so you don't. You lower your shoulder and wedge yourself into an already too small space with hopes and pleadings of 'excuse me'.

The bathroom is the same basic four stall, because all girls go in pairs, with a matching number of sinks. The white veneer is chipped, hinting at the age of this place, or at least the abuse of it. Black sharpies don't tell lewd jokes here. There's random shapes and letters with too many swirls spread across the deep green paint scheme. Some of the diagrams around the mirrors seem to almost glimmer, as if there is glitter, or some light source reflecting the overhead glare in the ink. I catch myself staring at them in the continued, constant state of confusion I have been in since arriving.

Sighing, I pinch the bridge of nose, closing my eyes against the stress headache I feel building. I thought I knew magic. I thought I was pretty well taught about the ins and outs of what I am and what it means. If anything, I just discovered the only thing I know is nothing at all.

"My, my, isn't she a pretty one?"

Snapping my head back up to stare into the mirror, somehow, while I wallowed in my brief moment of self-pity, I missed the entrance of three men now standing behind me. My heart does its little panic shimmy up into my throat before I can swallow it back down to its normal resting spot. My stomach, still not happy from earlier, joins in with my heart's demand for attention.

Trying to talk through the desert spreading through my mouth, I do my best witty, brave girl routine. "Pretty sure you forgot what the symbol for a penis owner is. Or maybe you're so used to having such small ones you identify with the other symbol?"

"Oh," the one who must have obtained the lucky title of leader says stepping closer, "she even has jokes. Dressed like a boring in all that polyester, she has jokes."

I self-consciously tug on what I thought was a cute, cotton shirt and squirm a little in my denim jeans.

"Must be all that red hair giving her some fire," another one states. "Carpets match the drapes, I wonder?"

Encouraged by the taunting of their leader, all three are now growing brave. Their shared looks whisper of this being a previously hatched plot and not just a spur of the moment thought process. I turn, watching and pleading with my brain to quickly think of something, as my hands search for anything removable from the sink behind me.

"Do you?"

All of our heads turn to see a fourth guy none of us had noticed. His black jeans are fitted and boast of being not a brand one would find on a rack of a store. His dress buttoned up shirt is a deep, charcoal grey. Black hair frames a face of pure mischief with eyes seemingly almost excited by the chances of a bar fight.

"Is that really all that you choose to wonder? Maybe not about how I shouldn't be causing such a scene in a well-known place? Or is it wise to draw so much attention to myself when I'm such a low rank on the rotting food chain? But no, you, and yours, went right for the wonder about what her most secret of places must look like? Bravo," he adds clapping with false enthusiasm. "You've set demon-kind back years of evolution."

"This isn't any of your concern," the thinker of the three answers. "We are allowed to have a bit of fun."

"...aaannndd I'm allowed to rip your heads free from your bodies. Who wants to debate which one would have more fun?" he looks around, as if there are more people in this small room than just the gathered crowd. "Anyone?"

He asks as if someone is going to answer him. No one does. It sets his smile wider.

"So, gentlemen, and I use the term loosely, what will it be? Your fun or my fun?" he asks the room.

"You don't own everywhere, Jedrek," the thinker replies. "Someone is going to call your bluff one day."

Their leader may have the courage to verbally taunt him, but he doesn't have enough to be the one to call his bluff. He motions for the rest of the crew to follow him out. I take note when none of the three make any kind of eye contact with him when they slide out the door Jedrek holds open.

"Not the best ambassadors for our kind," Jedrek makes an embarrassed expression with his explanation. "Sorry about that."

Skipping right over the label to avoid asking more questions in a place I am learning it might be best to shut up in, I shrug, since it's the universal language which might not land one dead. "Jedrek, huh?"

He smiles, lifting his eyebrows in a wide arch as his answer. "And you must be the littlest witch. Happy to meet you."

The way he smiles causes the annoying little girl side in me to sigh. There's something about those steel blue eyes which may even have the ability to charm GiGi's fire into something more than sarcastic embers. Remembering the scene at the bar, I clear my throat and belittle myself for being so weak.

"Witch. Necro. Confused kid," I say with an exhausted smile. "It's been a long list on a short trip."

Folding his arms, he almost melts onto the wall beside me bracing his body. "Yes. You're quite the talk of the place."

Groaning, and for some reason not at all suspicious of a conversation in a bathroom with a stranger at a strange place, I ask, "How can I be so worthy of such conversation?"

"Because you don't belong," Jedrek whispers in a teasing tone.

"That obvious?"

Jedrek's smile grows even wider with my question. The humor reaches his eyes as he says, "Let's see. Almost lost your lunch with the travel. Tripped at least twice on your way to the bar. Charmed by a gorgon, which was super sexy to watch by the way." He pauses in his long list of my failures to wiggle his eyebrows at me before continuing. "You shook hands with an energy reader, bad move if trying to fish out information. You asked about a very taboo topic like a naughty little girl and then, just to win the newbie of the day award, you slip away into a closed off space, filled with people waiting to torment you some more for their own enjoyment. No. Wasn't obvious at all. Your secret is safe with me."

Listening to him, my face must show all of my thoughts.

"You have no idea what a gorgon is, or an energy reader?" Jedrek asks. He's at least still wearing his amused look to soften the blow. "Tell me about the source you were asking about?"

There's a warning bell chiming away in the back of what's left of my brain. "I thought that was a taboo topic?" I ask him, still unsure why I am even talking to him.

"You can trust me. After all I did just save your life."

"Do those blue eyes work on everyone?" I ask, attempting to change the topic.

"Yes," he says without a sense of humility.

"You didn't save my life," I counter, making my way from the bathroom. "I was only in potential danger. Not real."

"So, I potentially saved your life." Jedrek tells me pushing from the wall to follow me. "Still counts."

"Potentially, it could count," I agree.

"Which means you could potentially tell me about the source." Jedrek leans against the door.

A part of me returns to the panic waltz, but another just finds his attempt to block me disgustingly annoying. "Or I could potentially not tell you. Really could go either way."

"What does a demon have to do to earn the trust of the littlest witch?" he asks, and I feel all the confusion return, again.

"Demon, huh?" I ask before I can stop myself.

Jedrek says nothing. He wears his signature smirk and one lifted eyebrow over my expression.

"Those other three demons, too?"

He presses his lips, shrugging with his face.

"What is this place," I whisper to him fearing even the walls will hear my complete lack of understanding.

"What did she tell you it was?" Jedrek leans closer with his question.

"She didn't. Just said to speak to someone named Charlotte about -" I stop myself, fearing saying too much.

"See?" He asks. "They work on everyone."

I had a sharp retort waiting somewhere on my tongue. At least I think I did, but the door being pressed open by team cheer stops it. Once inside, they look to me and back to Jedrek with sly smiles.

"Slumming it, Jedrek?" The blonde asks, pressing herself completely against his body while staring at me.

I'm not sure if I'm supposed to be offended or amused over how completely obvious, she is acting. I vote amused since I haven't had a death threat in a few minutes now.

"You wear desperation well. It completely covers the natural scent of your two hundred years of insecurity."

I knew as soon as it slipped from my mouth, I shouldn't have said it. It isn't because I just reminded myself that they are all over two hundred years old; it is due to the fact that their anger is melting their faces into walking corpses.

It started with the blonde trying to make herself a second shirt for Jedrek, but her friends joined her corpse bride look. I'm forcing my face to hold its unfazed posture, but I'm pretty sure the sound of my heartbeat is ruining my own attempt of a mask.

"There was a time," the blonde says with what my mind can only compare to oil running from the corners of her mouth, "when new witches would pay homage to their elders."

The glazed, pale eyes of a brunette glances over me before her bloated tongue licks her lips with her thoughts. "But what could she possibly have that we would want?"

"I have a thought," the other blonde standing near me pipes up. In her enthusiasm a clump of skin falls from her outstretched arm when reaching for my face. What was once perfect French tipped nails has turned into blackened talons. She cups my face as if trying to pierce my flesh. "We could take the little token she's so curious about."

The blonde pressing against Jedrek smiles, spilling more oil from her mouth. I don't want to hear her idea of my homage.

"Sorry, ladies," I offer, pulling my face free. I'm about to take a huge gamble and I hope it pays off. "I already promised it to Jedrek."

All three turn to him. If their flesh wasn't in such a state of decomposition, I may have been able to read their expressions. As it stands, it's just a trio of glazed eyes and rotting folds.

"Guilty," Jedrek says with his charming smile.

There's a moment when I fear the three will challenge him. I shouldn't have.

"And what will you do with it?" The brunette asks with sincere curiosity.

"Oh, don't you worry, Wens," he tells her, blessing her with one of his smiles, "I'll take good care of it." Slipping free from the blonde, he does his best to not stare at the mess of his shirt. "Ready, littlest witch?"

I take his outstretched hand without sparing a second of hesitation. My knowledge of demons may be short, but witches, angry rotting witches over two hundred years old who I have angered, seem more of a threat. I don't fight or struggle from his firm grasp as he leads us from the room, or even as he escorts me down the hall. He takes me right back through the crowded room I entered with all its ear rattling noise to stand in front of drawn door on the only wall without drapes.

"I bet you also don't know how to leave, do you?" Jedrek asks me as he pulls me in front of him.

I can feel his hot breath along my exposed neck. Once again, that annoying girl part of me wants to giggle with the sensation. Not trusting my voice, I shake my head.

"You really are the littlest witch," he tells me. "I'll see you soon, Harper."

I don't have time to turn to him to ask him how he knows my name. I don't have the chance to question his whole charade if he knew it the whole time. Instead, I'm spinning around in the same empty upstairs room from which I left. The sudden silence has a reverse feeling of suffocation. The twirling dust from my entrance is a poor imitation of the twinkling lights I just left. Hugging myself, I stare into the scrying mirror feeling completely alone in a different way than I have ever felt before. Just like the rest of the afternoon, I don't understand any of it.

"D iscover anything about your little problem?" GiGi asks the
next morning.

I had spent most of the night tossing and turning, hating
every sound from the house, in my debate over whether I should
storm up there and wake her up to demand answers or just pretend
none of it ever happened and keep our little false life going.

"You could say that," my temper, despite all the calming lavender
planted around our breakfast nook, is still not sated. "Want to tell me
about energy readers? Or why we don't shake hands? Or what a
gorgon is? Or about demons, witches, necroes and the many other
things you forgot?"

GiGi's face doesn't change during my whole rant. It might be the
pastel purple, smiley face PJs, or my fluffy robe ruining it for me. Then
again, it could be the squeaky slippers or the giant looped hairstyle
causing my hair to flop back and forth as I stomp towards her. Most
likely it is due to her general non-giving of cares over people's
feelings towards her, much less about how I appear, at all.

"See you found Charlotte," is what she tells me. Slow sip of coffee
and all.

"That's all? That's all you have to say?" My voice is the pitch of a
teenager being asked to clean her room. It annoys even me. GiGi
keeps right on sipping with her eyes bored and unmoved. "I could
have been killed. Potentially killed," I correct. "How did you not even

tell me these things? Even Charlotte is mad with you and that doesn't seem like a good thing."

GiGi scoffs, stirring more sugar into her coffee. "Charlotte is always mad. She runs a bar and is charged with keeping magic from happening in a place packed with magical beings. She runs on anger and caffeine."

"Let's talk about these magical beings." Sitting at the table, I place myself in front of her. "How many magical beings are there?"

GiGi lifts an eyebrow with an already exhausted look. "No one really knows. Hybrids are born all the time."

"There's hybrids? Okay, let's start with some basic. What are demons?"

"You act as if you've never had the bible quoted to you by frightened Christians?"

"Fair," I tell her. "What are they really?"

Sighing, GiGi places her version of morning salvation down. "Since all beings won't exactly share their secrets, the general idea is they are from the lower realm which some call Hell. They serve to keep their master happy, and who that is, well that's always up for debate with the many versions of the underworld. Their main goal is the constant tempting of mortals."

"Is there an order to them? Like high to low power-wise?"

She tilts her head, thinking. "I've heard that, but I haven't really asked one."

"And gorgons?"

Rolling her eyes, she says, "Overrated bitter women. Surely, you've heard the story of Medusa?"

"But I didn't turn into concrete."

"Well, of course not. Nothing is as strong as it once was. Now they are mostly parlor tricks using fundamental mind control. Quite sad really."

"Do I even want to know about energy readers or how Botox commercials could become decaying blobs?"

GiGi chuckles. "The Sinister Trio is still there? Oh, we didn't name them that," she tells me seeing my face over their title. "They did. They thought it sounded scary. Who knows? Maybe back then it did."

GiGi sips her coffee before speaking again. Maybe it's my nerves or my own lack of caffeination, but she seems to take forever. When she reaches for more sugar, I have to force my tongue to not move and my lips to press tight to see to the first demand.

"I probably should have told you about more than I have, but with you, the more I told the more you pressed to go find things out. I was worried what you would do with such information. To answer your question about that, witches have a wide range of abilities. You, for example, call the dead. It's not spell work. It's just what you naturally do. Charlotte can read people with a touch. She will know all your secrets, or at least your general truths. The trio are corpse walkers. They can rot on command, and if they want, rot things they touch. That's just the tip of the candle of what's out there."

She sips her sugar with some coffee without looking at me. I can tell by her deflated frame this isn't anything she had hoped I would have to know for many years, which makes me wonder my next question.

"Why send me there if you didn't want me to know all this? Seems counterproductive. You could have just gone yourself."

"It's time. Charlotte is right when saying you're in more danger not knowing than if you do know. She's also right about the danger to both sides should we not find this source."

Squinting my eyes, I ask her, "How did you know what she said?"

GiGi blooms back to her normal self. "Kid, all of us witches have our own secrets," she says, mocking the name Charlotte had handed out. "Did you sense anything powerful in the Torte's house?"

"Nothing. It was amazingly basic."

"Too basic?"

"What do you mean?" I ask her, amused by her constant amount of conspiracy theories.

"Like someone knew you were coming and cleaned house basic."
GiGi stirs her coffee as if she thinks she's suddenly blown the case
wide open.

"If a source is so powerful, I don't think a little sage or cedar
would make it undetectable."

"No," GiGi offers, "but if the one who gave it to her were to clean
their tracks to cover their own ass it would."

"How would one even do that? A house holds energy for years, if
not forever."

"There are ways. Not for someone like Miranda or the likes, but
there are ways."

"Let me skip along your logic. You're thinking when Bella told
her parents who she met at work, Miranda panic called who she got
the source from, if she has the source, and the owner of the source just
shows up on a moment's notice to not only remove it, but also remove
a dead girl and all trace of them both? Seems a stretch."

"Not if it was discovered by someone with magic. The owner
doesn't know how powerful or trained you may or may not be. You
could have discovered it, reclaimed it and therefore turned it in,
leading to the owner's death warrant."

"You do death warrants? Do magical beings in police uniforms
show up and arrest them? Put them in little magical cop cars?" I ask,
more amused than I should be.

"No. They show up and kill them." GiGi informs me of this fact
as if it's just the morning's weather.

"No trial? Just dead?"

GiGi chuckles, "Why need a trial when a simple touch can show
the truth? Saves a lot of time."

"You're telling me if I had found this thing, it would have meant
instant death to someone?"

"Most definitely. If not the owner, then to you as others fought to
claim it."

"Even knowing it's a death sentence to own it?"

"Even knowing," she nods. "Power makes people stupid."

"How do I find it then?"

"You're looking for the wrong type of magic. When do you go back?" GiGi asks as she collects the morning's dishes.

"Today, I suppose. I need to fill them in on what I didn't find."

"Good. When you go back, look past the air fresheners and the too hard of an attempt to look perfect. Don't feel for your type of pull. Feel for something hiding. The cleaning spell will be cloaked, pushed way down to hide itself among the energy of those living there. It may be a slight tickle, or a hum of something just a little off key, but it will be there."

"And when I find it?"

"Memorize it. The one who casted it will have the same feeling when you find them."

"It's just that simple?" I ask her, watching her clean and return things around the kitchen to their proper place.

"Wearing that, nothing is simple. No one would ever believe you're a death witch who wears nothing but pastels," she teases.

"I own other colors..." I self-consciously say when placing my cup in the dishwasher. "I just prefer to not highlight the fact of how pale I am, living in the south."

GiGi nods with false agreement when I walk past her, saying, "Wouldn't want anyone to think of a witch as pale and wearing black. The very idea..."

"You're such an ass!" I shout over my shoulder when her words trail off, letting me know she's wearing her trademark smile of sarcasm.

Her laughter follows me down to my basement apartment and I can't help but smile. We both know the reasons for my wardrobe. It has nothing to do with my coloring. Long time ago I was convinced if I did everything I could to not look the part then maybe the rumors would stop. Maybe, just maybe, I too would get an invite to the school dances or at least birthday parties. If I wore enough pastels, enough ribbons in my hair, then maybe no one would believe the things whispered when my name was mentioned. It never happened, but I had childhood dreams and teen hopes.

Despite all my efforts to blend in and be accepted, I never was. GiGi had told a sobbing preteen it was better that way. People are rude and at their core hateful for anything different than themselves. But the truth, the truth is people aren't always just what they seem. Sometimes people are just slow to embrace their truths and that I should accept mine and embrace them, even be proud of them. I am in my early twenties, and when walking past my bedroom mirror, in all of my attempted camouflage, I know, sadly, I still haven't fully embraced my truth.

Standing at the door of the Tortes, I have to softly sigh and if not completely laugh at myself. The conversation with GiGi has put all of my inner demons on full display with my blue shirt and cream-colored pants. We won't even mention the matching flats. Considering what I was wearing the first time I knocked on this door, I suppose anything is a fashion upgrade.

Lowering my walls, I push my magic around the little cement porch with its metal bench and seasonal coordinated colored pillows. At first there is nothing. No little 'hello' or small tickle left behind by someone. That's what gave it away.

A porch is the main entry way into a house. People stand, gather and travel through here several times a day. There should be something, some feel of life, if not magic, but there's nothing. If I didn't know better, I would say this house hasn't been lived in in years.

"Find anything?"

Jedrek's voice causes me to jump and break my concentration. Still wearing an ensemble of all dark clothing, he leans against one of the wooden pillars. His sunglasses aren't reflective. They are tinted and behind that darkened glass I can see he is watching me with more interest than his smiling charm wants to display.

"What are you doing here?" I whisper, figuring any moment the door will open.

"What are you doing here, littlest witch?" Jedrek is glancing around the proud house as if it's the last place he'd suspect to stumble upon me.

"My job!" My voice is still a hiss of aggravation.

"Wouldn't be that little thing we are both looking for, would it?" he asks will all mock sincerity and half smiles.

"Why would I tell you?"

"Because if it is, you're going to need me," he says this with an edge of caution to his mirth. "You see that little bird over there?" Jedrek points to an area of a tree behind my right shoulder.

Turning I see what he's pointing at, I just don't see why I should care.

"Yeah, it's a tree. That's where one would find birds. What's your point?"

"What about that lady down there who has been checking her mail for the last thirty minutes it has taken you to find the nerve to get out of your car and stand here daydreaming?"

Turning, I see the old lady. She doesn't appear to be watching us at all, making his question even more confusing.

"Oh, and my favorite, behind me, a jogger drinking from an empty water bottle."

"What's so special about a jogger?"

"He isn't wearing shoes," Jedrek whispers. "Sometimes they get things a little lost in translation."

"Who does? Upper class?" I ask him, feeling like I'm lost in a verbal maze or one of those posters one must stare at for hours just to see a glimpse of an image.

His half smile finally reaches both sides. "You really don't know."

It isn't a question. It's a realization.

"How do you know I sat in my car?" I ask him, unwilling to further be a source of his amusement, at least this time.

He doesn't say anything. He just wears the same smile and mirth filled eyes.

"Whatever." Is the only reply I can muster. "Just behave?"

"Wounded you would think otherwise from someone who keeps saving your life." He covers his voice in false sentiment.

"Potentially," I correct.

He does an eyeroll, lifting his eyebrows as well with the motion. Pushing from the painted pillar, he maneuvers past me to ring the doorbell. When Miranda opens the door, he's standing right beside me.

"You must be Miranda," he says before she can open her mouth, but that isn't what's the most shocking.

Miranda smiles, something I have never seen her do. Her hand almost flutters to her chest, hovering like something from an old southern romance movie. If she had pearls, I'm sure she would be playing with them at this moment. I glance to him and it's my turn to roll my eyes. There, on full display and wattage, is Jedrek's smile and blue eyes peering over his glasses at the oddly, agreeable woman.

"Come in," Miranda offers him, never looking to me.

"Thank you," Jedrek tells her, but to me he whispers, "Always," before slipping into the house.

I follow him with my face covered in disgust and annoyance. He strolls through the place draping and dropping his mask of flirtation each time Miranda turns away or turns to face him. He's doing the same thing he had done earlier. His face may seem all for Miranda and every item she shows him, explaining every overly drawn-out explanation about it, but he's actually looking for deeper hints of what the house may hold. Don't blame him. How many painted bowls can one really care to hear about?

"You know," he stops Miranda's next avalanche of descriptions, "I could sure use a nice glass of water. How about you, Harper?" he asks turning to me with an innocent inquiry. "Do you need more water?"

"I wouldn't want to put her out," I say to them both, ignoring his jab about the bar.

"Oh, it's fine," Miranda almost coos, "I'll be right back."

Jedrek tilts backwards to watch the woman to be sure she's completely gone. I know when she's reached the corner of the room. Jedrek plasters one of his charming smiles, doing a little wave until she is fully out of sight and he can drop the act.

"Do your thing," he whispers, still leaning to watch.

"My thing?" I whisper back.

"Yes!" Jedrek hisses, finally showing an emotion other than mockery and flirt. "That thing where you look like you're daydreaming but doing something witchy."

"I already did," I tell him with a little annoyance and pride slipping through. "When you two were fawning over some painted egg, I searched the place."

"And?"

"Nothing's here."

"You sure?" he asks, finally turning to look at me and not in the direction of the missing woman.

"You don't understand," I start as he turns his attention back to the path to the kitchen. "There's *nothing* here. Not the family. Not the memories. Nothing. It's a blank slate."

Jedrek stands upright to fully turn towards me hearing my words. "How is that possible?"

I'm not sure if he's asking me or just the space around us with spoken musing, but I choose to answer him since the chances of the house doing it is slim. "I was told, if someone wanted to be sure no one would find what we are looking for, they would be sure no one could find not only it, but any remnants of who it belonged to."

"She wiped it so clean it's a void," Jedrek says with amusement and curiosity.

"She?" I ask, wondering just how much more he knows and isn't sharing.

Jedrek shrugs, putting his smile back into place. He must have heard Miranda before I did for it's all stage play and 'thank yous' when he turns.

"Harper here says your family has a little rumor issue?" Jedrek asks, sipping slowly from the glass of water. "Something about people thinking your daughter is back?"

"So silly isn't it?" Miranda offers, as if he simply asked about what play her son was a part of for the past holidays.

"People will talk, won't they?" Jedrek says, with a voice heavy with scandal and a face to match the claim.

He's sitting on the large couch holding the glass like its expensive wine. With all of his dark clothes and dark hair you would think he would stand out like a glaring error, some décor glitch, but somehow, he seems to fit perfectly.

"How would one even do such a thing?" Jedrek asks, and when Miranda's eyes swing to me, he sits up, pulling Miranda's attention back to him saying, "I mean, obviously there are ways," he drops his voice as if mocking someone right of ear shot adding, "so people say, anyway."

Miranda, for the first time, looks nervous. With how she fidgets, I'm almost holding my breath waiting for her to confess everything to those staring blue eyes and disarming smirk.

"I wouldn't know," Miranda states. "Chad will be home soon."

I watch her switch from flirtatious, to eager gossiper and now she has changed roles again becoming defensive. Unfortunately for Miranda, a little mention of a husband doesn't faze Jedrek.

"You think he would know?" Jedrek asks, pulling on her fear of having too many conversations shared among too many people. "The strong husband and father dabbling in the dark arts. Positively scandalous." Looking to me with more mirth than the situation deserves, he asks, "Whatever would the neighbors say?"

I'm out of my verbal league. I've been out of since I met him. Sipping my water with a raised eyebrow of a bluff, I stare at the woman whose mental battle is portrayed upon her face. I would love to tell the neighbors what a naughty little girl Miranda has been, and she knows it. In fact, the rest of the Ripples' money cleared today. I may get a billboard made.

"You've seen the site." Miranda turns to me, hoping our gender will seal us in some form of camaraderie. "Tell him there is no way I could do that. Tell him!"

"Your husband or Jedrek? Because honestly it's only one of them you should care about." I sip the water again as if I've won some medal of wit.

"Both!" Miranda's hands are working harder than her face to implore me. "Tell them both."

"You have no idea, not even an ounce of understanding, how your daughter's grave keeps..." Jedrek pauses, looking at the ceiling as if the words he wants are upon it, "...becoming tossed like someone, or something, just crawled right up and out?"

If I had phrased it such, Miranda would have come unglued. Jedrek's smile earns him a free pass.

"None," she says. "Not a clue."

"Well, that's a pity the gossip mill just won't let you live your life in mourning." Jedrek's face melts to one of compassion but his eyes still hold the mischief of a little boy. He shrugs with his whole body before standing. "Thank you for the visit."

His smile is for Miranda, but his eyes are for me and they aren't very friendly. I'm not the only one who doesn't believe a word she is saying.

"You don't have to go." Miranda is almost running to follow Jedrek.

"Oh, but I must." He turns to her as if the hardwood flooring is ice, smooth and without a pause in his path. "Just think of the neighbors. A witch and now a man in the house of a wedded woman? Unaccompanied?" He shivers as if suddenly cold or frightened. "The scandal!"

Miranda had forgotten her one vice for a moment. Image is everything to her, and the thought of having it tarnished snaps her back to focus and less into his newest fan girl. She doesn't say anything as Jedrek holds the door for me. He waves a little finger motion to where she has stopped, frozen with regret over his departure.

Once outside his act only dims a few wattages. Placing his sunglasses back upon his face, he strolls right to my parked car before I can ask or even invite him along. With one lift of his eyebrows, he makes himself at home in the passenger seat, watching me and waiting.

I want to scream with my frustration. This 'demon' has settled right into my life by a chance meeting. Now, he's become my shadow and stalker all in the one.

"Coming?" He shouts out the window and I want to yell no.

I want to walk instead of riding in my own car with him. I want to demand he gets out of my car, that he takes his smirk and his blue eyes and gets out of my life, but I don't. I won't. I won't do any of those things my mind is screaming for me to do and it's becoming an annoying habit of mine.

We ride in silence. Me, seething in my frustration. Jedrek wearing his normal mask of a smirk while watching the view as if it is a scenic route. The ghost in the back is watching us both in her normal frump of a mood.

"Is she always this depressing?" Jedrek asks after another one of her long sighs.

"Is it so unbelievable not every woman is charmed by you?" I ask this but I keep my eyes on the road ahead. I don't want to glance back and have Myrtle disagree with me. There has to be someone other than myself who is not moved by him.

"Actually, yes," Jedrek says with that same annoying smile I was just mentally hating upon.

A thousand words are fighting to escape. A thousand rebuttals are waiting to try to dim the gleam in those eyes, but I don't. A part of me knows he'd just enjoy the verbal battle.

"Home sweet home," he says with a wide smile when I park the car in front of Great Hexpectations.

Slamming the door to the car, I don't argue with him. I don't even look to him, or invite him to follow me inside the shop. I know I don't have to. He'll do it anyway.

"GiGi?" I shout through the store when entering. "We're here." I drag the word 'we're' so I can fully fill the syllable with contempt for having a sudden partner for this case.

"Making new friends?" GiGi Jo asks from beside me, chuckling when I jump hearing her voice.

"Maybe," Jedrek answers before my anger could. "Tell me, how are you doing, Jo?"

GiGi doesn't let his question stall her from rearranging the many decks of card on display. She's adjusting them to her own measure of sorting with such concentration she can't be bothered by him

"Same as I was when you asked last time and the same as I'll be when you ask the next time," she tells him, still balancing her display.

"You two know each other?" The pitch of my voice annoys me.

"I know all the witches," Jedrek shrugs and begins to walk around the shop randomly touching items or tilting books by their spines.

GiGi shrugs, still fascinated with her attempted display.

"Nothing, huh?" I ask her back as she walks away.

"It's like he said. They know all the witches."

GiGi says this with nothing more than half interest, leaving me more confused. Which seems to be my pattern as of late.

"They?" I'm following her with my continued lines of questions. I swear she's walking faster hearing me following her through the wooden shelves and to the counter.

"Oh, this one," Jedrek mutters with mirth. "What a naughty thing you are not teaching her about her world."

Something about his tone sets GiGi into an almost lectured child look. I've never seen the woman let someone belittle her before. She's normally filled with more sarcasm than one should hold, and yet Jedrek somehow, with one sentence, has robbed her of all of it.

"Tell your grams what was in the tree today at the Torte's house." Jedrek is still roaming the store with false fascination.

"A bird. There was a bird in the tree," I say with my arms raised in confusion. "Birds live in trees.'

"What color?" GiGi asks, finally finding her voice.

It's my turn to shrug, but with confusion not avoidance. "Dark. It was a dark colored bird."

"Did it sing? Make any noise?" GiGi's face is one of concern and worry when she asks me.

I make a sound of confusion, unsure of what the bird did, or was doing. "It's a bird!"

Jedrek smirks, almost chuckles and I have a feeling it's not over the book in his hand. "Or the lady checking the mail, but my favorite," he says, turning to face the two of us, "my favorite still has to be the jogger with no shoes. Just classic."

He ends his statement with a smile so wide it almost looks genuine, but I've learned enough about him so far to know it's not. It's another toying, taunt at my expense.

GiGi sighs and it pulls her shoulders with the effort from it. "You've really stepped in it this time, haven't you, Harper?"

I lift my arms in confusion and aggravation. Before I can open my mouth to defend myself from some unknown, at least to me, fuck up, I notice something I hadn't before. The ghosts, normally roaming the store with peaceful ease, are hiding on the false upper floor. They are staring down where Jedrek stands in an almost fearful gaze. All except Janice. Janice is watching me as if I just betrayed her, as if I broke some best friend code.

"They can wait," GiGi mutters, knowing well what my silent moments mean. "Tell me about what you found at the house."

"Tell me why I should care about a bird." I counter, still watching their strange behavior.

Jedrek flops most ungracefully into a reading chair. "Yes, tell her why we should care about a bird."

GiGi glares at the man. "Because it wasn't a bird, she wasn't checking the mail and the jogger wasn't enjoying the newly edged sidewalks."

She sighs again. It sounds as if someone has stolen her favorite book and now, she has to come to the realization it's gone. I have a feeling I'm the book.

"It was a magpie. She was a shade. He was a ghoul." GiGi holds her hand to stop my stream of questions. "Magpies are used by witches to copy conversation and tell them what was said. Not the most reliable, but still used. Shades are servants to demons or other such beings. They are literally a shade, or replica, of someone who is real, or still living, so people don't question why they are there. It's the ghouls which have me worried. Why would vampires want to know what you're doing?"

I look from Jedrek to GiGi waiting for one of them to start laughing or some kind of 'just kidding' moment. They don't. GiGi has her concerns etched in every line of her age but Jedrek is still sitting, sprawled out over the chair's wide arms watching us both with great interest.

I feel as if my head may explode. I knew there were others like me. There had to be, but a whole paranormal world, and not simply just sitcoms or sparkling remakes, but a real world all around me this whole time.

Before I can question her further, she flashes me a look of warning. It's not just those above us who are holding mixed feelings about who is watching us.

"Now, your turn," GiGi says hoping I picked up on the hint to change the topic. "What did you find in the house?"

"Nothing," Jedrek shouts from where he sits. "Weird, huh?"

"Like he said, nothing. Not even those who are currently living there," I add to his answer.

"Not possible," GiGi whispers it, but how she whispers it tells me it's very possible.

"Exactly," Jedrek states, standing with the same invisible thread-type of style as before. "Which means we aren't dealing with a simple little housewife spell, not that a simple housewife could summon her daughter in full skin suit, but here we are ladies."

"Why do you keep using the word 'we'?" I ask him with more acid than I had meant to escape.

"Because we need him." GiGi confesses as she wilts in the chair beside her. "We really need him."

"Do we?" I almost shout to the woman who is normally ready to fight the world with angst or fists, whichever works best.

"You do, littlest witch," Jedrek tells me, and for once he isn't wearing his trademark smile.

"And why is that?" I ask him, wearing a mockery of his expression.

"Because I'm the only one who can keep you alive."

There's no flattery to his words. No boasting. No exaggerated gesture. He's almost sad to admit it, which is what causes my stomach to twist.

"And this time, Harper," he says, using my real name, "not just potentially."

13

"W hat does that even mean?" I ask them both. "How are you the only one who can keep me alive? Better question," I pause gesturing with my hands in a wide arch, "why would someone want me not alive?"

Jedrek is watching GiGi again. He's holding his head between his hands in an almost boy like way. I'm starting to learn he does these types of things when trying to disarm someone. It's the whole 'look how harmless I am' routine I'm sure serial killers do to lure their victims astray.

"Because you know, and now they know about you," GiGi explains.

"Know what? About who? Me? What's so great about me?" My voice sounds like a teen girl, again. It keeps hitting higher octaves with each word.

"Oh, this is where it gets good. Hold on!" Jedrek rushes to drag one of the reading chairs over to the counter. He settles himself before readjusting a time or two for better comfort and sight. "Please, continue."

GiGi glares at him. "Are you sure?" she asks. "Shall I fetch you some pillows for your feet or how about a nice virgin?"

He makes a disgusted sound with her last offer. "Virgins are so boring. Way over valued. Isn't that right, Janice?"

He shouts his question with a slight backwards tilt of his head. Until now, he hadn't even given the slightest of hints he knew they were there. My eyes are pulled instantly to where they have huddled, searching for the one he called by name, but she's not there. She's slipped away to wherever they go when I can't see them.

"Don't worry," he tells me seeing me searching for her. "She'll come back. Nowhere else for her to go, really."

"I'm so over your fucking riddles," I half whisper with my mental exhaustion taxing my patience level and manners.

"It's not riddles, my littlest witch. It's facts. Facts you just don't have, making it feel like riddles to you. Which is, in fact, not my riddle, but yours." Jedrek is pretending to examine his nails, searching for any dirt much like a cat would sharpen their claws.

"What do you remember about your lessons on magic?" GiGi asks, skipping over the little dramatic scene.

"Which lesson?" I'm laying my head against the cool glass of the display case with my answer. They are giving me such a headache, I'm not sure even the smoothest of tequilas would be able to chase away the pain.

"The one about abilities versus affinities?"

"Abilities are how good one can be at general magic. Affinities are natural born gifts, or a type of magic which answers best to a witch." I repeat the phrasing as best as my brain allows.

"Your affinity is one of the strongest. Every spell," GiGi says with emphasis, "is based on some degree of life and death. Energy, in some form, must always die. You, should you actually take this hocus pocus shit serious, can control it all."

"And that makes you either very valuable or very dangerous." Jedrek finishes for her. "If you did something very bad and suddenly this very dangerous witch is on to you, what would you do? Or, if you wanted to control very bad things, what type of witch would you want to be able to control yourself?"

"One of the strongest affinities," GiGi tags in, in some verbal ping pong game of reasoning.

"I wear pink and trip over air. No one would believe any of that about me," I tell them with a less than enthused voice.

"Well, one, that's just because you're weird," Jedrek says with a straight face, adding more judgement than a face should hold. "Two, that's because she's kept you hidden. That is until you flopped your first entrance at one of the most powerful watering holes we have. Not the best idea you've ever had, Jo."

GiGi flips him off and I'm starting to see some of her color return. "She wouldn't have stayed behind if I had gone. I needed to know if Charlotte knew about anything landing this way."

"And you think if she had, she would have told midget witch here?" Jedrek motions in my direction with his question.

"I thought I was littlest?" I ask with my face half smooshed against the glass from my resting position.

"You're sinking by the second," he informs me.

"You're sinking by the second," I return, mocking him like a toddler until realization hit. "I just sunk further, didn't I?"

They both answer in tandem, "Yes."

Lifting my head from the glass I tell them both, "Whatever. What you're both telling me is I have half the supernatural world after me because of who I don't know and what I don't know. What I do know is that there's a source out there, somewhere, that I innocently stumbled upon and they either want it, want me dead for knowing about it, or just plain want me so they can control it? Is that about summed up?"

They both answer again, once again annoyingly in sync, "Yes."

"Great! I better find it before they find me finding it or I'm found out for the fraud that I really am."

When they both open their mouths at the same time again, I lift the nearest heavy book and threaten them with it. "Don't do it," I tell them both.

"Feisty." Jedrek shivers as if my threat provoked a response. His wink tells me otherwise.

"Does anyone on this lame *Scooby Doo* team have a plan?" I ask either of them, realizing we just became a very real we.

"Of course."

It's Jedrek who answers, as it would be.

"Let's take my car, though. Yours has that creepy old lady."

"Nuh-uh," GiGi Jo says, crossing her arms to add finality to her refusal. "You don't really think I'm just going to hand her over to the likes of you?"

"Well, you did send her into a mystical lion's den. So, yes. Yes, I do." Jedrek is holding the door open, making a grand gesture of it even. His mirth is gone. His blue eyes aren't dancing anymore, but they are drowning in a color of warning. "This is going to get done, Jo. With me or without me, they are coming. We both know it."

"I know it, but I fear you more than I do them. I know what they want. It's what you want which has me worried," she tells him.

"Well screw it, I know nothing about what anyone wants so let's go," I shout with my frustration of feeling like an ornament in the room versus being allowed to be part of the conversation.

I don't wait for GiGi to answer my off-colored declaration. I won't waste my time asking about any more of their riddles, or their hidden meanings to their observations about my life. We have a little girl to put back in the earth. This I know. This I know well, and as per what the last hour has taught me, it's about the only thing I do know.

"Feisty!" he says again when I pass through the doorway.

"Asshole!" I label him with the same hint of amusement coloring my words. Except I'm not amused. Very much not amused.

Waiting for him to follow me out, I watch as he becomes the playboy flirt again. Just like my pastels, this act is his armor, his way of projecting how he wants the world to view him. But I saw something different. Whatever is coming has him worried.

"Who is coming?" I ask, but I hold low hopes of getting an answer.

Winking at me, he places one finger over his lips. "How do you know they aren't already here?" he almost whispers it, sending a shiver of apprehension, and something else, along my skin.

I hear his deep chuckle when I glance around us, trying to see what he sees. Everything looks as it always has. Even down to Ms. Dreberry pretending to sweep the sidewalk in front of her shop as an excuse to snoop on her neighbors. Nothing stands out to me. Nothing screams, or even tugs, for attention. It's just another day, in a small town, with a little dead girl roaming around. Nothing to see here at all.

Jedrek doesn't offer any explanation as to where we are going and I'm following him across the street like a stray, hoping for the best but unsure of where this will lead me.

Opening the door of a nineteen seventy Camaro, he tells me, "Get in."

"This is your car?" My voice doesn't hide my shock.

"One of them," he says with a voice so stuffed with ego it ruins my appreciation of the machine in front of me.

"And it just happens to be parked right in front of the shop, but you were standing at the house?"

"I'm not seeing the problem. How about you get in so we can go?" His smile is forced. It's not for me. It's for someone, or something, watching us and his little suggestion, as polite as it sounded, was more of a command.

Before I can turn to see what has him insisting upon our departure, he grabs my arm, pulling me to him in an embrace. I can feel the warmth of his body pressed to mine. I react, stiffening my body in his arms with shock, whispering mentally to a part of me to calm down, a part I'm slightly ashamed of at this moment.

Tucking his face close to my neck he whispers into my ear, "Get in the damn car."

When he releases me, I do just what he asked. Never turning to look at him or what is behind me, I slide into the leather seat confused with my body's betrayal.

"Thank you," Jedrek says with relief before shutting the door of the car.

85

I don't turn my head to follow his path around the car to his door. My eyes do all the work. They watch every motion of his body. The way his black hair flirts with the slight breeze. Even the way he sets his face to stone when he glances around the area one last time, they memorize it all and I hate them for it, but I can't seem to make them look away.

Starting the car with its deep rumble, Jedrek thankfully doesn't start conversation after he slides in. He doesn't spare the tires, letting our exit become obnoxious. I giggle like a little girl before I can catch myself.

"What?" he asks again, trying to sound mirthful, but his eyes keep glancing to the mirrors ruining his attempt for casual.

"How did you just happen to have a car waiting?"

"Where else would a car be?"

I do turn to him now. "Where you left it?"

"Well, that doesn't seem always practical. Now does it?" Jedrek doesn't force his mirth now. He's back to tight smirks and lifted eyebrows. He's back to enjoying my confusion.

"You know what?" I hold up my hands, trying to stop a conversation which will only hold more questions than revelations. "I don't even care. So, you have magic cars? Not even the weirdest thing suggested today." Settling back into my seat, I cross my arms with the pouting I feel headed my way. "How am I supposed to save the world from mystery people when I've just found out there are mystery people?"

"You're not," Jedrek is almost laughing, maneuvering the car through the slower traffic of the streets.

"Isn't this what that's all about?"

Jedrek is laughing now. Sharp, male sounds of amusement fill the space around me before he says, "My littlest witch, the only thing you're going to save is the abused dirt around a child's grave. Maybe the sod, as well, but not the world."

"And the source?" My voice is high pitched again, almost shrieking with his dismissal of me.

Jedrek makes a face of compromise, shrugging his shoulders a little. "The source is my problem, but yes, I will need you to recover it."

"Why me? There must be other witches you're more familiar with?"

"Oh, I'm very familiar with many witches."

The way he says it wrinkles my face with disgust. "That's not what I meant, but okay, why not one of them?"

"Long answer or short?"

"Short."

"Fair enough," he says, shifting the car into a different gear when he merges into traffic. "I can't make mortals do anything. I can tempt them. Persuade them. But the whole free will thing given to mortals has a bunch of boring fine print I have to follow."

"You have rules?"

"Everyone has rules." He doesn't bother to disguise his annoyance. "It's an understanding, per se. I need a witch to stop a witch, but most witches are aligned with a coven, or house, which means even more rules. You are not."

"Meaning?"

"You have a different set of rules, but basically, and plainly speaking, you can go against any house because you don't have a house. You're not aligned or governed."

I nod my head as if I understand everything he is saying. "Right. What's the big deal about what I do?"

Jedrek sighs, sounding bored, but he doesn't answer.

Catching the clue that he is over the Q and A part of our trip, I settle deeper into the seat. "I feel like one of those annoying cast types where she suddenly finds out there's all this stuff about her that she never knew. Like I'm just going to magically become this thing to save the world."

"You're not going to save the world," he tells me again with laughter. "You're going to piss off a bunch of very powerful things, as you call them, which will want you dead or controlled, but saving the world is not on the to-do list."

"Or part of the rules?"

He smiles at me and I hate the little twinge it strums along my skin.

"Like I said, the rules are different for you," he repeats with an unusual amount of joy.

"Why do I have a feeling we are about to break a few?"

"Because, my littlest witch, we are."

"My name is Harper," I tell him with the angst of a toddler being mocked.

"Oh, I know your name," he says, chuckling his deep laugh. "And soon they will know it, too."

I want to ask him who 'they' are and why 'they' matter so much. I want to know why the thought of them angry makes him mentally drift off to some place of amusement. Like a spoiled child, I want to stomp my feet, demanding to know the why me and the why of it all. Out of all the witches he knows, why won't he tell me why it's me?

I want him to tell me why GiGi was casted in such shadows of fear from their meeting, and the riddle filled conversation. How does he know her? What's their past? Instead, I listen to his amused sounds wondering where the hell my life is going, and if I should have worn better shoes, or maybe even boots, for how over my head we are about to become.

fter riding in a car which would have paid for most of my life's expenses, forever, the shock of the red brick building we pull in front of shouldn't have been so jarring. But it is. I'm not only wearing the wrong shoes; I missed the whole wardrobe memo for our little day trip.

My eyes roam the ivy-covered columns supporting the portico. I can smell the still flowering jasmine with its reluctance to admit the season is changing. The white, waxy, petals seem to stare at me just as hard as I'm staring at the building. They, like me, know I'm out of place with my unkept ponytail and sensible, pastel outfit. Suddenly I'm even ashamed of the panties and the bra I picked purely for comfort with their worn cotton fabric begging to be retired from rotation.

"Madam?" the gentleman who opened the door asks when I hesitate to exit the imagined safety of Jedrek's car.

"Excuse her," Jedrek mockingly whispers to the man. "She's a tad shy, but wow, when you get her talking there is just no shutting this one up!"

Jedrek is laughing at his own joke, making it as if we have known each other forever. The valet doesn't join the laughter. His face never molds into any visible sign of any emotion. He is standing in a red suit jacket and black slacks, staring at Jedrek with such disinterest,

Jedrek may as well be another flower on the climbing vines around us.

"Tough crowd," Jedrek says, turning to me with an outstretched hand.

He is wearing a smile upon his face, but it doesn't reach his eyes. He's trying to do that thing again where he thinks I can read and understand his hidden clues or messages. It's flattering, but apparently, I'm not as smart as he thinks I am, or as smart as I'm supposed to be. I haven't had a clue about what's going on since meeting him.

He wiggles his fingers, either coaxing, or close to demanding me, out of the car. Rolling my eyes, I accept his help. The gravel crunches under my feet. Something about the sound seems to be a louder, hidden clue about what is about to happen than any eye contact Jedrek has offered. But it's not the gravel which has my heart catching speed. It's not the flowers, or Jedrek, or the valet who now watches me with a blank face, but interested eyes stirring the whispers in my head I always fight to keep silent. There's magic here and it's playing with me, tasting me, testing my walls with a curiosity of a living thing.

"Oh good!" Jedrek almost shouts. "I was afraid she wouldn't be in today."

The valet isn't fazed by the outburst. He simply opens the giant, thick wooden door with its arched frame for us to enter, but my feet are doing that annoying thing where they don't listen. I'm stuck, frozen in place as this force surrounds me with an almost warning. The owner of this magic is all but pushing me back into the car, removing my walls to my own magic as fast as I can replace them. I've never felt anything near this strong, this stubborn before. I'm curious, like a cat willing to risk its remaining lives to discover what's moving just beyond the door. I want to explore how this is possible, but when I allow the spell in far enough to taste the magic, my curiosity becomes confusion.

"It's not possible," I whisper, as my shock slips from mental observation to verbal dismay.

"What's not?" Jedrek has turned to enter the once grand house turned into a spa as if he's been here a thousand times. "That the witch who just happened to be poking your patience in the graveyard just happens to be here poking it now?" Turning towards me, he smirks, lifting his eyebrows, he says in an exaggerated style, "Shocking!"

"How long have you been following me?" I almost yell at his back, rushing to catch up to him. I can only imagine the show we are causing to what is normally a very well repeated day for those we pass.

"I have no idea what you're talking about." Jedrek is answering me, but that's all the attention he is sparing for my question.

He is searching for someone, or something. He twirls his sunglasses by the arm of one side, lost in his observations of the large lobby with its shining hardwood floors and perfectly crisp painted walls. Oversized couches are placed in perfectly random locations, filling the large room with seating for the rich, and not humble about it, in white robes thicker than my comforter. My little unicorn robe seems rather pathetic as I watch the many people float to and from the lobby. My fingers almost itch to reach out and touch one of the soft robes, but years of being the target of social awkwardness keeps my urges safely at bay.

"Is she here?" I whisper, still watching those around me with what can only be called, robe envy. "Wait. How did you know she'd be here? Do you stalk all the witches?"

I want to sound offended when I ask. His soft laugh hints I failed.

"Did you think you were special?" he asks, looking to me with a mischievous look.

"Never a day in my life," I reply before I can stop myself.

Jedrek places a finger to his lips. "Shhh," he says. "Your trauma is showing."

"Being an ass is an art for you, isn't it?"

He shrugs, returning his attention to his search. "You do make it rather easy."

Tugging me to him, he spins me to face down one of the hallways joined to the lobby. He whispers in my ear, "Look familiar?"

I would answer him if all logic wasn't just stolen from me. A second ago I was ready to match his remark with one of my own, telling him how easy he makes hating him, or something along those very witty lines. Now, I don't even remember my name as the heat from his body wraps around my own body, tighter than the clinched robes I was craving to feel.

"Well?" he whispers again.

I'm fighting to remember why we are here and what his impatient voice is asking of me. When I see her, deep in a fake smile of conversation with a man, I remember everything. There, in all of her purple hair and casual demeanor, is the witch from the night with the Ripples. Seeing her brings her taste to my throat, tickling it with her signature tartness of the aftertaste of her powers.

"I'm going to take that sharp inhale as a 'yes'," he tells the concave of my neck and a part of me wilts when he withdraws from our embrace.

"You're just going after her?" I hiss, chiding myself for being so ridiculous, mentally listing all the reasons I hate him to chase away the butterflies he has caused.

Jedrek smiles at my agitation. Ignoring my question, he asks one of his own. "Coming?" he asks, and his smile widens when I feel my blush spreading from my cheeks to my chest.

"Just do us both a favor?" he asks me when I finally catch up to him. "Act like you're a real witch."

"What does that even mean?" I hiss again in an attempt to try to not have the whole place watching us. "Want me to cackle? Find flying monkeys? Sing a song to coax children into the woods?"

"How about just not talk?" he asks, wearing his face framed with mirth.

"I really hate you," I tell him, but I'm mostly telling my vagina, who is doing her best to argue that I don't.

He shows me one more smile before turning into the flirting bastard act I've watched too many times already.

"Regan!" he shouts down the hall as if he owns the place, completely not interested in the many who stare at his invasion of their tranquility.

I watch as she quickly dismisses the man glaring at Jedrek. Her body holds a similar posture as GiGi when Jedrek arrived. Her smile is forced, fake and curved with trepidation. The way her eyes bounce from him to me following is his wake portrays all the falsehood of her painted smile.

"Jedrek, how nice to see you again," Regan coos with her lie.

I mentally give her points for her voice being mostly steady.

"Am I the only one who hasn't met you till now?" I ask, risking betraying my own false bravado.

"Now, darling," Jedrek turns to me with a smile of warning. "I thought we agreed you'd let me do the talking?"

"No, darling," I repeat the pet name with a touch more sarcasm than he used. "You agreed I wouldn't talk, and I agreed you are an ass."

For a second, his face flashes a look of contempt, a quick coloring to his natural calm behavior, but either he saw something upon my face to change his mind or another mood swing hit him. "She's so adorable, isn't she?" Jedrek asks Regan. "There are days I could just kill her with how stinking cute she is!"

Regan is looking from him to me with her fake smile still proudly boasting of her unease. She says nothing to agree or disagree, much as GiGi had when we were at the shop.

"Now, Regan," Jedrek's voice pulls her eyes fully to him. "Tell me why you were sneaking around and peeping on my little witch here."

Jedrek is completely calm, almost playful with his question. He's leaning on a cleverly placed side table covered in pamphlets and brochures of the spa. He's all smiles and gentle eyes, reminding me of a cat toying with its prey before fully launching into an attack.

"If you're here, then you know why," Regan tells him, her smile never slipping.

"I know someone has been very naughty," Jedrek whispers playfully.

"We have our rules," Regan quips, almost sounding insulted.

"And the Ripples?" Jedrek asks, grabbing my arm in a fake motion of tenderness when hearing my inhale.

Regan shrugs. "And they have their rules."

"Which are?" I ask, trying not to wince from the pain of Jedrek's hand tightening on my tender flesh.

"To stay out of your way. No one wants a war again."

Jedrek's grip lessens when hearing Regan's response. "No. No one wants that again. So, if you, who very much follows the rules, were to know who is very much not following the rules, you would have to tell Harper?"

It isn't a question as much as fact check. He just phrased it open ended for Regan's pride.

There's a pause, a momentary tick of the second hand on the clock keeping track of the day where it sits on the table. It's just enough of a mistake for Regan to panic and Jedrek to attack.

"If I were to find out you're being naughty, Regan," he almost purrs. "I would have to be naughty too. Very naughty."

The last part he drops his voice to a husk of his normal pitch. Deep inside those two words vibrates a fear which reaches down my throat to clamp around my heart. I can feel it skipping beats, tossing me into a small panic I can't explain. I'm not the only one feeling it. Regan is holding onto the doorframe near her for support. Her eyes are wide, seeing something only she can see. The gentle apricot coloring of her skin has faded to a grey pallor. With breath, shaky and uneven, she nods, no longer trusting her voice.

"Long as we understand each other." Jedrek returns to his playful, sarcastic self. "I so hate when we don't all get along. Do tell Deon I'm taking extra special care of their father for me?"

Whatever I was feeling is slipping from me the way a thick lotion cools on the skin, slowly and chillingly. My heart is returning to its normal pattern, unlodging itself from my airway.

"Oh, darling," Jedrek calls me his mockery of a pet name when seeing me recovering from whatever the hell just happened. "You look positively chilled."

He doesn't ask the man who has remained near enough to be seen but not hear our conversation for his robe. Jedrek just takes it, twirling the man with his action. To my surprise, the now nude man, doesn't offer any resistance, or seeming humiliation, over the treatment. He's now standing unrobed, cupping a very ungroomed area, as he rushes further down the hall into an open room.

"Here, he insisted." Jedrek is draping the robe around me, enjoying my look of discomfort and shock.

With the grand show he has demonstrated to those around us, he waves, not waiting for me to follow his path of exit. He doesn't have to wait. He knows I will. Once again, not because I want to, but because what the hell else am I to do?

Glancing over my shoulder to Regan, still grasping on the wood of the door like it's a life raft, I see she still hasn't fully collected herself. Whatever I felt was just a brush of what Jedrek somehow did to her. She isn't wearing her smile anymore. She's let the mask fall away and now I'm staring into grey eyes filled with a warning. Unfortunately for us both, I'm still not smart enough to read the invisible words she's trying to share with me. I have a feeling, that inadequacy, will be the death of me, literally.

Neither of us speak to the other for the ride back to Great Hexpectations. Jedrek is humming some tune he seems to remember. The only tune he seems to remember because he does it over and over again. Even if my nerves weren't already frayed while wearing a robe once worn by a nude man, and the other many cherries of the day, his repeat of the same notes would have sent me over the cliff of annoyance, to the gulf of manic, even on my most non-hormonal days.

It wasn't until he steered his car behind my own, he spoke his first words.

"I'm sorry for what happened back there."

He's hidden by the early shadows of the faded sun. They encompass him, shielding his face with their blurring of his features. I've never heard this shade of his voice before. Normally he's flaunting and full of flirting colors like a peacock strutting through the landscape. Now, he's timid, shy with his slow, carefully thought out words.

I hear this new voice of his say, "I didn't think I could even influence you. It's comforting to know I can," he says with a touch of the familiar ego I know, "but I didn't think it would happen."

"Why wouldn't it?"

He sighs, moving in his seat as if uncomfortable by the complaining leather. "Because I'm not supposed to be able to. Not even one as old as I, an original if you must place a title on it, should be able to."

"So, it's a good thing, I'm sure for your ego, to be able to? Or is it supposed to be a good thing for my ego you shouldn't be able to? I really can't keep track of all of these side notes." I can hear the exhaustion in my tone. My mind is as over today as my body.

"Neither, Harper," he says, still using the same sad pitch. "It means we are fucked if they really want to test you. You're not strong enough to fight them and we just rang their doorbell with an invitation to try."

I laugh. I can't help it. "I don't even know who they are and if I remember correctly, I didn't ring anything. I wasn't even supposed to be allowed to talk."

"You're right," he sighs again. "It was someone else who dropped into the crowded, most popular bar, with nothing more than a loudmouth and naïve outlook."

"That was a mistake, maybe, potentially," I add in a slight agreement. "but not a full grand invitation into my life."

"What did you think would happen?"

"I thought," I start swallowing my emotions back down into the depths where I try to keep them. "I would find an answer for a grieving family."

"Have you?" he has the nerve to ask me.

"No! You know I haven't!" I scream my frustration into the car. "All I've learned is I know nothing about what I am, or who 'they' are, or what 'they' want but 'they' are coming because of everything I don't know about who I am, what I am, or who 'they' are!"

Jedrek's little laughs pull me from the edge of my building emotional break down. "Better now?"

I'm not. I can feel the tears sneaking their way beyond the will of my self-control.

"If it were up to me, I would tell you everything. As it sits, it's not."

"Why not?" I ask, fighting my escaping maturity.

"Because a part of me doesn't want you to know."

"Shouldn't I know if not knowing means we are both fucked?"

He chuckles again. "I suppose that's a question for Jo."

"Then I'll never know," I grumble, getting out of the Camaro.

I shut the door to the sound of his masculine laughter, and smile, despite my best efforts to stop myself. He doesn't leave until I am in my own car, still covered in the stolen robe. I ignore the sounds coming from the back seat. I can already picture the scowl of disapproval Myrtle will be wearing.

I shouldn't have. I should have checked but I didn't. I don't until I see her sitting in the seat beside me and not in her normal spot in the rearview mirror. She's staring straight ahead, focusing on something far away or at least beyond my line of sight. But the noises are still coming from behind me. There are moments when you are almost positive your heart will break your ribs, tearing through your flesh to escape the panic your brain is whispering. I'm on my second one today.

"If you turn, or give any signal..." the male voice leaves the threat in the air, letting me form my own conclusions.

"I don't have any money," I weakly whisper. "And to be honest, for a good time, you're probably better off with your hand and a good porno."

"I wasn't sent for either of those."

"Well, that's good, I guess. For both of us."

I'm stalling. Trying to find a way to escape the predicament I have stumbled into. Growing up on B-flick horror movies with GiGi, yelling at the females on the screen for their stupidity, I normally check for such situations. Not because, until now, I believed they would ever happen, but because it was set in my mind to do it. I could almost hear GiGi berating me each time if I didn't.

"Why were you sent?" I dare ask, hoping Jedrek figures out something is wrong as we both sit here in our cars on an empty street.

"She has a message for you," the voice whispers.

"...and it is?"

"Forget about all of this or risk it all."

"That's not much of an option."

There is only silence from the back seat now. A stillness which seems thicker than should be possible in such an already small space. I strain to hear a breath, a movement, some clue as to what the man behind me is doing now that he's stopped talking, but there is nothing. My passenger still stares out the windshield with no interest in what is happening around her. Easy for her. She's already dead.

Slipping my hand to the door's latch, I wince with every sound the cloth seat makes, positive at any moment the man will speak again, or worse. The release of the metal latch sounds like shrapnel, spreading its damage through the car, but still, he remains silent behind me. I don't wait to test my luck. Without any grace, other than the goal to escape, I almost throw myself from my seat, sure at any moment the threat he left hanging in the air around me will tighten like a noose around my throat.

Tripping over my own feet with my fear, I land as a most ungraceful heap in the middle of the road. Still, I wait to hear my attacker rushing for me. When he doesn't, it is almost more unsettling than if he were.

"You're that afraid of her?" Jedrek has exited his own car, leaning against the high gloss of its metal frame. He's looking with unhidden amusement from me, where I lay in the middle of the road like an attempted roadkill, and to the woman who is also watching me from the passenger seat with her normal annoyed face.

"No," I tell him, still catching my breath. "Not her. Him in the back seat."

Jedrek moves before I have finished my explanation. I reach for him, knowing he is unarmed and not knowing the same about the man in the back seat. Sidestepping my outstretched arm of caution, he seems to glide towards the car, pulling, without hesitation or worry, open the back door. What he sees doesn't stir the same sense of urgency as was stirred in me.

"This is what threatened you?" he asks, turning to unblock my view of my car.

Stretched across the beach styled seat is dead man. A very obviously dead man. In his hand, he holds a wilting yellow carnation. The bright coloring of its petals contrasts sharply with the greying pallor of the man's skin. The stench, which I somehow missed until he opened the door, rolls out as if it's a physical cloud, mocking me even more.

Jedrek pulls the body out, bouncing it against the pavement. Standing over it, he chuckles, but not from amusement. His laughter is thick with disgust and his eyes hold a fire of anger.

"He was not dead a moment ago," I insist.

The ground feels like quicksand underneath my feet when I stand. I'm sinking into confusion and fear. I know this man was just talking, threatening me, sent from some unknown woman with a riddle of her own. Now, he lays before me, rapidly rotting in the street. The yellow flower has slipped from his hand. His extended fingers seem to reach for it like a lost token.

"He is very dead." Jedrek kicks the man, sending him rolling forward with putrid fluids left in his wake.

"He was speaking!" I raise my voice trying to convince him I'm not as insane as I feel standing here watching as the man slowly stops rolling.

Jedrek laughs again, louder, and still tainted with disgust. "And what did this dead man say to you?"

I repeat his threat. "Forget about all of this or risk it all."

"While holding the yellow carnation?"

I can't tell if he's asking me or making an observation about the current situation.

Jedrek turns his full attention to me. "Do you understand?"

"No!"

Letting out a frustrated breath, giving it almost a sound, he stares up into the night sky. "This, littlest witch, was a test. You see," he says, slowly walking towards me in such a way to set my stomach with unease, "if you really are what you say you are, what Jo says you are, what everyone thinks you are, you should have sensed him in your back seat. Even if you didn't," he stands in front of me, touching my face with just the tips of his fingers, "you should have been able to control him. For that is what you are, death, and he is very dead."

"I raise the dead." My voice is just a whisper of strength. It floats away from me before I can muster any conviction.

"And then you?" Jedrek asks, almost matching my whisper.

"Control them," my whisper admits.

Jedrek's fingers are tapping my cheek bone. It's a forceful touch but also like a feather caressing my skin.

"The flower?" I ask, hushed and concealed with worry.

"The message."

Jedrek slips from me. Without his fingers, my cheek feels chilled. I watch him retreat to his car with an almost sadness aching inside of me. I feel like a child saddened for not meeting someone's approval. My mouth moves with the urge to speak words to win back his smile, but I have none.

"Go home littlest witch." I hear him say. "Go tell Jo everything which has happened. Tell her, her little lies are going to kill you. Tell her she knows now. Tell her she's coming and I'm not sure even I can keep you safe anymore."

I watch his car until there is nothing but the red haze of his taillights. Standing here in the night, with a corpse beside me, I feel raw. My life is no longer my own. It now belongs to those who ply me with riddles and hidden threats. To those whom I do not know, but whisper about me in some strange way I cannot comprehend. I'm Harper Buckland. I'm a simple witch, trying to make sense of what that means. I can't possibly be what Jedrek wants me to be, or what GiGi hints I may be, but yet as I stare at this forsaken and discarded man, my fingers twitch with a foreign feeling.

I gather the fragile flower wondering how something so simple could cause such a reaction as I once again sit behind the steering wheel.

"Aren't you the same as the flower?"

I lift my eyes to the rearview mirror when I hear her familiar voice.

"Such a simple thing, causing so much a reaction."

Her eyes bore into mine much the same way Regan's had earlier. This time though, I understand completely.

iGi is waiting for me. She's trying to look as if she hasn't been. She wants me to believe she's been sitting at the kitchen nook, sipping something warm, and no doubt laced, but the swinging, hanging plant she must have rushed past to make it to the table destroys the illusion, despite her best efforts to keep her face empty and her eyes glued to a magazine.

"Go ahead," I coax her, coming to lean on my normal spot. "Ask."

GiGi puts a false surprised look upon her face hearing my voice and entrance. "I didn't hear-"

The old woman moves from behind the table with speed I rarely see. The problem is that speed is heading right for me.

With her eyes wide, she clutches the robe I still have draped around me. Her hands roughly search for something along its collar, and when she finds the artistic scroll work of a logo, her coloring makes me look tanned.

"He took you there, didn't he?" Her voice is a soft hiss, something a cat would make from a dark corner of a room before streaking across it to trip you.

"He took me to a fancy spa, yes," I tell her, pulling away from this woman who seems to have become possessed by demons I don't have names for. "But that's not even the best part of my day."

I sidestep her, walking to the fridge with my body suddenly remembering food hasn't been a top priority today.

"It gets better than going to a spa where the rich pay the supernatural for their powers?"

I don't have to turn from my foraging to know her arms are crossed and she's five seconds from speaking rapid Italian.

"Thought that place was weird," I say in agreement around a mouthful of chicken cutlet.

I still won't look in her direction. I busy myself with the plate of leftovers like it's my last meal. It may be with how she's simmering, waiting for just one reason to go full warpath. When, without thinking, I place the crumpled flower on the counter beside me, I may as well have launched a grenade.

"What is that?" I hear her feet moving before her questions dissolve into a rapid avalanche. "Where was this? Who gave it to you? Why do you have it?"

"Which question do you want me to answer first? You threw out a few there."

GiGi Jo never struck me growing up. She had other ways of steering me back to the path she felt was correct. She strikes me now. Swatting the back of my head with her open hand before spilling forth the language I still haven't fully decoded.

"All of them!" she declares with an open palm hanging in the air.

"It's a flower. In a dead man's hand. The dead man, technically. Not sure." I tell her all of my answers between chewing, not caring about table etiquette.

My answers intrigue and worry her, but at least the Italian has stopped, and she seems calmer. "Elaborate."

Sighing, I begin the retelling. "He was in the back seat of my car. I didn't know he was dead, and that seems to really have pissed off Jedrek. The flower was in his hand and I'm supposed to ask you about it. I'm supposed to tell you, your little lies are going to be what gets us all killed. Well, mostly me it seems, but 'she' is coming, and I failed some grand test of hers."

GiGi's eyes may be casted in my direction, but it's not me she is seeing. It is not even this room.

"Who *is* she?" I ask.

"That doesn't matter. It doesn't have to, anyway. Not if we find this source and return it. She'll have no use for you then." GiGi says with her normal style of answering with a riddle she has taken to, as of late.

"Why would I be of use to her when it comes to this source?" I ask, still eating from the plate of leftovers. I too can pretend to be calm and uninterested while inside being churned like an angry sea.

"Because only one who can control the dead can use the magic inside it. The witch who is using it now, has stayed under the radar by manipulating humans to use it. I doubt she even really understands what she has done, or awakened, by her greed."

"You talk like you've figured out what it is. Last we talked it was just this mysterious source of magic."

GiGi pulls on the robe, stripping it from my body, and storms into the living room amid our conversation. I follow her, lost as to her sudden change in emotional lanes with her action. She has stormed into this room, tossing the robe of amazing fluffiness into the old brick fireplace the home was built around. I'm not shocked to see her dousing it with the lighter fluid she keeps on the hearth. Nor am I moved into action when she pulls the matches from behind a dust covered photo.

When the robe becomes an inferno, I ask her, "Did you even open the flume first?"

"Damn it," she mutters.

"I really liked that robe."

"You have others," her voice tells me, but she's watching the flames eat the fabric with a fascination.

"Why was that even necessary?"

"What did he tell you about that spa?" she asks me, still with her voice distant.

"Nothing. We went to see a witch name Regan."

GiGi sighs, leaning her head against the wooden hearth. "I told you to stay away from them, didn't I? I warned you about this."

Crossing my arms, I try to remember her ever mentioning Regan or the spa. "Pretty sure you've never talked about Regan or this spa."

"The Ripples, Harper. I warned you about the Ripples."

I feel as if I've been drinking cheap tequila for days. My head is swimming, lost and unable to connect the dots before me. Even when so many are placing them, I can't figure out how they are connected.

"Look, I'm going to need you, or Jedrek, or someone to just start at the beginning and then move to the ending. Right now, you two are in the middle of the book and I don't even have chapter one, much less the prologue to read, to understand what the hell is going on."

"Sit," she says motioning to the couch.

It feels like story time and the book is going to be filled with ghosts who haunt her. Sitting beside her, I can see the flames reflected in her glasses. She doesn't say anything. She just sits, staring into the fire of a robe which seems to be burning for an impossibly long time.

"Should that still be on fire?" I ask her, putting a voice to my thoughts.

GiGi shrugs. "Who knows what that thing is made of. I just know I hate them. I hate that place and I hate the Ripples. You didn't work two cases that night, Harper. You worked one, the same one. I figured most of it out today while you were away. There's only so many things on this plane which can wake the dead. Most are accounted for, as far as Charlotte can tell. Which means, the ones which aren't, aren't from this place."

"When Jedrek showed up, panting after you like a wolf in grand mom's house, Charlotte did some asking on her end. The source we are after is a crossroads demon's box."

I asked for chapter one. This doesn't feel like chapter one. Listening to her, I think she's still pretty far into the book of explanations.

"You know you're still speaking gibberish to me, right?"

She lifts one eyebrow quickly as her answer. "If what Jedrek says is true, we don't have the time to go fully into it like I should have years ago. I didn't want this day to come. I thought I could keep you hidden, keep my promise to your mother, but even she didn't fully understand what you would become."

"You say that like I'm going to grow horns or wings. Maybe a tail? Will it be a cute tail? Maybe with a little curl on the end?"

"Enough with your jokes," she turns to glare at me, "You must understand: the Ripples own the witches. Jedrek owns the Ripples. Jedrek owns everyone, and if Jedrek is scared or worried, we are as he says, fucked."

"GiGi, the Ripples own half of the town, and most likely other towns, but how does a family own a whole coven?" My hands are doing that annoying thing they do when I'm beyond frustrated. They move with each word, stretching outward, or flexing my fingers to add punctuation.

"Not just a coven. All the covens in the area. Every witch which answers to a house answers to the Ripples. All except for one. They are the last true house of unbound magic." GiGi corrects me.

"How is that even possible?"

"Because it's the deal they made with the vampires long ago."

"Wait," I almost shout, standing to pace the room. "There's vampires? Here? In town? Don't tell me they sparkle in the sun or chase after teenage girls filled with hormones and daddy issues?"

"You with the jokes again."

"If I don't joke, my head will explode. Basically, what you're skipping over is everything is real? These things just blend in and walk around?"

GiGi laughs dryly. "You're a witch who had her dead parents ringing the doorbell one night after staying up too late to watch a horror movie and you're shocked vampires are real? It's going to be a long year for you then."

"Why is that?"

"Because the Ripples are werewolves, and now they have your scent. There's nowhere you could go and they wouldn't find you. Nor is there any place you could hide from them. You didn't raise their father for them to ask questions. You raised their father for them to ask about you. At best, it's one of their witches who has the box."

"At worst?"

"They think you're the witch with it."

"Who is 'she'?"

"The collector."

"What does she collect?" I ask fearing I already know her answer.

"Witches, Harper. She collects witches. She sleeps until something stirs her. Something so powerful, she leaves her world of dreams and nightmares to torment us in life. She's the reason we sleep with a dream catcher woven from hair of every generation, to confuse her and keep her eyes from us. She's the reason we craft our poppets, stuffing them with cloth holding our blood so she will search for them and not for us. She's our boogey man."

"But *who* is she?" I ask, pushing harder for something more than just old tales and whispered rumors.

"Enough, Harper. To speak of her is to summon her. Leave it be. Focus on what is before us, and with any luck, she'll go back to sleep."

"Jedrek said I failed her test."

"Good," GiGi says in her sigh. "Then maybe she will think she was mistaken and lose interest."

"I have to visit the Ripples then?"

"You have to visit the Ripples then," GiGi repeats. "Preferably before Jedrek does."

"Why?"

"Because if you find the box first, Charlotte can hide it, keep it from doing any more harm. If he finds the box first, he will kill every witch who dared to use it and return it to the demon it belongs to, to further collect souls."

"No pressure," I tell her with my own sigh as I collapse back to the couch.

"None at all," she says, still watching the robe burn.

"Seriously, how is that thing still on fire?"

"You don't want to know," GiGi says, and maybe I don't.

Her voice is heavy with ghosts haunting her. She's lost in the memories of some past I never asked about and one she never spoke about, either. Watching her, hearing her, she's right. I really don't want to know.

Parking my poor Honda along the rows of cars with more vowels to their names than should be allowed, she's a blaring contrast. Her paint isn't the high gloss of what's around her. Her color isn't as dark, but she's paid for and sometimes that little fact can make a car the prettiest of the lot.

It took me hours to find my outfit for today's little meeting. What does one wear to the house of the richest people in the town who just happen to be werewolves? Toss in the fact they also seem to own a couple of covens and suddenly you have the most interesting game of monopoly ever played. I'm about to try to pass go, but I doubt I'll collect my two hundred. After hearing more of GiGi's stories over breakfast, I'll be lucky to keep my head.

Standing on the obnoxious porch, which I'm pretty sure is made from some style of swirling granite, I regret picking the mauve dress. I should have gone with the slacks. Slacks are easier to run away in, or recover when tripping in the forest, or whatever it is you do when being chased by rich werewolves.

While standing here, preparing a speech consisting of balanced proportions of questioning instead of accusation, the door opens, ruining any imagined perception of any authority I thought I may have, having been caught talking to myself. The woman stares at me, reading my startled face perfectly. She's the perfect platinum blonde the Ripples boast of with the matching body and bright eyes. The town jokes of them being vampires with their time evading beauty. I guess no one thinks of werewolves. I hadn't.

"They are expecting you," she tells me with a playful smirk of a warning.

"They?" I ask hoping to be given the rundown of names waiting at my execution.

"Yes. They. He said you would be coming," she tells me, stepping away to allow me to enter. "I guess he was right."

"Jedrek?" I ask, saying the name like the curse he's become.

She nods, still flashing her smirk. "Are the rumors true?"

"There's just so many of them to know which ones you are asking about."

She leans in to not be overheard with her question. "That he's amazing in bed."

My face reacts like a preteen being told what happens between adults. My stomach answers differently. "No," I tell her. "That one is not true, or at least I don't know if it's true," I quickly add, floundering with embarrassment.

"Pity," she says, answering other rumors she has heard about us.

She's all hips and sways while I follow her through the house. The walls are covered in wood paneling, casting a warm feel to the grand mansion. It's the only warmth. Everything from the tall oil paintings of past relations to the furniture feels cold, empty of the joy such furnishings should provide. All this finery and not a single smiling face amid it. The holidays must be draining.

"Through there," she motions at set of sliding doors.

I wish I was wearing the same smile as she. I wish I felt even an ounce of her confidence. Taking one last breath, I nod for her to slide them open, like a curtain of a play, I convince myself of my role I will play.

"Littlest witch!" Jedrek shouts with mirth when I enter. "You're only slightly late."

Jedrek makes a show of checking an invisible watch upon his wrist, before looking at me again. His eyes are dancing with blue mischief. He's wearing his normal black on black ensemble with black pressed shirt and slacks. His shoes almost glow as deeply as his car's paint, which I somehow managed to miss among the many outside.

"I wasn't aware there was a meeting time," I reply.

"It's generally understood one arrives before noon." Deon is sitting in an oversized chair, watching me like I'm a small animal she may toy with if motivated. "But it is also generally understood witches answer to a coven, and I've been told you don't understand any of the rules we have among us."

"You mean answer to you?" I hide my nervousness behind a voice stuffed falsely with steel. I'm strolling the large room with its fireplace empty and black with soot, doing all I can to avoid Deon's eyes which keep pace with me.

Her hair is pulled high into a bun upon her head. The blonde shades of her hair almost glow, absorbing the light from the room. She balances her cigarette between her fingers. It smokes like incense, filling the room with its heavy scent.

"In time," she tells me, "you will. They always do."

She says this with such off-handed certainty, all I can do is lift my eyebrow with a silent mocking.

"Now, ladies," Jedrek interrupts the mounting ego game. "We are all here for the same reason."

"I doubt that," I sigh, knowing the reason we are here may be the same, but the many options after the reason are not.

Deon says nothing. She sits as if the chair is a throne. The only movement she makes is that of her foot, slightly swaying in her black leather pump. The red bottom flashes like an underbelly of warning before a serpent strikes.

"Well, at any rate," Jedrek aimlessly walks to where I have come to sit on a wooden desk, "it's not here."

"Here, as in this house, or here as in the possession of this family?" I ask him, matching his calm exterior.

He purses his lips, lifting his eyebrows before slowly casting his eyes to where Deon sits. "Both."

"But it was here," I loudly whisper to the room.

My strolling wasn't simply something to do. I had spent the little tour sending out my magic, pushing it through the walls and into the grounds saturated in the blood of witches which surround this home. In the midst of all the horrors I discovered, of all the secrets buried under rocks of lies, there was also a tickling, a soft tugging of something heavy, something foreign. It was an old magic, dark and tasting earthy, like a decadent dish.

Jedrek's eyes float back and forth across my face, trying to read any doubts or uncertainty. When seeing none, his mask of a jokester melts as he turns to where Deon sits. Without any words said between them, they exchange looks holding a whole conversation in a short span of seconds.

"It may have been," Deon admits, "but I have no knowledge of it now."

"Is that what Daddy told you?" I hear myself ask.

"Actually," she says turning her attention from Jedrek to myself, "Daddy said I should kill you the next time we meet. He had a thing for burning loose witches." She says the word 'Daddy' with enough acidic sarcasm to melt her own tongue.

"Trust me, Deon," Jedrek chuckles. "She is anything but loose."

When the joke isn't well received by either of us, he holds up hands in surrender.

"I know," I tell her, pushing a pen upon the desk back and forth. "I felt them. They told me all your dirty little secrets. They also told me the box was here, used by one of your own who once worked at the spa but is now, how did you phrase it? Oh yes. Loose."

I strike a nerve with Deon. I can see the soft twitch of a corner of her mouth.

"Where is this witch now?" Jedrek asks. His hands are spread out for either of us to answer.

"I don't know of the witch she speaks of," Deon insists, but I saw through her. "None of my witches would dare it."

I saw through her porcelain face, sculpted with its blank expression. She knows exactly who I speak of, but what she doesn't know is so do I. Jedrek is correct. I can control the dead. I can speak with the dead and they speak with me, and the dead here have plenty to say. In fact, they told me everything.

I smile at her, giving her much the same expression as Jedrek does when he knows a secret, he is not willing to share.

Jedrek presses his body close to mine. He leans in for a false kiss to my temple. Whispering into my ear, he asks me, "Are you sure of this?"

Some version of me, some part I know but am unfamiliar with, lets her fingers trace along his chest, testing each button along the trail. I let my magic stroke his skin, wrapping its tendrils of power around his ribs and taunt stomach. Whatever he sees in my eyes, catches his breath, removing his composure for a moment before he can collect himself.

"You could have just said yes," he whispers with a breath hot and shaky.

"Where's the fun in that?" I reply.

"Didn't take you for a girl who likes to have fun," he whispers to me, but for Deon he announces, "Well, then I guess there's no reason to be here anymore."

Draping his arm around my shoulders, he steers me away from the waiting beast in the armchair. Her foot is swaying a little faster now. Her cigarette, clinging to its last spark of life, drifts only a thin line of smoke, but I'm not done, yet.

"Have you gotten any yellow flowers as of late, Deon?" I ask her over my shoulder.

I can feel Jedrek's grasp tighten on my body. He sighs a sound of disdain.

"Daily," she tells us. "She's coming, isn't she?"

Jedrek doesn't answer her. He's staring at me with questions upon his face. I don't answer her, either. He firmly takes me from the room before my mouth can cause any more trouble. He nods at the perfect blonde replicas we pass. Each time he feels me begin to say something, his fingers dig into the flesh of my shoulder, warning me with bruises upon my flesh.

When I step into the soft grass, I can hear the whispers. Voices urging me with their desires of vengeance, pleas of help and the general mental caressing of finally having someone to speak with after so long. I can feel each one of their emotions merging with my own until it's hard to tell where I end, and they begin. They are showing me their deaths, their lives, their sorrows, and their joys until I feel as if I am them.

"You need to slow down."

I hear Jedrek's voice from some long hallway. It's covered in warnings and apprehension. It pulls on a part of me still scared with all that has happened; a part of me which knows something is wrong but ignored by the part of me reveling in this feeling.

He's shaking me, jostling me to gain my attention. "You need to slow down!"

I touch his lips, pushing them gently with my fingertips. They are soft, damp with his tongue nervously darting over the warm flesh. I pull his face towards mine, entangling my hands in his dark hair. I let my tongue mimic what my fingers just were. I test his lips with this new feeling, sucking on them gently before fully pressing them against his. He doesn't resist me. He lets me toy and play, giving as much as I am to this new venture. Only when my hands begin to roam low on his body does he pull away from me.

"You are power drunk," he tells me, whispering the words against my neck. "You must slow down."

He kisses my forehead, pausing as he presses against me. I can feel the cold chill so familiar from the day at the spa creeping through my veins. Like a chilled river, it flows inside my body, stealing the heat of my magic. When his lips leave my flesh chilled and aching, my head is my own again. The voices have simmered to a dull roar, but they're not overtaking or demanding. I can already feel the flush rushing to my face over my behavior.

"Don't," he whispers against my forehead. "Don't apologize. Don't make excuses. Never feel shame over what you are."

Cupping my face between his palms he pulls it even to his. We stare at one another for a moment in which time seems to stand still. I forget about the dead little girl, unearthed against her will. I forget about this mysterious woman whom everyone fears. I even forget about the hole I keep festering in my heart from the loss of my parents - as a warning to the suffering that loss can cause from those you let get too close. I only see his eyes, feel his warm hands, and remember the taste of his mouth against mine.

"My littlest witch," he whispers to me. "You will be my undoing."

There's a heavy silence between us now. It sits as thick as fog and as heavy as a winter quilt. Jedrek isn't humming. He fidgets with the old radio display of his car, trying to find anything to fill the void, as we once again head back to the spa.

"What will you say to her?" I ask with a voice hesitant to speak first.

"What should I say to her?" he asks, still shuffling through the radio noise. "I really wasn't going to say anything. She lied. She knew."

"Regan may not have," I offer in the defense of a woman I don't know. "Not fully."

He makes a sound of disdain upon hearing me. "No one keeps such a secret. What she had to go through to get it, no one would keep such a secret."

"I told you, it's not her. It someone close to her. They whispered her name, but I couldn't hear it. It was soft. Almost like they were afraid to say her name too loudly."

"She has to have a touch of necromancy in her blood to be able to handle the box," Jedrek muses as he drives us back to the spa. "They may have been afraid of her or known she could have been listening."

"Without being there?' I ask with full amazement.

Jedrek looks to me, smirking. "Yes, without being there."

"You're right. I do have a lot to learn."

"You have no idea." Jedrek says with flat honesty.

The building still has the punch of grandeur. As we drive through the swinging iron gate, I can't subdue the gasp of shock. It seems to stand even taller, the bricks a deeper hue and the vines thicker than when we were here before.

"It seems different," I tell Jedrek as we park and exit his black Camaro.

Jedrek sniffs the air. Shutting his door, he shrugs. "Mortals must be very bored." He holds up his hand before I can ask what he means. "Part of what the witches take feeds the building. The more 'clients'," he says the word with sarcasm, "the stronger the illusion. This place was an abandoned mansion before the Ripples took it over years ago. They found it easier to remodel with the many covens' magic than to actually pay a crew to come redo the whole place."

"I have so much to learn," I mutter behind him as I follow him up the path.

The same valet meets us at the door. Without a car to help me out of, I lacked an excuse for my reluctance to enter again. If warning bells and red flags were visible, this place would be decorated in them from every window to each proudly standing pillar. They would be displayed like banners or framed art upon the walls on the interior to clash with the white textured wallpaper hung to make the place feel upscale. The illusion shimmers in my mind, flashing between what is present and what was the past.

It wasn't the crumbling exterior causing my heart to flutter behind my fragile ribs. It was the blood. Blood streaking down the red bricks, painting them a dark shade of almost black. The handprints, pressed and smeared, screaming of those who were unable to escape, but there are no dead here. There are no screams from those souls locked in their purgatory, reliving their last horrific moments for all eternity. There's not even a shade of a ghost, or a shadow figure roaming, trapped between this world and the world it knew. Seeing what I am seeing, it seems impossible.

"This isn't right," I whisper out loud, to no one in particular.

"Ma'am?" the once silent valet asks.

Jedrek spins, wearing an amused expression. "Lookie there. Igor speaks," he contemptuously tells me.

I'm not looking at Jedrek though. My eyes are centered on the man who once stood tall in a red jacket and black slacks. The skin upon his face has shrunken, clinging to the bones of his cheeks. Eyes which once watched with intense scrutiny, are now pale globes, almost floating, rolling in rotting sockets. When he smiles at me, his lips are pulled too thin, cracking the skin to ooze a black substance down his chin and dripping onto his no longer pristine red jacket.

Jedrek's eyes swing from me to the man, mimicking the motion with his finger, pointing in the direction each time. "Why is he smiling at you?"

"Because I finally see him," I explain. "The real him."

"Well, I'm sure that's quite the bummer for you, but how about we move this little event inside?" Jedrek asks, unmoved by the fact that I'm seeing past the façade of the place.

"Sure," I reply. "I can't wait to see what's inside!" I fill my voice with such false cheer it borders on sarcasm and frustration.

I don't want to step through the entry way. I have already seen what awaits just beyond the grinning skull of the valet. I don't want to know what other truths are waiting to be whispered.

"There's no need," Regan's voice breaks through my mental prison.

Unbeknown to me, she has been leaning on the building's column, watching our arrival and all which came after. Her purple hair, fashioned in random braids, is held high, cascading around her face to frame it with the various shades. She is running her fingers through the grout of the bricks, toying with it like a pouting kid or a bored teen. Her white sock displaying the spa's logo is tightly tied around her waist giving the only hint of her shape with her black scrubs hanging loose in a bell-bottom style.

"Ah, there she is," Jedrek walks slowly to come stand by me. He's doing his performance again and I roll my eyes, drained by his many mood swings. "We were just looking for you. Weren't we, Harper?"

Staring at her, I listen to the many voices tilting my head with their whispers. Someone is looking for her, definitely, but I'm not sure it's us.

"This is where you agree with me," Jedrek says from the corner of his mouth nearest to me.

"Who is Johanna?" I ask her, not surprised to see her head snap in my direction.

Jedrek claps, rubbing his hands together in his emoted glee. Regan's eyes are cast from me to him, wondering what we know and trying to attain those answers from our faces. Hers is filled with fear. It caresses the color of her eyes, turning them into a deeper shade than their normal color. Her breath catches and the coloring of her face seems to fade for a moment upon hearing the name.

"Johanna?" Jedrek asks me, making certain he heard the name correctly.

"Why does she want you?" I'm ignoring the instigator beside me. My attention is for the whispers, spilling their secrets, and the blanched face of the witch in front of me.

"How do you know that name?" Regan pushes from the wall to take a small step forward, whispering to me as if the house will hear her. "We don't speak her name."

I lift an eyebrow, asking why without putting my question into words.

Regan shakes her head, refusing to answer.

"She's exiled," Jedrek answers, making a great show of whispering it to me. "As is her name. It's a witch thing."

"To say her name is to admit her ties, thus allowing the ancestors to know her once more," Regan whispers.

"But it's not a witch thing," I press, repeating the voices in my mind. "It was a Deon thing."

Jedrek's head spins towards me with such speed I fear he may have broken his neck.

"Johanna failed Deon. This was all Deon's idea, for if she could find a way to raise the dead, the war could begin again…" my voice trails off

"….because Johanna deals with the demons. She has their magic," Regan continues when I drift.

Jedrek takes a dangerous step towards Regan. He is staring at her with a face awash in rage. "She does what?"

Regan is visibly shaking. Her fingers almost twitch with it and the witches who died here swallow her emotions like a rare nectar.

"I didn't know!" Regan exclaims. "None of our coven knew. Only Deon and the wolves knew about what she was doing at the time."

I don't know why I moved. I don't know what little tickle of ancient instincts spurred me into action. I just moved, almost tossing myself behind Jedrek. The pain was red hot and instant. My back is seared with the sudden attack, stealing my breath as I collapse from it all.

I don't know what Jedrek did. Or even what Regan did. All I can see is the crushed gravel I have crumpled upon. Through my hazed vision it seems to almost have a glitter-like coating upon the rocks. My head swims, wanting to desperately escape the pain coating me. The gravel fades, as if time herself has returned to an earlier date. There's wet ground, almost mud under my hands now. It's cold, damp, thicker than anything I remember from my youth.

There are voices. There's a woman urging me to get up. Her voice is gentle like a caress, coaxing me to do what I don't want to do. What I don't think I can do. When a male voice covers hers, I know it's not me to whom she speaks.

"What is the point?" he asks her, and I grunt in agreement.

"So that we don't die!" She almost shouts with anguish.

"We all die eventually. At least this death would be quick."

"This death will be the death of all of us," she tells him. "Not just us, or those we know, but our descendants, too. If you don't get up, everyone who should ever be, will never be free. You must get up!"

Lifting my head, I see the two who have been speaking. They are hazy, like a water-colored painting with soft colors and blurred edges. Around them lay so many people, bleeding and dying, strewn about like discarded dolls. The dolls cry out, begging for help or mercy, maybe both. It sounds all the same.

"If we survive this," the man says, "we will never side with any faction again. Witches are to stay neutral or risk becoming enslaved."

"Agreed," the woman says, offering a hand to help the man stand.

I know, without knowing them, they both die shortly after this memory which is lodged in this thick mud. The clay of the land cradles it, holds it, keeping it safe like a treasure long since buried. I know he got up. I know they tried in some long-lost war. I also know they failed for witches now seem to be very much enslaved. At least the ones who listen to the rules, that is.

A cold chill is crawling along my skin. It prickles and pokes, pushing a thousand needles into my flesh. Even as this chill is pushing me to my already tested limits, I am calm, welcoming it. This is Jedrek pulling me from this world around me and back into the world around him, the world I somehow slipped from with my fall.

The pain in my back is the first sadistic welcome party when I arrive back on the gravel. "What happened?" I ask the man whose magic still travels along my skin.

"You, being stupid, made a meat shield out of your back against the doorman," Jedrek's voice holds a touch of concern, but it's mostly amusement to cover his worry.

"Why would you do such a thing?" Regan asks.

I don't have to see her to know she is examining what is left of my back. With the amount of searing pain, my mind has already imagined it to be nothing but gaps of hanging flesh, cut raw and ragged.

"We were supposed to stay neutral," I mutter more to myself than those around me with my thoughts still marred in the images I saw.

"What is she talking about?" Regan asks Jedrek.

Her fingers are like molten lava, pouring into each space of flesh. They burn with such searing pain my head fights to stay clear. My body crumples to the cold earth wishing to show me so much more of those who still linger in this place, this prison for witches.

I know it's Jedrek who has lifted me, carrying my limp body back to his car. Each rocking motion of his gait rekindles the fire consuming my body. My vision is trapped between what is around us and what was before us. It rolls my stomach with an almost motion sickness of a sensation. Their voices are growing, roaring, lamenting my departure, begging me to stay or at least return. I cry, not only from the pain, but the pain of those who are now just shades lost forever within the red bricks and wet clay of the mud.

Reaching my fingers to touch their outstretched hands, I tell them, "I'll come back. I'll come back for you."

"Great," Regan's voice floats around theirs. "Now, *who* is she talking to?"

"I don't really want to find out. The dead should learn to stay dead, littlest witch. Let them stay dead."

Jedrek's voice is the last thing I hear before the darkness finally wins. I succumb to it, sinking into it, finding joy in my escape. Except, it's not an escape. Not really. I learned long ago, in the darkness is where the voices are the strongest.

I know where I am before I awaken. I know the smells of her kitchen like the perfume of a mother. I can smell the herbs, the potted plants with their seasonal blooms and a heavy, sauce covered meal. It would be all very welcoming if the warm fuzzy feelings weren't stalked by rapid cursing and the sounds of wooden spoons bouncing off walls. That sound I know well, too. I'm home, but hopefully not left alone, with just the lone witch waiting for me to open my eyes.

My vision is still blurred. Not by the swimming visions or the swallowing darkness, which lingers in the far rim of my sight, but by waves of my red hair. My hair which has been tossed, and unforgivingly pushed aside, to further expose my back.

I have created a small lake of drool on the pillow which was shoved under my head. Which is impressive with my mouth now feeling like it's coated in sand and a throat so dry I doubt there's enough water in the town to bring either back to life.

"Nice nap?"

Of course, it would be Jedrek who is waiting for the first verbal jab. Considering the volleys GiGi holds in her armory, I almost prefer him. Almost.

"You're welcome," I somehow mutter with a throat fighting to work.

He laughs softly, amused by something I've said, or done. It's hard to tell between layers of thick red hair and the many horrible decisions I have made. Pushing myself up on my arms, I feel every angry muscle voice their thoughts with the effort.

"Wouldn't..." Jedrek offers. "Best to just lay there and rest, Harper."

"Oh, my first name. How incredibly kind of you, Jedrek."

I watch as he makes a wide gesture with his arms. He smiles, and even in the pain I am in, my eyes roll with his mockery of the situation.

"Look who is done muttering in her sleep!"

I wince. Not just from the obvious reasons, but the reason who just appeared with a voice sounding like a red flag of warning. Knowing what is headed my way, I collapse back onto the couch in defeat.

"All back in the land of the living, are we?" GiGi asks, and I tell myself there's concern somewhere in there swirling with her scorn.

"Lucky me," I mutter into the damp cushion.

"Lucky for you Jedrek was there to finish the ghoul!" GiGi shouts.

I don't hide my glare from the still smiling man. His eyes are dancing, shimmering in mirth. Taking a sip from his cup, he lifts one eyebrow daring my next move, and I accept.

"I'm sure there are lots of witches so eternally grateful he was there in their time of need. In fact, I believe I saw a few today." If my words could scald, I too would dance with mirth. But if they hit their mark, the mark just smirks with that arched eyebrow taunting me.

"Whatever are you talking about?" Regan's voice comes from somewhere near me.

I have either missed her entrance or missed the fact she's been sitting here the whole time. Not that either would have changed my tone or my avenue of verbal travel.

"The ones who fought to keep us out of all the drama. We were never supposed to be toys for others." I say this through gritted teeth, determined to sit up before anyone else should suddenly appear.

"Seriously, what is she talking about?" Regan rushes to me when hearing my not so lady like sounds of determination. Her face is a mixture of confusion and a warning. She's doing that silent eye communication thing again. "Maybe you should just rest?"

Her hands are like warm water, soothing away my aches and spite-fueled thoughts. The pain of my back is still present, but I don't really care about it. It's drifting somewhere beyond my list of give-a-damns. My mood is melting, sliding into the warm pool she's created in my body. Every muscle is relaxed, except my brain. It's throwing red flags and caution lights faster than a strobe at a rave and I only slightly care.

"This is wrong?" The words flow like a question from me, meek and unsure.

"You need to rest," Jedrek tells me.

His eyebrow isn't as high, but it's still there in a different way. With my neck refusing to work, I can't turn to see what Regan is doing exactly, but whatever it is, Jedrek is enjoying the show. Which is exactly the last flag to fall into place.

"Nope!" I shout, sliding as best I can away from the embodiment of warm fuzzies sitting beside me. "This is definitely weird."

Now that I have squirmed an inch or so at most, my body reluctantly begins to answer my demands. Looking to her, Regan is staring at her hands with wide eyes. Everything about her says there should be something shocking covering the flesh of her hands, but if there is, only she can see it.

"What are you?" Regan whispers, still staring.

"Tired of being asked that," I reply, gathering all the scorn back like a flower girl who has lost her petals. All of my issues are mine and I don't want to share.

"She doesn't even know?" Regan's having a rather in-depth conversation with her hands.

"What are you?" I counter, still wondering what it is she is seeing.

"Regan," Jedrek begins, with GiGi watching it all from where she still stands, silent and cataloging everything which happens, "is an energy witch. Boring people, mortals per se, pay the spa to have her absorb all their cares and pains. She can pull from them every ounce of depression, or anxiety, or whatever it is they don't want to deal with and convert it to power for her."

"Then she pours it into that building to feed it," GiGi finally speaks, but her voice is filled with lost thoughts and locked emotions.

Not willing to even dive into the explanation he just offered, I skip right over it, letting it soak in some part of my brain until I'm ready to plunge into whatever depth of crazy he just wrapped around the room. "If witches keep the place running, why are there so many dead ones trapped there? But not as ghosts or even souls. They are almost embedded in the place."

"Because witches do keep the place running," GiGi answers still speaking in her tormented whisper. "If you don't escape, you won't escape. You will never escape."

"How did you escape?" I ask GiGi, wondering if she will finally admit what she hasn't yet put into words.

"I didn't sign the book," she tells me, letting it be her confession.

"Fuck me," I mutter, thinking this headache is not so much from today, but from all the days since taking this case. "There's a book? Why is there a book? Can't werewolves and a haunted spa be enough hocus pocus shit? Now, you have to add books and sources and demons? Oh, and let's not forget the one who shall never be named just lurking around, looking for her next trophy?"

"You forgot the bar you enter through mirrors," Jedrek sips from his glass again with a curved smile.

Lost for words and patience, I send him a one finger hello. "I don't want to do all this right now. Later, I know I'll have to, but not right now. I made a promise to a family to put little girl back to rest and nothing is being done to fulfill it."

"Hasn't it?" Jedrek asks, standing to stretch. "We've narrowed down where the source is and who has it. We know now the wolves are somehow involved and Regan here is going to take us right to the very thing we both need." He's strolled over to stand in front of the still dazed Regan. "And now, our little syphon is all charged up and ready to find it for us."

"Canker sores and whores!" GiGi exclaims. "You can't dangle that little girl like that. They will tear her apart!"

Jedrek turns just his head to look over his shoulder, "Now Jo, I wouldn't do that." He almost coos the words with false empathy. "All I need is for her to find this Johanna. It's Harper I plan to dangle."

"What is it you said earlier, GiGi? Lucky me?" I ask her, forcing my wobbling body to stand. "Let's go get lucky!"

"Sorry Harps, but we won't be bringing anything battery operated with us tonight." Jedrek pats my head. His smile is enough to make me want to tear it from his face.

I didn't feel the gathering of power in my hands. I was too lost in my fury over his mocking face, an emotion I don't normally jump to so quickly. I'm tired. I'm hurting. My nerves are exposed, almost bleeding with emotions I can't contain or conquer. I have one thought, just one little urge, or fantasy, if one will – tear that smile from his face.

"Stop it," Jedrek whispers, straining to say the words.

"Stop what?" a voice not my own asks.

"Harper, don't do this," GiGi pleads, but I have no idea what she's upset over.

I watch, oddly numb and fascinated, as Jedrek begins to peel his skin from his face with his bare hands. His eyes are locked with mine. There's no mirth. The only thing dancing in those bright blue orbs is anger.

Regan is screaming when the blood begins to pour from where the corner of Jedrek's mouth once sat. I'm not screaming. I'm watching it from far away, uninvested, as if he is nothing more than the frogs in biology class, with their bones and tissues exposed for all to see.

"Harper!" GiGi is screaming, shaking me. "You are not your mother!"

I'm jolted awake, blinking from some slumber I wasn't aware I was lost in. Her words carve a hole in my heart for reasons unknown. We never mention my parents. We never speak of them in death or in life. She just did. She did with sledgehammers.

"You are not your mother," she repeats again, staring into my eyes with a different emotion than Jedrek had. Hers is desperation. It colors every inch of her with a flush as she pleads with me. "You can control this!"

My mother is just a rumor, some slip of past knowledge locked and forsaken. I was seven when I walked into a living room covered in what I had thought at the time was thick paint. It wasn't and that image is creeping along my spine now, crawling its way to my far, hidden memories to display everything GiGi and I work so hard to deny.

"Stop it," she whispers, softly. "Call it all back."

I'm not sure how I know to do what she's asking, but I do it. Like collecting a lost emotion or regaining control, some part of you lost in a moment, I inhale deeply with my eyes closed and call everything back, shoving it deep inside of me where secrets and lies dwell. My hands seem lighter. My head is a dense fog, swirling and tossing me with waves of nausea. Even as my stomach threatens to let loose what little I have eaten today, my back is silent, no longer demanding attention with every inch of movement I take. It's my turn to arch an eyebrow, touching what was tender, angry flesh. My fingers tap along what I can reach, testing it, and there is nothing. Not the slightest twinge.

Unfortunately, for Jedrek, it's not the same. His face is half torn, his lips hanging open from where his fingers had dug into the thick flesh and pulled it apart. If it hurts, he doesn't show it. All he displays is anger, and honestly, I don't blame him.

"Sorry about your face," I acknowledge awkwardly. What are the correct words for, 'whoops, didn't mean to lose it there'?

"Enough," GiGi tells him, trying to pat some of the still streaming blood from his shirt and chin. "Put yourself back together and stop with these theatrics. She didn't do it on purpose."

Regan, no longer screaming, does a slow cat-like walk to where Jedrek still stands, soaked in blood and anger. Poking the ragged flesh, she asks, "Did Harper mind fuck you? She can do that?"

"You seem to be pretty fascinated with what I am and what I can do," I mutter, crossing my arms and playing the don't blink game with the mute Jedrek.

"Dude," she says, smiling like a teen whose friend just did something very naughty, "you just mind fucked the top of the food chain demon! Like an original!"

I'm waiting for her to start clapping, bouncing in place with her purple hair bouncing with her.

When I don't join in with her glee, she asks, "You don't know what that means, do you?"

My face must have displayed the words I know better than to say with GiGi so close to hand swinging range.

"You really are a lame duck," Regan whispers with wonder.

"A what?" I tilt my head with my question. I've been called so many things, but this one is a first.

"A lame duck. A witch who is lost in the water, just spinning in circles, getting nowhere," Regan is poking the dislodged lips of Jedrek as she explains.

His blood coats the tips of her fingers from her exploration. When his eyes swing towards her, the fury roasting inside them is enough to quench her desire to keep touching him. Shrugging, she walks back to the couch, but not before smearing her fingers on his once pristine black shirt.

Lame duck she called me. Spinning in circles. Getting nowhere. If my life was a t-shirt, that would be the Pinterest vinyl displayed across it in some swirling font.

Jedrek, either done with his display or plotting his next, begins to reaffix his face. He matches the edges of the wound to where they once were. His skin appears to crawl over the gaping lines, pulling this missing flesh back together. It's like watching it all in reverse.

"Fancy," I tell him, refusing to let him know how bad, and somewhat nauseated, I feel.

"How's your back?" he asks with lips slow to form the words.

"Seems all better. Do I dare ask why?"

"He's dead. Just like every time you cut yourself to wake someone, you pull from their energy to heal." GiGi offers as if saying what's for sale in today's paper.

"You're welcome, but if you ever try that again-" Jedrek begins, but Regan's laughter cuts his words.

"She just had you rip your own face off without breaking a sweat. What exactly are you going to do, oh unholy one?" Regan asks between giggles.

Jedrek is watching me with a new expression. There's so many emotions rolling through his eyes, his mouth moves with unsaid words. They are empty of mirth and jesting. This blue is a blue of pale intentions - intentions walking a thin line between hatred and fear with a touch of curiosity.

I know I should be alarmed with what I have done. I should be scared, wondering how it happened and how to never let it happen again. A thousand apologies should be rolling from my tongue, but my jaw stays locked unsure of what to even say or how to begin. What is the proper apology for influencing one to do such a degree of self-harm? A part of me knows it's useless even if I knew. I just became a possible dead duck and there's no Pinterest shirt with trendy font for that.

My unicorn robe is of no comfort this morning. The dancing horses seem more of limping casualties. With my mother riding my dreams all night, I tossed more than I turned and definitely more than I slept.

"Long night?" GiGi asks, sliding a mug of liquid caffeine to me.

The deep, dark brew smells delicious. Little wisps of steam pet my senses, promising to help me through the day. Coffee often lies, but I enjoy the hope it offers.

"The longest," I reply, sipping the first taste of what salvation must taste like.

"Her again?"

I don't have to ask who she means. The pronoun instead of actual name easily gives it away. We don't ever say my parent's names aloud. At least, we don't anymore.

"Yup," I tell her, tossing the red curls, so like my mothers, away from my face.

"Wanna talk about it?"

We both know I won't take that offer. It's most likely the only reason she does offer.

"Nope."

I watch her nod and exhale the breath she was holding. A part of me wants to change my mind just to watch her squirm. Seems fair after the last few days.

"Where would one find a witch, who is hiding from werewolves, and has the balls to trick demons at their own games?" I ask her, not willing to ask what I should be asking.

"If she's as good as she sounds, you won't," GiGi offers but I can tell she is in deep thought trying to think of a place.

"What if she's not good?"

"She smoked a whole house, leaving nothing behind," GiGi reminds me. "She's good."

We both sit in silence at our customary breakfast nook, our thoughts traveling in different directions. GiGi wants to believe this woman is powerful, but if she's dealing in powerful toys, maybe she's not that good. Maybe it's her toys making her good.

"Would a demon have a trinket to smoke a house?" I ask her.

"Absolutely!" shouts Jedrek as he enters our space and we both jump.

"Peasant's piss!" GiGi shouts over his entrance, her racing heart, and the spilling of the sacred brew.

"I see your face is working again," I tell him, not as creative in my angst as GiGi Jo.

Jedrek's face flashes rage for a second before he leans down, wrapping his arms around me from behind. "Only took a few virgins and some impressive sins," he whispers this in my ear like a snake would, hissing and warning me to back away. "Speaking of virgins, I guess I could have just used you?"

Lifting my mug much in the same manner as he had last night, I smirk, saying with complete false bravery to hide my guilt and shame over the event, "You could have tried."

"Children," GiGi complains, still cleaning the coffee from the table.

I don't even question when she twists the little rag she seems to always have hidden somewhere over the hanging fern. Nor do I ponder what her whispered words may be saying. I'm way past that level of curiosity.

Being the first to hoist the white flag, I ask still holding the warm mug like a shield. "You're thinking what I'm thinking?"

He's still leaning into my hair, whispering, "Dunno. What kind of naughty thoughts might you be having?"

"Gross," I say before I can stop my middle school like attitude towards sex from verbally erupting. "I meant, she's using toys, not spells." I can feel his next comment before he says it and I lift my hand to stop his game. "She's using stolen trinkets and not abilities," I correct, avoiding the mess of innuendos I know he was about to vocally spill.

"I did a little digging," he says, taking my mug and the seat next to me. "Jo, if you're going into the kitchen, Harper needs a new round of coffee and you might want to change that robe, dear. You got a little something on it."

He's actually smiling as he talks to her. I suspect he could remark on the color of the sky and somehow make one feel degraded without any effort. I had a friend's mother who could do such things. She blessed my heart a lot and she was always excited to see people on Tuesday.

"So, you did a little digging? Maybe your own grave if you keep taunting an Italian witch?" I ask him, filled with regret that I allowed him to steal my morning precious.

"She's a green witch. At worst she may command some vines to ensnare me," he whispers into the mug.

I want to remind him what I can do, take some of the confidence from his voice, but that would be the opposite of the whole white flag thing I started before I knew he would steal my only morning motivation.

"How did you really heal your face?" Is not the question I meant to ask. It escaped all on its own. I blame the lack of caffeine.

His eyes go dark for a moment. Without turning his head, he stares at me, reading my expression as innocent curiosity and not antagonistic before he says, "It just does."

"And my back?"

"More shredded meat than a hot pocket, suddenly all better?" he asks, knowing it's exactly what I already asked, just with less visionary efforts. "As GiGi said, you took power from my moment of weakness and your body used it to heal itself. I will give God five stars for how reliant He made your bodies. It's like He knew you would all be stupid."

I chuckle. Not because I find him amusing, but because it's nine a.m. and he's bringing up Divinity. I still have to figure out a spa, a book, werewolves and a magical bar Potter never prepared me for. I'm not about to step on into the quicksand of religion.

GiGi returns, all scorn and wearing a new robe. "We don't preach His name here. In this house, we respect all the powers which be, as it should be."

Jedrek lifts his arm, palms out surrendering to her building wrath. "Mea culpa. Mea maxima culpa," he says, taunting her even further.

I wait to see if she will respond with some creative explosion. She doesn't. She strides to her normal chair, and even in such a short distance, her robe flares around her, saying everything she didn't.

"Where is she getting these trinkets?" I ask Jedrek, trying to return his focus.

"Crossroad demons," he tells the dark liquid of his cup. "She's using mortals to trick demons. Once the deal is made, the items given over, the mortal has thirty days before the clock expires. Once it does, the demon returns to collect the trinket and the soul."

"But she's showing up first?" I ask, trying to follow along, but the bouncing ball is missing.

"Exactly," he confirms. "Once mortals know their time is up, they panic. They try to renege on the deal. How would a mortal find a witch strong enough to help?"

"The spa," I say with wonder over how simple and yet smart it is.

"Yup, the spa."

"Where this Johanna used to work for the Ripples who own it." I connect the dots. The lines are crude, but all the dots are slowly getting touched. "Which is why it attacked me."

"Mmmhmm," he says after a long sip of what was my coffee. "They are the watchmen, men who long ago sold their souls to keep the witches confined and the owners safe."

"Regan met us outside thinking the watchman would keep her safe, too." The dots are connecting faster. "But why would Johanna go against Deon?"

"Because she was sleeping with Richard. Richard promised to wed her, but instead just kept bedding her." Jedrek smirks. "When he died, she was supposed to be freed, and given a nice little chunk to live her best life."

"Guess none of that happened?" GiGi sneaks verbally in with her question.

Jedrek just smirks, sipping from the ceramic mug.

"Why would Deon want a source of magic to control the dead?" I ask, confused over why it's something desirable.

"Vampires," both GiGi and Jedrek say at the same time.

"Oh, right, because they are real too. Sorry. Forgot." I throw my hands up with irritation.

"Stop being petty," GiGi swats at me, missing but not by much. "This is the part you need to think about. If Deon was willing to risk hell itself, " she gestures to Jedrek, "coming after her for abusing one of their own sources, what do you think she's going to do to you now that she knows you can do the same thing?"

"She didn't want her father raised that night, least not entirely," he tells us with pride over knowing the hidden agenda we didn't know. Leaning back in his chair, he continues, "She wanted to see if you could raise their father that night," Jedrek tells me this as if what he really said is Santa isn't real. "She had Regan there in case you were more powerful than she anticipated. Regan would have drained you and dragged you back. Your enslavement to the spa, and the Ripples, is what was supposed to have happened."

"But it didn't." I remind them.

"It almost did," Jedrek corrects. "But you were too strong for Regan to force herself upon you. Your walls and your will kept hers out. Otherwise, this little story would have held a very different outcome."

GiGi has exploded in rapid Italian. The few words I can pick out lets me know someone is in trouble. Not completely positive it's not me.

"Didn't I tell you to stay away from them?" GiGi shrieks.

The coffee-soaked rag misses my face by inches. I'm not sure if she missed or was just venting rage in a healthier way than I seem to, as of late. I'll take a rag to the face if I get to keep my lips.

"To be fair," I offer as a false flag of peace, "you told me they were vampires."

"To be fair," GiGi mocks, "I told you the town joke!"

I pause, unsure how to counter her truth. "That's fair," I agree before moving on. "The family who owns most of our town is werewolves with a fetish for power over the dead. I must have missed that chapter in all the teen half-dressed book covers."

"Well, that's because most of those books are written by middle-aged women who think putting the vibrator on a setting above a three is risqué." Jedrek is flipping through the morning paper with half interest in it and in the conversation. He wears boredom as well as he wears mischief. "You said last night all you wanted was to help the family put the little girl back to rest. Is that still true?"

The warning bells in my head are chiming again. He's not looking to me, giving me any clues to what hidden games he has plotted depending on my answer. Looking to GiGi Jo, I can see she too has concerns.

"What are you slinking around about, demon?" she asks, her voice a warning in itself.

"Oh, Jo," he says almost playfully. "You and your trust issues."

The flipping of the paper's pages is like a whip to my sanity. Until now, I didn't even know it was possible for a newspaper to make so much noise. Even the font of the pages with its block style of lettering disgusts me.

"Oh, shit," Jedrek says from a far hallway even though he's sitting beside me.

This time, I know something is off. This isn't me. I'm sarcastic, maybe a touch witty, but not hostile. Not really. Yet, somehow, all I want to do is tear through the house, screaming with my rage, throwing a tantrum over the lies and the secrets. This isn't me.

"You can fight it, Harper," I hear GiGi whispering near me. "You're stronger than them."

"Them?" I ask, trying to find something to focus on. Any little thing instead of my building rage-inspired desires.

"Jo…" Jedrek's voice is filled with shock and disappointment.

I'm missing something again. Some little silent conversation they are having with their eyes. A conversation about me.

"Would you two just stop it!" I scream and the bookcase behind me hurls its paperbacks.

The room becomes a mockery of a winter scene as the pages are freed from spines, floating through the air to land randomly around us. Books which held themselves together are launched as if from a canon. They become small fragments of weapons, tearing through anything fragile in the room.

"I got this," Jedrek tells GiGi, keeping his eyes on me. "You go."

I tilt only my eyes to see the woman who has raised me for most of my life torn in the moment. Her sadness should reach some part of me. It should be the cold water to my inner bonfire, but it's nothing. It's almost as if I don't know her, or have any connection to her.

I watch as she takes his advice, glancing once to the man who urged her to leave. "She's all I have," she tells him, but it feels as if she's speaking to so many more.

He nods, sharing one last look before he's truly alone with me.

"I know you don't want to hurt me, but, at the same time, you really want to hurt me," he says with a face of disarming amusement. "You're going to hurt me, Harper, and I'm going to enjoy it. We both are."

He's right. I'm going to hurt him and I'm going to absolutely enjoy it.

He moves as if at any moment I may strike. He's treating me with caution, never turning his back to me, keeping his eyes locked with mine as he walks away from me. I follow him into the living room still stained with his blood. Like a ghost of a perfume, the copper scent is still dancing in the air.

"That rage you're feeling," he tells me, keeping his voice low, "is the rage from the witches yesterday. You brought it all home like a used coat, wearing it and now they are wearing you."

Somewhere, deep in what was once the rational side of me, this makes sense. The part of me awash with emotions, too abundant to pluck apart, ignores the logic, embracing only the feelings I am having with gleeful anticipation of what's to come. They care only for the wreckage and the restoration.

"You should have been taught how to ground, to remove all that baggage, but you weren't. Or maybe you were," he shifts his words when my eyebrow does a warning lift, "but just not to the degree to handle all this. We have two choices here, my littlest, deadly witch. I'm really hoping you pick door number two. Door number one won't be as much fun for me."

"Why is it always about you?" a cold octave of my voice asks. "It always comes back to you."

"Just a lucky guy like that," he teases, daring the embers to keep feeding the flames inside of me.

140

"What's door number one?" I hear myself ask.

"That's where I miss part of my body again, and as you can see," he says as he slips the dark grey cotton shirt over his head, "it's a rather nice body."

Even as deep as I am in this pit, my stomach tightens in agreement. My breath rolls from my mouth slowly with my eyes following his hands. With an expertise he's learned long ago, he trails just the tips of his fingers over his smooth abs before resting them on the top of his black jeans. I watched all of it yearning for his hands to keep going.

"Ask me about door number two, Harper."

His voice tightens things low in my body. My breathing has quickened, lifting my chest with each breath as if there's not enough air in the room for us both. The rage I was feeling is drifting towards a different delicacy. It's still red hot, but fed by a different type of fire.

Without any verbal prompting, those agile fingers unhook the button at the top of his jeans. The zipper seems agonizingly slow. Tooth by tooth the metal bondage slips apart, but he keeps it tightly clasped, unwilling to allow me to see more than he wants me to see.

"Ask me about door number two, Harper," he repeats.

I hear his breath catching between his words. The sound of his labored breath reluctantly pulls my eyes to his. Their dark blue shade paints his desires. The way he unconsciously licks his lips coaxes me closer. I want to taste his mouth again. I want to feel that tongue in my own mouth, on my neck, and lower. Every little dirty secret I have kept locked away from this man is pounding through their cage, timing their beats with that of my pounding heart.

He doesn't resist, or pull away, when I push myself against him. His hands are as hungry as mine to feel the hot skin of the other. Our mouths are starving, dining off what we can as clothes are discarded with no care to their stitched seams. He is everywhere, and nowhere, at the same time making whimpering sounds escape my throat with a need I have no name for.

Walking us further into the room, I still follow him, refusing to allow his body to be too far from mine, and when I can no longer handle the few steps which seem to be becoming miles, I lift myself onto him, wrapping my legs around his waist to be carried.

He settles us onto the couch. I waste no time. He slides easily inside me, stretching me to the point I cry out with so much more than just pleasure. There's a razor's edge of pain as he fills me, rocking my hips with a need of his own. It's perfect, pulling moans from both of us, but for me, I'm pulling something else, as well. I'm pulling from the ghosts with their secret agendas who are riding me as hard as I am riding Jedrek.

His tongue is hot, trailing along my neck, paving a path for his lips. He's sampling every curve, every nook of my neck, exploring the spaces thoroughly.

"Your turn," he says, huskily, holding a tone in his voice men can only find in the depths of passion.

I'm confused, not sure of what he's teasing me. Until his hands slip from my hips, slowing our frenzied pace. It's my turn, because for once, this isn't about him.

His speed was frantic. Mine is slow, deep and rhythmic. Where he rocked, I now roll. Leaning my forehead to his, we stare into each other's eyes knowing what is building deep inside each of us. Our breathing becomes entwined, panting, with our bodies begging for release.

"Let it out," he whispers to my lips. "Let it all go. Take me instead."

I don't know what he's talking about, but my magic does. Whatever he invoked, stirred with his demand, answers his request. It's slow, inching up my body with a heat that tilts my head back. I wait for it. Cry out for it, but it's not fast enough for Jedrek.

Latching onto my arched breast, he pulls the tender flesh into his mouth, surrounding it was a different fire. A fire he tosses more heat to when the tip of his finger reaches down to dance, push and roll along my most sensitive parts. He pushes me deeper into the inferno consuming us both. The slow, deliberate rhythm I started with is gone. Destroyed but this hunger to be consumed by all the different fires lapping at me from so many directions I fight against the screams wanting to be released.

"Let it out," he commands between taking turns tormenting each of my breasts. "Let them out and take me, Harper."

I'm bucking, fighting to keep a pattern as the magic surrounds me, filling the room with a green hue. My skin is glowing as if there are lights randomly flashing inside of me. There is nothing I can do now but scream. Scream with the eruption of pleasure and scream with the suffocation of the magic.

"Take me, Harper!" Jedrek shouts with his own orgasm. "Take me instead!"

Fed by the magic and his commands, lost in the moment, my hands travel his chest, dipping into the concaves of his ribs before sliding back to cup his face. Some ancient part of me, bred from years of knowledge, does as he asks.

Sliding impossibly deeper upon him, I coax the last of his orgasm. I feed upon the energy of it, taking it inside of me, pulling it into the core of me where scream after scream of his is stored. His back is arched, lifting, almost bowing his spine and I still take more. When there is nothing left, not even the slightest pulse of power, only then does my hands travel to run my fingers through his damp hair.

I'm breathing just as heavy. My skin is just as damp, but it's my skin again. My head is clear, tired, confused by what just happened, but clear.

"You will be the death of me, my littlest witch," Jedrek manages to say between heavy breaths.

I giggle. I legit giggle before I can stop myself. Rolling my eyes, I climb away from his lap, as the feelings of shame creep in, as they always do after I have sex.

"What was door number one?" I ask him with my back turned to play the game of 'where did I leave my bra'.

I can hear the couch protest his departure and I still jump when his fingers reach to help me fasten the clasps of my bra. He grazes the path of my spin, lightly coming to rest on my shoulders before he tours where his tongue had made a playground. I know he's inhaling the scent of my curls. I picture his eyes closed, hiding for a paused moment in the red waves. It causes me to shiver.

"Let's always stick to door number two." The heat of Jedrek's words calls forth goose bumps, tickling me from my neck to my toes.

"Fuck buddies with a cause?" I ask, trying to deflect the situation, and my questionable feelings, with sarcasm.

He laughs. It's a short sound and completely male, tugging on the part of me which is completely female.

"As strong as I am, I'm not sure I can do that often. We will need to teach you how to better protect yourself. Besides," he says with his normal voice and I know the tender moment is gone. "no one would believe it, anyway."

I'm glad for the exit plan. Not only are the endorphins wearing off, letting my body remind me it's been a long time since my last escapade, but also, I was willing to dive through the closed window if he had started to talk about feelings or a relationship.

Slipping back into what somehow feels like the least romantic lingerie ever invented, I ask him, calling him on his comment, "Why wouldn't they?"

"Because I was supposed to kill you, but I've decided I rather like having you around." He is redressing, not concerned with how his statement may affect me.

Throwing my hands up in frustration, I ask without really wanting an answer, "Is everyone supposed to kill me?"

I expect him to laugh, to mock me, reply with one of his normal riddles painted with ego and smirks. Instead, he glances at me over his shoulder before coming to help me pull the tangled red mess from the neck of my shirt.

Floating his fingers through the jumbled red mess, he tells me with an honesty I only have seen a few times from him. "Yes.

Everyone will try to kill you. You have the potential to be too powerful. You'll tip every scale, of every house, and there are houses who won't stand for it. If they can't have you, they will kill you to be sure you can't rise against them."

"What am I?" The soft question comes from such a place of vulnerability I can't stop the first tear from falling.

Jedrek cups my face with hands of warmth and comfort. "You are amazing. A witch like you is born only of blood and death, a source of magic all on her own. I was there when God first pulled the rib from Adam and never have I met a woman as powerful as you."

"I don't feel powerful," I confess.

"The magic knows what to do. It's there like a twin flame, waiting to show you everything which is possible." He's staring intently into my eyes as if he can see it flickering behind them. "Trust it. Trust me."

"The man who wants to kill me?" I mockingly jest, trying to recover from my emotional walls crumbling without my permission.

Jedrek smiles, placing a soft kiss upon my forehead. "I am no man, Harper. I never was, but for you, I wish I were."

"I wish I were a lot of things," I tell him, pulling from the moment before I cave entirely to years of regrets. "Now what?" I ask him and I'm not entirely sure if I'm asking about us or the wicked witch roaming around with a trinket everyone wants.

"I'm going to raid the fridge while smiling at Jo over having sex with her ward, while you put on something an adult would wear and not a child," he tells me with more honesty than I honestly wanted.

"And then?" I ask, continuing to push my luck.

"With you all super charged and smelling of naughty things, I'm going to dangle you in front of the ruling house of werewolves."

"Can we revisit that trust me part again?" I ask him as I leave the room.

His laughter follows me down the steps to my little cave I call my own. A part of me feels shame for what just happened. I'm not going to boast about being wholesome, but I'm not whoresome either.

Standing in front of my full-length mirror, glaring at my dancing unicorn pajama pants and the matching pink tank top, how can anyone be afraid of me? As if on que, the lights behind my skin flicker, letting me know Jedrek is right. The magic is alive and waiting inside of me. Just waiting, as it has been my whole life.

Leaning closer, there are stars in my eyes. Their beams stretch to my irises making them glow a brighter hue than normal.

"Who are you?" I ask my reflection, and the lights glow more, and I swear, the reflection smiles back at me, winking a glowing light with a taunt.

"You are dressed for dangling," Jedrek compliments when I emerge from the house.

I was rethinking my tight jeans and black halter top. I was in complete debate over the knee-high boots. With his eyes touring every curve, maybe I made the right decision.

My hair is pulled high, wrapped tight into a bun. The product slicking back all the wild strands has made the normal bright red into a shade darker. I felt powerful in the darkened room, lining my eyes wider than I normally would. Under the sun, I wasn't so sure.

"Are you actually being nice?" GiGi is finding reasons to be outside, watering the many roses and other plants she has planted in perfect rows. "Guess the sounds make sense then."

I can't hide my blush. My morning after walk of shame is in broad afternoon and I'm dressed perfectly for every step.

"She's better, isn't she?" Jedrek asks, full mocking bow displayed.

The Italian muttered almost under her breath are phrases not of the kind sort.

Like a child running from a scolding, I rush to the open car door he is holding for me. The black Camaro may be my only salvation. Which in itself should worry me.

"Guessing you don't bring many male visitors' home?" Jedrek asks with amusement since GiGi's words are still flowing when we pull away.

I don't want to talk about my failings of last relationships. Not even Cass with his bloated belly and sweating seem worth the effort of an explanation.

"Back to Deon?" I ask, covering his question with one of my own.

Jedrek scrunches his face. "No. I want to play a new game."

"I thought you wanted to dangle me in front of her?"

"No. I said I wanted to dangle you in front of the ruling house of wolves. Not Deon."

"Always riddles with you," I sigh, turning to stare at the town we drive through.

"Deon is the head, yes," he begins, "but she is not the ruler. Wolves are a pack. Their alphas are only allowed to be so as long as the pack allows it. They are one of the few houses where most, if not everyone, has a voice."

"Sounds like the better of the plans."

"Has its pros and cons, I agree."

"Where are we heading then smelling of naughty things?"

"To the local coven."

My heart stops when I hear what he has said. I was prepared to face off against Deon and her judging eyes. I am not prepared to stand in front of so many I should call my own.

"I'm wearing almost spandex jeans!" I tell him, my thoughts freeing themselves from my panic. "Shouldn't I be in a robe? Or a hat? Maybe something a little more formal?"

"I said the local coven. Not Gandalf."

I don't have to look at him to know he's rolled his eyes, arching his brows wide with a comment he finds utterly ridiculous.

"Does GiGi know?" My voice is higher than I wanted it to be with my question. It almost squeaks with fear.

Jedrek laughs. "Are you in the car?"

I don't have time to ask any more questions. His car pulls in front of a large gate. The metal bars are a haze with inscriptions. Most I can make out, a few I can even read, but there are many I cannot. These are the words which worry me.

I'm still trying to decipher them as the car rolls through the gate. A desperate attempt to try to understand what Jedrek is throwing me into now. It's useless. They swim, hiding and swirling their symbols the harder I try.

"You know you're pretty much ringing their doorbell, right?" Jedrek asks offhandedly.

"What?' I ask him with the same level of interest. I'm turning, struggling to discover any insight before they are too far away to see.

"The words you can't quite grasp, there's a reason for it. They aren't real symbols."

Spinning back to face him, my face doesn't hide my shock. "Then why put them there?"

"Because, littlest witch, only something strong in magic can see them. So, when something pokes them, a seer inside knows it. It's like Ring for witches."

"Something?" I half ask, watching the white house come into view.

"Witches always think only witches can do magic," Jedrek sighs.

I don't ask him for an explanation. There is something far more interesting than him and his half comments: the house before me. It sings with a lullaby a mother would whisper to her child, lost and scared. It calls to me, that part of me I didn't know I held inside me until just a few days ago. Unlike the spa, this place is honey and milk, soothing the scars the world has put upon those that live inside. The song promises safety from a world of cruelty.

It's a spectacular contrast of white and black with the wood accents blending the two together. The round picture windows hold the dark paint of stained glass. Even the old weathervanes perched on top of the black roofed towers are perfect.

"It's beautiful," I whisper, pressed against the door's window like a child at a holiday light display.

Jedrek makes a sound tossed between amusement and wistfulness. "They always say that."

"What do you mean?" I ask, exiting the car in a daze of wonder.

Coming to stand beside me, he tells me while staring at the house, "Once upon a time my job was to bring witches here."

"Why?"

"Because I was told to." Jedrek is already walking away from me with his typical style of answering without answering.

"I hate when you do that." I shout to his back and he flashes me those blue eyes of mischief over his shoulder.

"Better hurry, littlest witch. You're going to miss the show."

I almost run up the wide, white stone steps upon hearing his jeer, thankful for every thread of spandex the jeans hold.

"What show?" I ask when I catch up, my voice caught still with child-like curiosity over the place.

"Yours," he whispers, before opening the arched door and pushing me inside.

The place smells of sweet sage and soot. The same lullaby I heard outside is no longer a hum. It's a full song with its words just out of reach of hearing. The same black and white melding of a color theme carries to the inside with the crisp white walls framed by black molding and baseboards. It presents the illusion of the hallway expanding for miles ahead of me.

"Hello?" I call out to the empty space unsure of what the proper protocols are for entering a coven's home. GiGi always keeps loose tobacco in a pocket of her purse which she leaves in random places. Unfortunately for me, after raising a client with a tracheostomy, and all the many things which climbed out from it, I quickly gave up smoking years ago.

"Did you really just call out 'hello'?" Jedrek asks, strolling past me, trailing his fingers along the smooth wall.

"Sup bitches, seems a little rude?" I shrug, following him.

"We are about to paint these walls red and you're worried about proper greetings?" Jedrek turns to me after his confession. "So precious."

"We're killing the witches? We are not killing the witches!" I hiss as if someone might hear him.

"No, silly girl. They are killing the wolves. We are just the match."

"And why would be we killing wolves today?" a woman gliding down the grand stairs asks.

My heart does that annoying thing where it drops to my stomach before rushing back to wedge in my throat. She's beautiful in a manner which makes you fear for your life. Her deep brown hair is half pulled up to fall in floating waves down her back. Her face holds no expression, but I know those flat brown eyes see all.

"Winnik!" Jedrek exclaims. His voice has turned soft as melting butter and as sweet as caramel.

Still holding her face an almost cold neutral, she lifts her hand to stop Jedrek from talking. "None of your games, old one. What have you brought to my house?"

"I think she's asking about you," Jedrek makes a show of whispering over his shoulder to where I am standing.

"I'm not," Winnik corrects. "This is the necromancer who was never told. I know her well. In fact, she should have been mine at birth, but I was overruled."

"Why?" I ask her, ignoring Jedrek.

"Your mother promised us she would groom you to be what you should be. She would teach you our ways, keep you safe, but she never brought you. Now, you are here without her. Which can only mean she has passed."

"She did. When I was seven," I tell her, not sure of why the words won't stop. "She went mad with her power during an argument with my father. I came home from school to find them both."

I gasp, hearing one of my most locked away secrets flowing so willingly. This is a topic normally hidden deep, shoved into the darkest of caverns in my mind and heart. It's a dead end, never acknowledged or spoken of growing up.

Winnik's face almost moves, before asking, "Who raised you?"

"GiGi Jo."

"And with hopes I suppose she has now passed away, too?"

Winnik almost sounds as if she is reading from a book instead of having a conversation, a very boring book. Her face sits as cold as she holds her voice. If she ever held any feelings for GiGi, or my mother, there are none over their suspected death.

"Oh, that one is very much still kicking. She just doesn't know we are here. Well, not yet." Jedrek leans against the wall when telling her this. His all normal all dark outfit almost places him seamlessly in the home.

"Interesting," Winnik muses, coming the rest of the way down the stairs.

Jedrek follows her into the large den as if invited to do so. I pause, attempting to sneak a glance up those steps, hoping to see a row of strong women staring back at me, but there's no one. It's empty and I can't fight the feeling of disappointment when I follow the other two.

He has stopped beside a glass case, staring into it as if the pictures and trophies fascinate him. Exhaling his breath to fog the glass, I watch as he uses his finger to clean away the word 'no' before swirling over it to remove it.

I may have failed in every silent eye lock of conversation casted my way so far, but this, this I understand. Sort of.

He motions for me to seat myself on one of the burgundy couches placed for conversations. It's stiff as if newly purchased, hinting this is not a room used very often. Winnik is standing at an old-fashioned tea station. She's adding the cubes of sugar to petite cups on matching saucers. If it weren't for the three cups being prepared, she hasn't acknowledged we have followed her at all.

"Would you like some tea?" her cold voice asks over her shoulder.

"No," I say politely but proud I put the clues together.

"Jedrek?" she asks.

"Love some!" he enthusiastically tells her with a smile.

I put my confusion on my face, trying to get his attention before she turns around. He ignores me, but I know he knows of my attempt.

When she hands the set to him, he smiles at me when taking his first sip. "Let's talk," he tells the older woman.

Winnik does nothing to start the conversation. She's ice, empty and simply here.

"I need to punish a witch who once belonged to the Ripples," Jedrek informs her.

"And you need my permission."

"And I need your permission."

I'm watching the two of them verbally volley back and forth.

"Why does this witch no longer belong to the Ripples?" she asks, finally moving to taste the tea.

"They want her punished, too," my mouth says. When they both turn to look at me, I wish the couch allowed me to sink further down.

"She ran from them," Jedrek clarifies, but I notice he isn't mentioning the reason we are really looking for her.

Winnik sips from her tea with almost passive, hostile flair. Her hair doesn't move. The soft plaits of waves sit as bored and uninvested as she does with her spine so straight, I'm self-consciously adjusting my posture. The self-confidence rolls off of her in waves of authority and power.

I'm trying to recall every witch movie I have ever binged for 'rules' no one has yet to tell me to best judge how to address such a woman. How did all the other girls react to discovering everything is real, and not just lines from a favorite book or show? Did they sit mute, wearing a dumb smile? Why did I open up so easily to the ice queen who I've just met when I've kept people on emotional lockdown whom I have known for years? How am I supposed to act being the necromancer who was never told? And what the hell kind of title is that? And why am I spiraling mentally?

"We tend to not get involved in such matters. If she was a witch of the Ripples, she is already lost to us. She is beyond my reach and interest."

I hear Winnik say with the same winter chill, snapping me back into the present. Her teacup doesn't even clink when she places the pair back on the table between her and Jedrek. Nor does her spine bend or head tilt, but her eyes are very invested in mine.

I've missed something again. Jedrek is all teeth in his smile before he nods to her.

"As much joy as that brings me, you may change your mind," he says, still wearing smile so wide it's unnerving, bringing her attention back to him.

Winnik arches one of her perfect sculpted brows. "I doubt that."

The little tea game is fraying my nerves. When she opens a little tin of flat cookies to offer, I'm pretty sure we have reached supernatural domestication hell. I'm almost grateful when the whispers start. Like a soft breeze, they almost tickle my neck, lifting the little hairs on my arms. Since anything is better than sitting here watching this complete disappointment of meeting a powerful witch, I listen to them. I invite them, and as if I flung open a window, they flow through.

I try to keep my face as present as I can, nodding when I feel the conversation requires it, but I can't really hear Winnik and Jedrek playing verbal chess. I can only hear the many voices screaming for attention. Their screams aren't of their past lives. Their urging is for my present situation. Jedrek was right. We are about to paint the walls red. The Ripples are here.

We have a problem," I throw into their polite conversation. "If you two are done jerking each other off with whatever this is, the wolves are here."

Winnik stares at me as if I just grew another eye in the middle of my forehead, or maybe a complete other head, but whatever she is seeing finally puts a crease in her milk white skin.

"Impossible," she scolds me. "The wolves are not allowed beyond the gates without a formal invitation."

"Someone forgot to remind them of that, then."

I don't waste time arguing with her or trying to convince her they are here. If she's so powerful, let her discover it, or maybe someone else lurking unseen upstairs. For me, I prefer to meet Deon and her family standing at a door I can close if I need to.

"Where is she going?"

I hear Winnik demand of Jedrek when I leave the room. I don't even know. Not really. In fact, now that someone has asked, I falter, realizing I am moving to confront, standing on the front lines, and not do my normal one line volley from somewhere safe.

Jedrek doesn't have time to answer her. The knock on the front door is loud, demanding, and not something one would hear on a casual drop by from a friend. This is a drum of war announcing intentions with three solid strikes.

"Don't worry. I'll get it!" I mockingly shout to the two powerhouses still sitting in the other room. "It's just a bunch of angry werewolves, who aren't allowed to be here, but are here, demanding their witch back, who I thought only lived in bad teen movies and Netflix shows focused more on more dick than plot. No big deal. Just another Thursday."

"Isn't she fun?"

I hear Jedrek ask before he appears beside me. His face may be his trickster signature, but it doesn't reach the blue of his eyes or his stone set shoulders.

"What's the plan again?" I whisper, trying to cling to this false bravado I'm displaying. My mouth is always brave. It's my brain who is late to the party.

"Don't die?" he offers in jest.

"Is that a possibility?"

"Death is always a possibility," Winnik's voice interrupts our exchange. "But not today. Not for us, anyway."

"Just to be clear," I ask them both. "Wolves are bad? Witches are good?"

"Today, yes." Winnik smiles and I'm shocked to see it possible. "Tomorrow may be a different answer."

"Glad to see everyone talks in riddles," I mutter, not quietly, but not as loud as GiGi would.

Winnik and Jedrek are too focused on the door to pay my attitude any attention. They seem to both be listening, but in different ways. I can feel Winnik's magic filling the space around me. In fact, it's the first sense of magic I have felt from a house which is supposed to hold the witches of this area. Only the house felt powerful. Not a sense of a person. That annoying alarm bell is chiming again, but it may be too late.

Whatever Jedrek is doing has made the corners of the house dark with shadows that seem to move when watched from the corner of your eyes. There's a chill in the air, waking feelings of fear and of being watched.

It feels as if I, too, should be doing some type of prep, but when the glass smear of a word forms again on the hutch, I take the unspoken advice. I do nothing. Waiting and unsure of what my role is supposed to be in this supernatural stand-off of broken rules.

"Open the door," Jedrek requests.

The door opens on its own. Swinging slowly, those on the wide front porch come into view a few at a time. They are all dressed the same. Forsaking the Ripples' normal high-priced look, the family, and a few too many who were not at the graveyard that night, are all wearing jeans and tank tops. From torn to worn thin, their jeans were not chosen as fashion. Nor were their faded tops. If I were born with an IQ, this would worry me. Instead, that easy to amuse part of my brain is hopeful this means I'll get to see their other side and something other than tea and cookies.

"Not a good time to smile," Jedrek whispers.

Dropping the corners of my mouth, I nod, trying to replace the eager smile with some sort of 'game face'.

Deon emerges from the center of well-built men. She, too, is dressed in the same attire with a ponytail pulled tight.

"Greetings, Winnik," Deon shouts from where she stands surrounded and protected.

"You're trespassing, Deon. You are not invited nor welcome." Winnik doesn't call out the way Deon had. With her magic flaring like the rattle of a snake, her voice is the same cold, collected tone.

"Hand her over and we will leave. No reason to risk your own for one who is not a part of your house."

Deon's words flutter my stomach. Stepping an inch further behind Jedrek before I can stop myself, my mind races for options for escape should Winnik agree.

"Slave trade is for the wolves. I do not participate in such things. If you want her, you must come take her."

"You would risk your own house, and all those in it, for this one witch?" Deon sounds disgusted with Winnik as she asks, but she hadn't prepared for Winnik's reply.

"You would risk your own house, and all those in it, for this one witch?" Winnik asks, turning the tables of logic upon Deon like the reversal of a sword, but she isn't done. "You would risk all treaties, past and present, voiding all agreements held, for one witch? Then if you must, Deon, then you must."

I hadn't heard the other women come down the stairs. I feel them. It's a wave of power with an undercurrent threating to drown us all. With so much magic surrounding me, pushing at me, I can feel my own awaken.

"No," Jedrek barks. "You don't have control."

I want to say that's an obvious observation. It's the one-word admission I wasn't able to admit in time. This twin flame Jedrek named as my power, flares to life while I stare at him. My skin glows the faint green with almost wisps of green smoke circling my arms and hands.

"Do not let your hair down," Jedrek pleads, but that, too, is too late.

My fingers have already found their way to loosen the tight bun, letting the spiral waves from being put up wet drop dramatically. Lifted as if by an unseen breeze, my red hair moves around me, alive and waiting.

"Do not kiss me right now," Jedrek suggests again and when I feel my face wrinkle with it, he nods before turning his attention back to where Deon stands beyond the door. "Good. For a moment there I thought you were just purposely trying to piss me off."

"I can smell the necromancer in there," Deon shouts. "Is that your little ace in the hole? Is she why you dare stand here to defy me?"

"She came of her own accord," Winnik almost giggles as she answers. "Seems you have more enemies than you are aware of."

"Powerful people always have powerful enemies," Deon shrugs. "It's the way of our world."

My feet are moving before I know they are. Jedrek does his best to sidestep, blocking whatever path I am on. With a simple twitch of my fingers, he is down on his knees, sighing and annoyed.

"You talk too much, Deon," I announce when I come to stand beside Winnik. "Your father was right. You're still pretending you have any authority."

My words sour her whole posture, but she still doesn't take the bait.

"Where is your twin brother?" I ask her. "Does he know you're here?"

The werewolves standing around her turn to look at her. There is whispering coming from those further towards the back. Just as the voices had suggested – Deon is here on her own, against the wishes of her family.

"What I do is none of his concern!" she shouts, addressing not just me, but those around her too.

"You're going to break all treaties without his concern?" I make a tsking noise. "Whatever would Daddy say? Shall I go ask him? Shall I bring him back, and bring him to you? Shall I parade him down main street, shouting ridicule for you and your grab for power?"

Clenching my fist, I pull the slumbering dead from the unmarked graves around the house. These protectors who sacrificed their eternal rest so long ago, awaken easily, eager to protect those inside of this house. They don't stand as shambling corpses. They stand around the wolves as if it were the day of their death, wide awake and ready for whatever road Deon takes us down.

"Or maybe I should just kill you now, where you stand. I'm within my rights," I tell her, not sure of how I know such things, but not willing to interrupt whatever this bitch trip is I am on.

I can see Deon weighing her options. Those around her have tensed, waiting for any command or signal. The ones on the back rows, not so much, but that could be because they are the closest to my new little friends.

"She's mine, Harper," Deon says through teeth so clenched I worry for their enamel.

"I will find her," is all I offer.

"And you will bring her to me!" Deon almost screams, rattling the nerves of those she has brought.

"I will find her," I repeat, not agreeing nor denying her request. My green smoke grows thicker responding to both of our building emotions.

We stand, our two sides for what feels like hours, watching and waiting for the other to change our standoff. This is more than just a test of power. This is a stand for survival and for today, as Winnik has suggested earlier, witches are good. Wolves are evil.

"Kill them all," are the words which turned our world upside down.

Three little words and the sky fell, and the walls ran red with blood.

The wolves on the front are running faster than I can react. Jumping in midair, their change is fluid, instant. I answer with adrenaline and instinct.

Those I had summoned are already falling upon the ones closest to them. Their screams are filling the air as their brothers and sisters fill it with growls. Their family doesn't turn to help those screaming their names, begging for some kind of help. They are left to die, already written off as casualties lost.

Shadows I had only thought were moving earlier now race past me. Jedrek pulls me back, away from the black curtain formed around the door and entryway. When the wolves crash through it, it steals whatever magic had turned them. Nude crawling men and women fill the hallway. They are dazed, shaking their heads as if to clear it, but still, the women lined along the stairs hold back.

When Deon finally walks through the dark barrier, she stands in the middle of the weakened crowd of her family. To say she is pissed does not fully cover the rage she is wearing.

"Now," Winnik nonchalantly says.

The screams from those along the floor are a mixture of howls and human pitches. They wither, clawing at their skin, their eyes, the one next to them, tearing flesh and thicker meats from bones and their bodies. Veins are sliced, arching blood in wide arches along the near walls. It soaks the carpet. It seeps into the wood floors as if watering

161

a garden. There's meat and blood everywhere and the sight of it steals my bravery. My magic seeps away as their lives are doing the same.

"Enough!" Deon screams, almost pleads as those who have been mauled try to reach her, stretching their hands out to their leader, the one who brought them here, for help.

"Is it?" Jedrek asks her. "I thought you were ready to risk your whole house?"

"Whatever would Roman think?" I ask her, but also myself.

"How do you know his name?" Deon isn't hiding her rage. It covers her voice, her face, and the tears gliding down her high cheeks.

"The same way I know he doesn't know about this. Nor does Gabreile. I know all that the dead know and the dead here know all about you."

I'm not bluffing. If she wanted, I could even tell her the shade of the thong she's wearing, but I don't think it would be the least bit helpful amid all the dying around me.

"Take the ones who can stand. The rest belong now to me." I say this with that voice that isn't entirely mine.

Deon stares at me in horror. She twists from where Winnik stands, blocking her any further entrance in the house nor near her coven, to face Jedrek. He rests against a wall dripping with the bright blood like reverse icicles along the white paint. Neither of them offers any argument, or expression of support, for Deon's nonverbal request for help.

"I won't just hand over my brothers and sisters to you!" Her voice has dropped dangerously low, warning of what her next actions might be.

"You already did," Winnik reminds her. "I asked you if this is what you must do. You had your chance to leave. Instead, you offered up your whole house to her and now your house she owns."

Deon's face melts from rage to shock. She was so confident in her plan, she never thought to consider the outcome of any other occurrence. Words are sacred with witches. They have been handed down from generation to generation to teach spells, bindings, and potions. When a witch offers you her words, she offers you her word and her trust. And thus, words are binding, binding them to you and you to them. Deon never stopped, lost in all her ego and anger, to think of what she was saying to the witches inside of this house.

"Unless I kill her," Deon muses.

I know the lights of my eyes are dancing. I can almost see them, little ripples in my vision which blur things around me and yet don't at the same time.

"Yeah," Jedrek tells her, whispering the second part, "Good luck with that."

"Go to your brother and sister, Deon. Go before you cause more damage you cannot undo," Winnik says, offering her advice instead of a taunt.

Those of her family who can stand, in some way or another, have already began to exit through the dark curtain of Jedrek's summoned shadows. The ones unable to stand are no longer moaning for help. They have accepted their fate. They watch with sad eyes as their leader backs away, before those same eyes fade to empty shades of death - but the eyes of Deon, those eyes are filled with anger and their color is only growing.

There's an audible exhale from the room once she is gone. The celebration is mild, mostly hugs shared among the nameless women behind Winnik. Jedrek, for all his worry before it began, is eyeing the collection of bodies with cold disinterest. His look reminds me of a toddler discovering a vegetable of their torment on their dinner plate.

With my magic gone, and my eyes back to my own, I feel exhausted. My muscles ache as if I have just run a marathon, uphill, in the snow, both ways. My head is heavy. Before I can put the many reasons I shouldn't before me, I drop to the floor in a less than graceful attempt to sit.

Staring at the many dead who are almost on the same level as myself now, I wonder why that part of me wanted to keep them. Remembering how I raised the dead outside without any ceremony, I wonder how I did that, too.

"You've always been able to," says one of the witches who has come down the stairs to stand in front of me. "You were taught how to restrain yourself. Not how to embrace yourself."

She's petite, almost fragile looking with hair as ashen as her complexion. Her drape styled dress hangs on her frame in the popular boho style. She's staring at me as if I'm some rare bug pinned behind a glass frame. It's weird, and unnerving. Mostly just weird.

"You're reading my mind, aren't you?" I ask her when the feather sensation trails along my skull. "Seems rather rude."

"I can only hear your current thoughts," she remarks, almost offended. "Your walls, even in this weakened state, are too strong for even me to pry the bricks loose." Turning to return to her post near the bottom step she says over her shoulder, "You're keeping them as pets to remind the Ripples of who you are and what you are capable of. You will need that."

"Why?" I ask, wondering why I keep insisting on pushing my luck.

"Because Deon's thoughts weren't hard to read," the witch tells me.

"Tell us where she is," Jedrek requests from Winnik. He's staring at his nails as if they are caked in something robbing them from their normal gleam.

"I don't know where the one you search for is hiding," Winnik says, throwing her hands up in the air when the shadows start to move again. "I do know where one is who may know. We banished her name when I discovered her dealing with a certain cursed necklace. She said she had received it from a wolf witch, not knowing its origin."

Falling backwards onto the carpet, hoping for a split second the blood hasn't seeped this far before I land, I ask with my exhaustion tinting my words with a southern accent, "There's more than just the one trinket loose? What the fuck does this one do?"

"I expect there are many, as there often is at any time. Normally, witches aren't the ones with them. We let the mortals have their little game of consequences. As long as the mortal agreed of their own free will, there is nothing anyone can do. It's how the demons have been playing their game for centuries." Winnik put scorn in every word, not hiding how she feels about the other side's tactics.

"Why do witches have them now?" I ask the collective staring at me.

"One witch," Jedrek corrects with an air of annoyance. "One very brave witch."

"Great, so back in the car to go somewhere else. I feel like all we have done this whole time is ride in your car somewhere or sit at my house. I used to have a day job. Maybe a little Netflix obsession, too. Now, just car and home to car and home."

"You done?" Jedrek asks from where he stands.

"Would it matter?" I return.

"Nope," he says with a genuine smile. "Tell me where to find this banned witch of yours, Winnie."

She almost smiles when hearing his chosen nickname. I'm surprised by the jealous lurch my heart does when I see it. I'm not surprised when the blonde witch snaps her head in my direction.

Winnik walks to a side table and writes on a piece of paper tucked inside one of the drawers what I hope is the address. I hate myself for watching her walk to him. I hate her when she does smile, offering the slip between two clasped fingers.

"Never a dull moment when you arrive," she tells him, and for the first time her voice has warmth in it.

"Aim to please," he tells her, and the smile they share makes me want to punch them both.

The dead man nearest me twitches a little, opening his glazed eyes to stare at me. "Shhhh," I tell him. When he falls back limp, an empty shell, I cringe a little.

"Playing with your toys so soon?" Jedrek asks, standing over me to offer a hand. "March them home, littlest witch. They won't all fit in the trunk."

"March them home?" I repeat his phrase. "Can I even do that?"

"You can do anything you ask your magic to do," the annoying blonde, as I have now dubbed her, tells me.

Standing, I stare at the many who have fallen needlessly for Deon's pride. Some with faces so clawed, they are unrecognizable. Others are missing vital chunks, leaking fluids darker than blood from their open cavities. I don't want to think about what they may look like waking from their grave of soiled carpet, much less trekking through the woods to Grandma's house.

"We will cloak them. No mortal will know."

I look to where the blonde is standing on her second stair. "That's getting really annoying," I tell her.

"It saves time," she returns with a shrug.

"Fine, let's do this so we can do the whole car thing again."

I'm still staring at the shambles around me, nude and stretched in such fragile ways it tears a part of me. I wonder who is waiting for them to return with Deon? Did they know when they crammed into the many cars to arrive, they wouldn't be going home? All of this over a witch with a forbidden trinket, a source of power so powerful it was never meant to have escaped hell.

"Tick tock," Jedrek whispers behind me.

Closing my eyes, I pull open the locked door I keep the magic behind inside of me, or at least the door I try to keep sealed. I feel it stir, stretching its many tendrils like an octopus testing the area around it. I feel those tendrils wrap around my heart, my mind, and a part of me I didn't know it could stir. It pulses with those organs, wanting to become a part of me like they are. It whispers to me such delicious things; I want to let it.

"Control," Jedrek whispers into my ear.

The image of my mother stirring a bowl of cookie dough knocks on my thoughts. I can see her as she was that day I came home from school. Her white blouse was ruined with the blood from her face where she had pulled her own eyes from their sockets after seeing what she had done to my father.

The tendrils relax their grasp, and I breathe a shaky breath before pushing it out into the fallen around me. Jedrek has made a point to stand behind me, far from the bodies I am focusing on. At first, it's little twitches, arms or legs jumping with a spasm, heads jerking with tremors before they fully awaken. Sixteen men and women stand facing me, waiting for whatever it is I ask of them to do, but they are empty shells. There's no true life in the husks before me.

"Change," I tell them, not really thinking it would work.

Some crouch low. Others bend as if to touch their toes before the many shades of fur erupt from where skin once sat. Their wounds look so much worse. On their human bodies it was unnerving. On their wolf form it's a different type of horror, a more pronounced desecration with whole muzzles missing and ribs sticking from shaggy fur.

Despite the change in form, it's the same empty feeling while they stare at me. I may have what's left of their bodies, but luckily the power which animates us has slipped away. Hopefully somewhere far enough away to not be bothered by the display I may need to make with them.

"Go to Great Hexpecations," I tell my new undead army.

Silently they shuffle away, following the command I gave them and any command I may ever give them. When the last grey wolf makes its way to the door, it turns, looking over its shoulders, raw with exposed bones and tendons. There's a light in those warm brown eyes. It's questioning me, as to why I am doing what I have asked them to do. I can feel the wordless question in my heart before it turns to follow the others.

"Why is that one different?" Jedrek asks me, as if I have any idea about half the shit I'm doing.

"Because she's the direct blood line of the Ripples. Her name was Isabell," the annoying blonde tells the room. "Roman will be most upset over this."

I imagine Roman will be most upset over it all, but I don't correct her. That would invite conversation and conversation is something I am over having.

I thought this house would hold answers. I thought I'd find my missing pieces stitched together by an invisible lullaby. Instead, I'm leaving with more questions, more holes and dark memories stalking just beyond the shadows of my mind. Behind shadows thicker than anything Jedrek could summon, a woman who had once sung me to sleep with lullabies waits. Except, in the end, she too, had just been a reanimated shell.

Neither of us spoke on the drive to the address on the little paper. Correction. I didn't speak. Jedrek wouldn't shut up. He commented on every make of car, billboard, song on the radio and even threw in random facts, as if any of it mattered to me. I've had enough relationships to know, the only time someone talks this much about random facts of life is because they are afraid you may ask about specific facts of theirs. We haven't spoken a word to each other, but he won't stop speaking all of his words to me. Even as we pull alongside of another house of visitation, his syllables never slow.

"Did you know the style of this house is called Tudor?" he asks, building up to another lesson fact I have no mental stamina to sit through.

"Great! Let's go kill a witch?" I ask him with a smile so false and wide my cheeks hurt.

I don't exit the car gently. The door slam is as much for my benefit as for the period on the conversation. I don't even care if whoever it is we are arriving for hears me.

"I think we may need to take this one a little slower than our normal pace," he tells me, rushing to grab my arm before I step on the lawn.

"Why?"

"You're doing that whole thing again where you are looking but you're not seeing," he says, gesturing with his hand in front of me. "Nice green lawn under the heat of summer? Do you hear a single bird singing or dog barking? Should we even remark on how bright the paint on this house is compared to the rest of the houses? As if it was just done yesterday?"

Reluctantly, I stop to look at the neighborhood. These houses were once the pride and joy of those who built them, but those days, or families, are long gone. Yards are dry patches or choked with weeds. What started out as well thought out paint schemes are now faded regrets. There's not a sound among the many structures. There's no life, and yet somehow the house before us looks fresh and brand new.

"Maybe she just keeps up with the place?" I suggest, not always willing to jump to the magic assumption. "There are people who find pride in what they have. Take care of it. Fix it. Keep things going."

He leans in close with his eyes still for the house before us. "Are you still talking about the home?"

"Of course!"

At least I think I am and to prove that I am, I walk right through the lawn and then double over with pain.

Jedrek sighs. "Tried to warn you." He strolls easily through the thick grass. Once again offering his hand to help me stand. "This is getting to be a pattern."

"Fuck off," I mutter through the pain and the amused expression on his face.

The yard seems the length of acres as it tears through my stomach. Every step takes more strength than I knew I had within me. The grass feels thicker with each step, tugging to secure my feet, rooting me in these waves of pain forever.

"Almost there," Jedrek offers, trying to hide the worry from his voice. "Soon as we get to the porch it will stop."

"How do you know?"

"Because there is also no driveway or walkway. That pretty little yard is a barrier spell against witches."

"Why witches?" I ask, trying to focus on our conversation and not the feelings of my guts being scrambled.

"If she was truly banned, no longer protected by her house, then she's free game for any harm she's ever done. No witch makes it in that coven without making a few frenemies along the way."

"Sounds delightful."

Jedrek lifts me, carrying me the last few steps. When he places me on the first red bricked step of the porch, the pain slides away. It pulls from my body instead of being an instant stop, leaving behind an ache to remind me of what awaits me when we're done.

"Better?" he asks, leaning over to look at my face.

"Yeah. Better." I nod, trying to tell myself I don't need a hug from the arms which were wrapped around me only hours ago. I almost convince myself it's true. Almost.

"Maybe I should go in first?" He's still bent over to read my floating expressions, trying to gauge which personality is headed his way.

"All you," I pant, still fighting through the dull ache.

He makes an exaggerated face of shock but takes the steps ahead of me. The cement porch is pressure washed white. The wooden door gleams with a polished look. Even the little row of windows at the top of it are free from dust or dirt. I've watched GiGi take a toothbrush to our home and never has it looked as crisp as this house does, but there's one thing ruining the perfect projected image. The smell.

I know that smell. I know it for many reasons, most I don't talk about, but I know it. It's the smell of a rotting body, fresh and most likely bloated and moist from sweating the putrid juices of the internal organs.

Jedrek turns to me, wondering if I smell it too. I cast him an expression of 'no shit' before leaning on the porch railing. Shrugging to keep our silent game of charades going, he kicks the door open, if not completely off its hinges.

It was a mistake. The type of mistake I have been making most of my life. What could have been a gentle entrance, easing our senses into the hot oven of a house which sits cooking whatever is dead inside of it, he ruined with ego and misplaced confidence. Now, the waves of it rush to the porch like an angry sea, battering us with the strength of it. It sticks in my mouth, lodges in my nose and even coats the walls of my throat causing me to gag.

"I don't think she's going to tell us where Johanna is," I tell him, not letting the irony of the situation escape me.

Groaning with frustration, he storms into the house. My stomach is begging me not to. It's been through enough, but my brain, the one normally shy to enter the fray, is listing all the reasons I too have to follow him into the house.

The first step is the hardest, that motion to defy all logic. The second step is slightly easier. The third your body caves, understanding you're not going to listen to its advice, anyway. By the fourth step I'm fully in the house, standing at the base of the wooden stairs with their runner in front of me, and to my side, a room Jedrek is standing in, still and waiting.

"She's over there, isn't she?" I ask him, draping my arm over my face to secure my nose in the safety of my elbow.

Jedrek makes a sound of agreement. It's the emptiest sound I have ever heard from him. My mind races with what condition she must be in. It paints a thousand rotting shades of her skin, to the list of insects devouring her. My mind spares no details. It hides no idea, no matter how unlikely it may be. It prepares me for everything, or so I thought.

She's resting on an ornate chaise. Her black hair is spread around her like a demonic halo, framing a face so deformed, and covered in crawling insects, it takes a moment for my eyes to bring what I am seeing to focus. Where her eyes once were, are now long furious rows, ripping open her face from her eyebrows to her cheeks. On either side of her mouth is also a long gash almost reaching the rows from her eyes. Her scalp is missing sections of hair. It's been pulled so hard there are missing pieces of her head. The bugs are so numerous, feasting in the mutilation, her skin almost seems to move as they burrow deeper into their meal.

"Explains the smell," Jedrek says to me, noticing my losing battle against it.

"Any idea why she looks like this?" I ask and then quickly add, "If you say because she's dead I swear I will punch you."

"Foreplay? Here?" he gasps, sitting on the chaise and patting a spot beside him. "If you insist."

His patting has made the body move, tilting the head to almost appear to be staring up at me. When a giant bug crawls from a socket, my stomach expels everything which was in it all over the hardwood floors.

"Could have just said no," he tells me, overacting a bruised ego with an eye roll and forcing himself off the chaise. "This is classic beauty gone wrong. Or right. Depending on what the deal was."

"The deal?" I don't bother to stand fully erect. My stomach is still taking bets on if it's done or not.

"A mortal would normally sign a contract stating for five to twenty years, depending on how good of a mood the demon is at the time, they would be beautiful. The kind of beauty mortals do stupid things once achieved, like make porn tapes and swear their ass is real. After the allotted time is reached, poof, mortal goes insane, killing themselves and most times others too. That part is kind of a bonus for the demon."

"Oh," I say not sure what else there is to say.

"Most likely, since I know of no contract enacting this little beauty of a curse," he turns to me, his face beaming, "no pun intended, I'm guessing this is the work of our little naughty girl."

"If when the curse is up, the demon collects the soul, what is she collecting from the deaths?"

"My littlest witch, you are a genius!" He kisses the top of my head after he claps, rubbing his palms together with excitement over whatever my question meant for him.

"Power?" I ask. "If a witch dies under her curse, she collects their power." My words are soft, the type of pitch when one talks out loud to solve a problem. Our problem just keeps growing. "Which is why she could clear the Torte's home so effectively. She's killing witches for their power."

"Ask her where she is," Jedrek suggests.

"Who? She's dead."

"Exactly."

His smile is one of a challenge and a dare, doubt filled that I will take him up on his offer, but excited to see if I will try.

"She's too gone. Who would want to return to that?" I ask, rudely gesturing to the state of the woman's body.

"Don't ask. Command." He takes a few steps back, retreating from the direct line of the magic. "Force her to come back."

"Seems rude," I whisper like a child being bullied. "I don't think this is a good idea."

"We are wasting time. Demons are disappearing, a family is waiting for you to help them and who knows how many others are just waiting time bombs for her to use. What is ruder? Sitting back because you don't want to bother a witch who sold her soul for a few years of beauty or waking the bitch to ask her how to stop it all from happening again?"

"You suck at pep talks," I tell him adding a middle finger to solidify my words, but he's right and that's the real reason the middle finger was added.

Fighting past my stomach's refusal to stop the war, I coax the dark tendrils out of their cage. They answer, slithering inside of me, easing down my stomach and whispering their words of bravery in my mind.

"Take it right to the edge, Harper, but no further," Jedrek warns, feeling the ripples of magic edge towards him, curious to taste him again.

I search for her in the beyond, seeking her little light as souls appear to me. I feel her light before I see it. It's rushing away, hiding and blending with the other souls she passes to conceal her. She's ashamed of the life she lived and the death she allowed. There is no desire to return to this realm.

The magic knows what to do. With the patience of a predator, it waits for her to run a little too close, and when she makes that mistake, she is snatched by green wisps encasing her. They drag her to this side, thrusting her so forcefully into her rotting cage the body bounces with the merging.

"Tell me your name," I command of the writhing corpse.

She fights me, trying to flee back to the other side.

"Tell me your name!"

Her mouth opens, spewing forth the many insects which have taken haven in the dark cavity. "Nia." The voice is nothing more than a dry whisper.

"Where is Johanna?" I ask Nia, clinging to the thread of connection we have made.

She starts to twist her body again, sending the bugs everywhere around her.

"Where is Johanna?" I ask louder, tugging on the magically created leash wrapped around her.

She stands, lurching her body forward in one impossible motion. Bugs and damper things are expelled towards my face, knocking me weak. The husk laughs. The dry sound taunts me.

"Where is Johanna!" I scream, and it's my turn to play.

My magic shoves its fingers into her skull. I pull from her every moment she wished to hide from, displaying them for her and me to see. Her body vibrates, rocking from my magic robbing her, invading her mind to gain what she is fighting to tell me. I watch the moment they met. Nia, a shy mouse of a woman and Johanna a temptress of possibilities, but Nia tries to block the image of Johanna from me, wrapping her in a hazy fog. The deeper I push, the clearer she becomes. I watch as Nia signs the parchment scroll with a moment's hesitation before being coaxed into it. I watch Johanna place the silver locket with a fragile chain around Nia's neck. There are instructions given and Nia nods before leaving the room. Forcing myself deeper into the memories, I memorize everything about the outside of the mansion Nia exits. I see through her eyes the white stucco and the numbers of the house proudly displayed next to the door. When I have what I need, I withdraw my magic, dropping the broken shell of the woman to the ground.

I know she's still in there. I can feel her shame still rolling around in what's left of her. If I left her now, she would forever be trapped, wasting away until there is nothing to hold her. Then this house would be her grave. She would roam the halls, searching for some means of escape for eternity.

"You are free to return to the other side," I tell Nia.

There's a soft sigh when she flies from her body once more. I can see the little spark swirling, unsure of where to go, but it doesn't carry any interest for me. The missing locket does.

"It was a silver locket. She took it off and this happened. She clawed her own face when she saw it once more, no longer hidden by the magic. Her mouth, which she always hated, she used a butter knife to "fix it'."

"How did she die?" Jedrek asks, stepping closer now that the magic is safely tucked away.

"The wounds on her forehead are from her slamming her head against the table to flatten it. Blind and unable to talk, she hit her head until it killed her. All she wanted was to return back to how she was before the locket was removed."

Jedrek and I both stand in silence, thinking about what this woman's death entailed and the suffering she caused herself. She was told lies to convince her to sign. Little lies which were based on the truth but omitting too much to make them the truth. Little lies to draw one in with hopes of their torment ending. The little lies which sneak past our defenses and leave us vulnerable. Johanna trades in little lies and souls. Unfortunately for her, Nia's little lies showed me exactly where she is.

Walking to the table coated in blood and bits of things I don't want to acknowledge; I open the velvet pouch laid upon it. The spark hovers, waiting to see what I will do. As soon as my fingers touch the chain to pull the locket out, a cold frost climbs along them.

"If I tell you not to do that, you're just going to do it anyway, aren't you?" Jedrek asks from behind me.

There are so many dead attached in some way or another to this piece of heirloom jewelry I don't need Jedrek's warnings. I see all their deaths, each worse than the other. I hear their screams of anguish. For a few, I hear their victims, begging them to stop before they too dissolve into the melody.

Without a word, I hand the locket, asleep in its pouch, to Jedrek. Without a word, he takes it. When we glance at each other, still without a word, we both know I just helped sign souls to hell, and we both know, I will never let him forget that fact.

Johanna's house sits behind a wide circular drive. Every plant and bush has been picked and pruned to accent every space of its exterior. Various different makes and models of cars are parked, some exquisite, some soccer mom style - complete with stick figures on the back windows - and yet others are the normal working class. They all sit, and they all say something different.

"She's making quite a little shop for herself," I remark as Jedrek and I stare at the assembled parking lot.

Jedrek says nothing, just lifting his brows the way he does when he isn't sure he can trust his words.

The home is grand and has a wide-open floor plan. She hasn't spared a penny on outfitting her new empire. The floor is gleaming. The white marble granite, with the grey lines streaked through it, has been polished to a shine the moon would envy. Everywhere, large bouquets of fresh flowers sit on tables. They fill the air with their perfume. It's sickly sweet, almost too much, just like the rest of the house with its portrait covered walls.

"Which one is her?" I ask Jedrek, pointing to the many faces watching us.

I know they are enchanted. I can feel their painted eyes watching our progress through the house. I have no doubt they report back to Johanna all who enter her home and all that is said while in it.

"None of them," Jedrek informs me. "She wouldn't be so stupid."

"She seems pretty stupid," I whisper, feeling their eyes heavy on my back.

"She's foolish. Maybe a pinch of brave, but not stupid. She has guards which cannot be corrupted," he gestures to the many paintings strategically placed. "She has plants which poison the air with a spell of beguile, making anyone with grievances forget them. Her floor is enchanted with a spell of enfeeblement, making people easier to manipulate. So no, she wouldn't be so stupid to put herself in a painting which could be used against her."

"I had no idea," I whisper in amazement.

"Don't worry," he tells me. "Neither did she till a few months ago."

Following the sounds of conversation, we find those who own the cars pacing the thick rugged sitting room. Men, and a few women, wait with tapping fingers or swinging feet with their anxiety written all over their bodies. All of them are here willing to sign away something they don't believe in until the bell tolls. Then they will beg, pleading for another chance. A chance they won't get.

"If she knows we are here…" I let my words trail off, wondering how to surprise someone who has taken every precaution to not be surprised and yet grateful her other precautions have not taken effect. I still cling to every intention to rip her trinkets away, despite what it may mean.

"Then we wait," Jedrek says, claiming a seat a short sofa nearest to where we stand.

The others in the room are doing their best to not look at us, only to fail and cast their eyes our way over and over again. I can feel their anticipation drizzled with fear. They are wondering if they are making the right choice. With every step on the thick rug, I can see the spell floating upwards relaxing their distress, easing whatever burdens they have placed on their minds about doing what she has asked as her price.

"She's good. I'll give her that," I say, watching the spell repeat itself over and over.

Jedrek rolls his eyes with an expression of one having to give credit to their sworn enemy. I watch him settle into a mental debate. As he stares at the closed door, I know where his dark thoughts are carrying him. When it slides open, Jedrek is up and walking towards it with a motion more fluid than a mortal could achieve. His eagerness to be the next through the door sets the room into motion.

"I was here first!" a woman shouts, almost climbing over the couch between her and the door. "I was here first!"

Jedrek gives her a smile which sets her feet to frozen. She inches backwards, clutching her bag to her chest as if it were a shield. The size of it, it could be one.

Rushing to keep up with him, I can see there is no one to stop us. There is no one blocking or keeping watch over who comes and goes through this last barrier. The doors open to a room filled with the smoke of incense. It rolls in the air with a life of its own. It doesn't part or follow any breeze made by our entrance. It hovers, waiting, reminding me of one of Jedrek's threatening shadows. It's as he said before. She doesn't need guards. She has protection made from her will and the stolen items taking the will of others.

"I was wondering when you would come, Jedrek," her voice comes from the very back of the room. "I didn't expect you to bring friends."

She emerges from the darkness she has created around the far corners of the room. Her black hair shines, catching the light from the many candles burning around us. Her makeup is artfully done, pulling colors to her ruby lips and darkened eyes. Everything she passes, she trails her fingers along, touching and caressing the items in her path. She moves like a serpent, but she walks like a seductress.

"This little witch?" he asks, mimicking her slow stroll through the room. "She's here for a different reason."

She lifts one of her perfect eyebrows. "And for what reason is that?"

"To convince me to not kill you," he says with a touch of boredom for the words.

"Others have come before you, Jedrek. What makes you think you can?" she smiles her question, enjoying the game of his ego.

Jedrek shrugs, making a grand gesture of extending his arms with the motion, but he says nothing.

Johanna's eyes travel from Jedrek to me. I can feel her testing my walls, pushing against my power to see how it answers hers. I can feel her in my mind like cobwebs trying to disorient my thoughts, to slow my magic's response. She creeps around my heart and mind trying to pry my deep secrets from their locked rooms. She gains nothing but my anger.

"How dare you," I whisper, hearing the voice which lives deep inside of me. It's my voice. It belongs to me, I know this now, but she's so different than me. "How dare you," I say again with the taste of her black licorice flavored magic coating my tongue.

"Or maybe *she'll* kill you," he states hearing my voice. "Maybe we'll *both* kill you." He's tossing his head back and forth with his contemplations.

"Or," Johanna counters, "maybe I'll kill both of you."

I didn't see the smoke creeping around me. I didn't feel her power coiling itself around the room. GiGi had warned me, but as always, I wasn't seeing. I was just looking.

The black smoke rushes down my throat, clogging and blocking air from reaching my lungs. My panic causes me to claw at my flesh as if I can make another hole for which the air may find entrance. Darkness clouds my vision. It blocks the room from me despite the many sounds reaching my ears. Lost in my own fears of death, I cannot tell if the screams are from Johanna or from Jedrek.

The pressure in my skull feels as if it is breaking bones as organs starve for air. With my life slipping from my body, the panic slows, and I can think. I can see. All around the room stands the many people Johanna has tricked. They are still, mute, unspeaking, and almost washed out. They are trapped between this world and the next where they belong. It's from them who she pulls her powers.

They feel my call. Their heads turn towards me, watching me fight to outlast the smoke invading me. With my magic, the magic which does not need to be awakened, but the magic which is always there, I push them, forcing them to the other side as I would not do with Nia. I separate them from her one by one, plucking her threads which tie them here. With each washed-out form slipping into the beyond, the smoke shrinks, allowing air into the narrow gaps now provided.

The room also comes into sight. Johanna is no longer the perfection she was when we entered. Her hair is rumpled. Her face has scratches with red streaks of blood ruining her composed appearance. Her bottom lip also bleeds, smearing a wide, red spot across her chin. The vibrant anger proves it's been a long time since someone dared to harm her. Much longer time since someone was able.

Jedrek is panting, leaning against a tall bookcase smiling at her. His ice blue eyes, even in the midst of this fight, are bright with excitement. The sleeves of his shirt are torn, showing where blood once was, but Johanna cannot keep up with his unhuman body. It heals faster than she can harm it despite her desperation and many newly acquired powers.

As the smoke grows too weak to keep me enthralled, I fall to my knees, panting and retching on the carpet. The spell she has placed upon it caresses my hands, stroking my face with gentle warmth to bring me comfort. Since it was the dead who gave her strength to empower it, it does more than just comfort me. It feeds me, opening the door to the magic I fear, but now need.

There was no coaxing this time. I feel the green mist wrap around my arms like vines, growing wild and quickly along my body. The lights of eyes merge with my vision, casting the room in a green tint. I can feel the dead here. They call to my banner like ancient knights of darker times, rallying to my side with a battle cry older than time herself.

"How dare you," I call again in the same voice which sparked Johanna's attack. The same voice she recognized as my voice of power. "You steal the power from the dead and think you can use it against me. Me? Do you not know who I am? What I am?"

Standing to face her, I can feel my fingers twitch with power waiting to be unleashed. The dead stand ready in their many wraithlike forms to do my bidding and eager to seek their revenge. They tell their tales of how she lied to them. She never spoke of what happens when the trinkets stop. She neglected to tell them of how every blessing has its curse. They paid her exorbitant price with more than just the money she asked. They paid her the exorbitant price of their souls.

"You cannot control what is mine, dark sister," Johanna shouts from across a table she's placed between her and I. "You have no power here."

"Jedrek had said you were foolish, but he was wrong. You are truly stupid," I calmly tell her as my skin begins to glow. "You can't control what you lied to. A contract is only as good as the words put upon it. You made a deal for their money. You never signed for their souls."

I watch as her face contorts with her thoughts. "When they die, they revert back to the item. I own the items!"

"You've stolen the items, naughty witch," Jedrek coos, walking to where she stands foolishly behind the wooden table. "They never belonged to you."

"Nor do those you lied to, but they do have a message for you," I tell her, releasing those waiting to inflict their revenge.

They tear into her, ripping her apart so she may feel the anguish, the torment she gifted them with for her own gains. To those who cannot see them, it must look as if she is carving her own flesh in her madness as she tries to cover her gaping wounds. Her face is ribbons, weaving rows of her tanned skin between lines of the exposed meat of her cheeks. Her eyes are hanging merely by the tendons attached to them. The slinky black dress she was so proud to wear hid nothing then and hides nothing of what is left of her now. They have torn her so deeply, bones are visible in her legs, her arms and whole fingers have been degloved, yet still, she lives, screaming in her agony.

"Enough," my voice catches, trying to call back those I unleashed, trying to stop what I have allowed to happen. "Enough!" I shout more from terror than strength.

"You have released them to do as they want, littlest witch. You can't call them back now. They won't stop till their rage has been sated." Jedrek tells me from where he is walking wide around the scene I have caused. He doesn't shrink from the sight as I am. He is fascinated, watching it all like it's a grand tour of hell herself. "I always wondered what would happen to souls not collected. There have been times I felt guilty for God's mortals in their foolishness. A time or two I almost agreed to let them stay here on Earth as they wailed over their dead bodies." He tells me all of this while Johanna screams, trying to run from the things destroying her with her body almost too broken to do so. "There were times those like me, those not yet twisted by hatred for His favorite little pets, did leave souls behind and they turned into the haunted places mortals now have become obsessed with." Reaching his hands to brace either side of Johanna's face, he wrenches her head abruptly, ending the screaming forever. "And now I know what happens."

The dead do not stop simply because she is dead. Her body jerks with their attacks. They drag her limp body from one side of the room to the other, lifting her high along the walls to further spread her blood along their new canvas. I once again fall to my knees watching it with guilt robbing my strength. The tears upon my cheeks feel warmer than the blood this room shall forever be stained with.

"There must be a way," I remark weakly.

"They are bound to the cursed objects. You simply summoned them, gathered them and used your will to release their motives." Jedrek is searching the room, throwing things randomly into the air if they hold no interest for him. "The only way to salvage this whole mess is to find each item and reunite it with the proper owner before they grow bored with her destruction and become something you don't want to learn how to deal with, yet."

"And then?"

"Then the object, and all those attached to it, will return to hell to be stored away."

"They didn't know," I plead.

"You're right," he tells me with aloofness. "They simply just signed a piece of paper offering them their heart's desire never questioning the real reasons behind it. You know," he spins to me with his latest thought, "there was a time when witches were thought to be hand in hand with the devil himself for their wicked ways. Somehow, you became the good guys and yet we still stayed the bad."

"They are under the floorboards under her desk." Too exhausted to play his verbal games, I point to the large ornate desk where she has kept all her secrets safe, until now. "All but the music box being used by Miranda."

It is nothing for him to slide the heavy desk aside. Nor did he struggle to lift the metal door from the safe. He doesn't cast a sideways glance with the sounds of bones popping from what's left of Johanna's body. I can't help but look. I can't help but stare with tears of regrets and guilty thoughts of what kind of monster I must be to allow such a thing to happen.

I can't hear his victory cry. I don't listen to his cheerful disposition. All I hear is the sounds of wet meat being butchered. All I see is the woman who stands watching the unnecessary destruction of her body. Her sorrowful eyes float my way, connecting with the magic which now hides in shame deep inside of me, deeper than it normally lurks. With that spark, I know he's wrong. He said so himself. I was born of death and blood. Death and blood are my calling card, my Hallmark greeting. All I have to do is accept it, embrace it and use it.

I let the green smoke wrap around me once more. I welcome it. I don't hide or try to let the inner voice take over. I merge us. My doubts. Her strength. My shame. Her glory. I bathe in it, all of it, no holding back or hesitation, and the world never looked so beautiful.

Everything is awash in shades of greens. From the deepest of jades to the brightest of limes, the room is alive in a way smoke is in a crowded room. The colors encircle and embrace each other to blend, making new shades with the energy of the room pulsing the colors past one another. It's not just the colors that are new. I can see the objects around me in their true stage of life. Fruit, which was ripe and tempting when we arrived, is bruising, browning as it sits. The plants are failing, wilting in their pots. I can feel all of those, alive and dead, who have traveled this room. I can hear their conversations rolling on top of each other as each person debated with Johanna, and themselves, over what they came to do. The room is alive, but it's also very dead.

"What are you doing, Harper?" Jedrek asks, and for the first time there's a twinge of nerves emerging from behind his words.

"What I do best," I answer him with a voice all my own. "Proving people wrong."

I can see every soul who is feasting upon her. They are lost in their frenzy of revenge, sinking deeper into damnation and oblivion as each act strips them of the humanity needed to anchor in this world and be allowed into the next. A few more minutes and all of them will be lost to a purgatory of their own making, an eternity of being housed in their madness.

"Enough," I command, pulling from the depths of my being to reach what small spark is left in the depths of theirs.

There's a pause, tilting of their heads, but nothing more.

My power is the pain of death, the torture of loss, grief, everything they are revealing, and I pull that emotion, much as one would a leash on a dog. I pull it to me and pull them with it. One by one they leave their battered trophy, confused as to why they are doing it, but obeying the pull just the same.

"Harper?" Jedrek's voice calls again. "What do you think you are doing?"

"Pissing you off," I reply with a version of a smirk to match his on his best days.

These people didn't deserve the trick which was played on them. Demons, from what I have gathered, have rules. There is fine print, read and agreed upon. These idiots just thought they found a shortcut in life. They didn't know it would cost them theirs.

Still clutching their leash tightly in my closed fists, I tell Jedrek, "If all of this means there is a God or Devil, a Heaven and Hell, or just something after we die other than the holding area I find them in, then let God or the other guy sort it all out. They aren't going to Hell simply because a trinket says so. Not today."

With the declaration made, I force their sparks into the beyond. I push them mentally through the veil before their flickering spark is spent, casting them forever into darkness. I do this as I watch Jedrek dissolve into a rage.

"Those were not yours to give away." Jedrek is staring at the spot the many were just standing. "We earned those souls. Demons were killed to steal them from us. A few of them were my friends. Most I won't miss, but that doesn't mean you can tip the scales on a moral whim."

His voice is calm and collected, but his face is not. His face tells of a war brewing, a war with me. Seeing as I already have that card played with the werewolves, I really shouldn't be amused by how undone he has become.

"I thought you couldn't manipulate free will?" I ask, tilting my head, and my red curls float with the soft movement.

Jedrek is silent, trying to figure out where I am taking this crazy train of mine now.

"They didn't give you their souls of their own free will. They gave their money, sure, but not their soul. Just as you told Johanna, you don't own the souls, just the trinkets." I turn my back to him, ready to leave this forsaken palace built on the damnable. "But I imagine, she had to sign a deal or two to start this whole scheme. What's the soul of a witch worth down there?"

I don't wait around to watch another round of torture Johanna. My stomach has had its fill of the gambit today. My mind and heart aren't far behind.

Those who were waiting are still doing exactly that, waiting with tapping feet and drumming fingers. How the screams and chaos didn't reach these outer rooms brags to the former mistress of this home's power, but she's no longer here. Just me and a demon with a score to settle. Neither of us are granting wishes today.

"Is it my turn?" the same lady from before jumps up to ask.

Her business suit is three different shades of black. Her heels have the visible signs of sharpie to attempt to cover the many scuffs from everyday wear. This is what the outside world sees. I see the many deep lines creeping along her skin, the thinning hair, the sunken eyes from long sleepless nights from stress and all the brown spots of southern sun damage just waiting to further whittle away her self-esteem. Remembering the rows of cars parked, the voices match her to the car with the words advertising her latest work from home failure. It's not hard to imagine what she came for, or at least what her goals are with being here.

"Sure is," Jedrek says beside me, causing me to do a very annoying little jump. He covers my mouth with his hand before I have the chance to argue. "She's waiting for you."

Leaving the sliding doors open, he pulls me from the room, spreading his cheer and warm smile as we exit. Flashing his baby blues to the room to keep their anxiety to a low rumble with the enchantments wearing off, his hand clamps harder around my mouth.

"Might be a good time to pull that magic back in," he suggests in a whisper.

I had forgotten. I had grown used to seeing everything in swirls and their expiration date boldly displayed before me. Yet, I can't see his. He looks the same.

We are in the main foyer when the screaming starts. The many large bouquets, without the magic feeding them, are now rotting stems, moldy in their murky water. The white marble has become slate-like flooring, showing its true state. Even the tall painting which once stood guard, watching and tattling on all those who entered, has aged, becoming thread bare and desolate. This whole place held Johanna's biggest illusion and her darkest fear. She was nothing without someone else's power, someone else's source. Her magic was slim, slipping further away each day. Using her own fears of being forgotten, being powerless in her own life, she drew the mortals in like a spider on her web, ensnaring her clueless victims before wrapping them so tight that death was soon eminent.

"What did you do with her?" I ask Jedrek once we are safely driving away from our second murder scene of the day.

"Found out what the current worth is for a witch's soul," he tells me without any joy.

He's back to answering questions with riddles but this time I can read between the unsaid words.

"And the objects?"

"Sent them back to where they belong."

"Except for one," I remind him. "But we'll go get that back tonight after a shower and some food before the spell ends and takes Miranda.

He's chewing his bottom lip over whatever thoughts he may be having hearing my reminder.

"Right?" I ask with his extended silence.

He tilts his head as he tries to pick the best way to start the conversation. "Not exactly?"

"What do you mean?" The way this day has played out, I'm not sure I really want to know the answer.

"Remember how all this started? Our little romance? Me saving your precious little life?" He asks, sounding almost nostalgic with his words.

"If that's how you remember it, sure."

"Feisty," he loudly whispers. "Do you remember the word 'source of power' being tossed around like condoms in a college dorm?"

"Never went to college, but sure," I tell him trying to block that mental picture.

"Well," Jedrek says with a nervous smile trying to be something more playful, "The one Mrs. Torte has her hands on isn't just another trinket from the dark side, per se."

"Per se?" I turn down the volume on the radio to better hear how much worse this is going to get.

He makes a grimacing expression of jest. "This little box of fun is from one of our strongest. Its magic was forged from the first magic. It was corrupted by the woman who wielded it when her lover changed teams mid war. The pain from his betrayal caused her to become a little hostel. Honestly, I never really liked him. Didn't fully understand her melt down over him, either." He turns to me pointing to his eyes. "There was always something a little off in his eyes. That one should have been cooked a little longer before the big guy pulled him into being."

Placing my hands over my face, I rest my suddenly heavy head on their braced support. "We have started a war with the witches and wolves. We just watched the slaughter of another witch after having a nice little visit with a rotting witch. Both of these witches, I might add, we desecrated their bodies, and now you want to have a little chit chat about Divinity?"

"Divinity is kind of an important thing here," he offers off-handily as if insulted.

"I don't even believe in 'the big guy'!"

"Not really important what you believe in. It doesn't change things. A few days ago, you didn't believe in half the stuff you've seen in the past twenty-four hours. Guess what was still there today? Mortals believe mostly in Potter and Santa Clause, it doesn't mean the real stuff isn't around. In fact, if things which were only believed in existed, half the people I know wouldn't. Which might not be a bad thing..."

His words trail off like my patience for the whole situation. I took what was supposed to be a simple plan, which somehow turned into a plot twisted into another plot by mere chance. A simple side job to make the debt collectors happy has been nothing but little lies upon little lies, turning into a disastrous event. This whole event, from start to finish, which we haven't even reached yet, has turned everything upside down, scattering locked memories like a used deck of playing cards and opening closed doors wider than their hinges normally allow. I wish I never agreed to that blind date. I should have stayed home, snuggled deep under my electric blanket and telling Netflix I'm still there.

"How do we fix it?" I ask the silent demon; lost no doubt in the list of names he wouldn't mind missing.

"Define 'fix'?"

I know what he's asking. He just thinks he's being clever.

"I don't want her dead. Her family has been through enough, Jedrek."

He drums his fingers with his thoughts while I stare out the window. I'm watching his reflection. None of the faces he is making brings me any positive vibes for a happy ending to this story.

"We're going to have to kill her, aren't we?" I ask his reflection, not willing to see the truth in bold colors before me.

"Or we could just wait it out," he suggests. "If she's opened the box, and obviously she has if the girl is back, then she's linked to it.

The dark magic is using her. It's her life which is giving the little girl life."

"Can't I just put the little girl back?"

"There's that whole 'linked' word you missed. Even if you do, the magic will pull her back as long as Miranda is alive."

"There has to be a way," I argue. "I might not know a lot about this shit, but I know every spell has a back door, some loophole worked into it."

"It does. Define fix."

"You define fix, Jedrek. Tell me, in plain English, how to fix this!" I'm shouting at the situation. I'm shouting at my exhaustion. I'm shouting because he's right. There's too much I don't know, but I'm here, waist deep in it all, watching the water slowly rise over my head.

Jedrek sighs, trying to find a way to tell me what has to be said. "There's two options, Harper. You're not going to like either of them, because both means you have to stop acting like a toddler and accept things." He pauses, waiting to see my reaction before starting again. "One, we let this play out. We let the mortal pay for her actions. She's brought suffering to her family, disturbed a soul at rest and most likely warped the little boy for the rest of his life. I'll probably be called back to collect him in a few years after what he's seen."

"Option two?" I ask, trying to keep him focused.

"You accept your role in the supernatural order of things."

I turn from his reflection to face him. As he mockingly winces, I ask him, "What does that mean?"

"It means you have to stop hiding, stop being afraid, demand Jo tell you everything, and then step into your powers. This is dead magic. It brings back the dead. You can break it, if you were powerful enough, anyway, and before you open your mouth to argue, or to list all the many things you did today, this is God magic, the first magic. Which presents another problem."

"Like we don't have enough of those you want to sprinkle in some more, just for fun?"

Jedrek lifts his eyebrows playfully. "Life has gotten a little more amusing since stumbling upon you."

"What's the other problem."

"You'll be marked for her to find. She won't want to pass up the chance to own a witch strong enough to break God magic. You'll be setting a timer for your death or at the very least, your slavery."

"I die or Miranda dies is the summary of all of that?" I ask, sitting back in the leather bucket seat.

"You die or she dies."

"Can we talk about how much I hate blind dates?"

There's a tremble to my voice. I wasn't ready to sacrifice myself. I was ready to fight, to learn, to accept, but not die. I was ready to do what I do, put the dead to rest. I didn't know when I met the Tortes there would be a chance I would be putting myself to rest.

"We could just let it play out, Harper," Jedrek whispers to the windshield, also not wanting to see me in bold colors of truth. "We don't have to tell anyone. We'll let it play out and then collect the box. It would be our secret."

"Our little secret," I whisper.

So many little secrets. So many little lies. So many truths simply not told to protect the one we love the most, ourselves.

"Our little secret," I whisper again, knowing it's not a secret I want to keep.

GiGi Jo is waiting outside the shop when Jedrek drops me off. He doesn't stay. He doesn't even leave the safety of his car. This time, it's not me of whom he is afraid. It's the old woman, with her face set to murder, waiting for us on the steps of Great Hexpectations who has him fleeing for safety. If I were smart, I wouldn't have gotten out either.

"Is your phone broken?" GiGi clips her words with her question.

It's worse than Italian. Her fuse is smoking with how short the wick has become from the fire of her rage. Whatever I've done is bad. Very, very bad.

"I've been a little busy," I tell her shifting from foot to foot in my guilt. I want to spill forth everything I have done today like a small child pleading her case for why she shouldn't be grounded.

"Oh, I know," GiGi tells me, swinging open the door to the shop like a dare and less like an invitation.

Like the idiot I am, I walk through. I almost stopped to think about it. Almost. I should have, because waiting for me is Roman and my army of undead wolves.

"This is the longest day of my life," I whisper to myself.

Roman is wearing jeans which never saw a rack from the moment they were created. Nor did his pressed shirt or shined shoes. His blonde hair is cut close, professionally leaving just enough to allow his blonde birth right to shine under the shop's overhead lights. His deep brown eyes don't have the warmth his smile is trying to portray. Those eyes are predator and I think I just became the prey.

"I see you've met the family," he jokingly says, spreading his hand wide to motion towards the large wolves watching me, waiting for my next command.

In this moment, I'm not sure who they would answer to if called. In this moment, being watched by so many death-threat filled eyes, I'm not sure I want to know. Which means my mouth opens like the idiot I am.

"Deon introduced us. It was a charming little visit. I even adopted a few," I tell him, regretting every syllable I spilled.

GiGi clears her throat, an audible warning of a sound. She's taken to the little reading nook, placing herself in between the little standoff in case she is needed to fix any damage my sense of sarcasm and habitual death wishes cause for the already tense room.

Roman's smile widens, showing teeth whiter and sharper than natural teeth should be. "Deon has been dealt with. I just have to deal with you now."

"Good luck," I tell him. "GiGi has been trying to deal with me for years. Just look at all that grey hair."

Walking into the shop as if I own it, because I kind of do, I don't let his open threat show how it made my stomach do a little tango. I fight to appear unbothered as my heart beats randomly with a new pattern. In my mind, I'm going over every lore I've ever heard about werewolves, just as I had earlier with witches and covens. Unfortunately, it too is all movie-based and filled with popcorn scented disappointment.

Roman is chuckling a soft sound of danger when he begins to walk in my direction. I'm used to the way Jedrek moves. He moves as if he is held together by strings and air. Roman is walking so slowly it's as if he's made of things which hunt you in the night. He embodies the types of things which cause you to look over your shoulder when walking alone. He's every warning label we are taught brought to flesh and he's headed my way.

"You know I can hear your heart, right?" he asks, with his head low, listening to something I cannot hear and tapping the pattern with his fingers on his leg.

"You know I can feel my heart, right?" I ask, admitting my fear.

"Then why play these games?" he whispers with his head still low.

"It's kind of what I do," I whisper back. "Or maybe I'm just bored with you and need something to do to entertain me."

GiGi rolls her eyes, tilting her head back to stare at the ceiling above her.

"I could kill you where you stand." Roman lifts his eyes, watching me with his threat.

I feel the smile come to my lips before I can stop it. The giggling I hear from me has my mind asking if I have finally gone insane.

"You find me funny?" he asks. He's started his slow walk again, watching me with those lowered, brown eyes of his.

"I find you insulting. We both know what would happen should you kill me. The little break in the treaty your sister did this morning can be handled in house. You kill me, and you invite complete war."

"Why should I be afraid of a war with witches? We own over half the witches in this town."

"And the vampires?" I ask, totally hoping my little grasp on the fragile situation works in my favor for once. "Do you own them, too?"

Roman's predatory face melts to one of caution. "Our treaty with them has nothing to do with our treaty with the witches."

Lifting my hand, I tug on the magic which has been pacing inside of me, like its own version of a predator, just waiting to spring forth. The green mist swirls slowly encasing my fist, twisting with a warning of what may come.

"I'm not an ordinary witch."

"She's a head of a house," GiGi says from her chair. "You kill her, and you've attacked a power base, opening yours to be attacked by any other head of house. The vampires have been wanting more area to control for decades. You might as well fly a banner letting them know to come on down."

Whatever remark Roman had, Isabell whines to stop him. He glances to her, reading something in those eyes so close to his own coloring.

"She brought back an army of supernatural beings," GiGi reminds him.

"And all before noon. You should have seen what the rest of my day entailed. I'm really tired so if you could just tell me what this little drop in is about, that would be great for both of us."

My magic has grown, answering my skipping heart's panic. It's wrapped its long tail around my body, filling the area around me with a green haze of light. I know if I don't stop my racing heart my magic will continue to grow, filling my eyes and skin with its glowing lights. It will push this verbal stand off to a level I'm not sure I'm ready to handle.

"I want my family members to be put to rest. What Deon has done is one thing, but this," he looks to where the wolves are standing in a line with their mangled bodies and blank eyes, "this is something utterly different."

"And if they are put to rest, how do we know you won't come and do something stupid?" GiGi asks, and I understand where I get my false bravado from after hearing her.

Roman sighs, letting the predator side of him slip away with the air from his lungs. Holding his hands in a surrender pose, he says with an honesty that reaches his eyes, "I don't want to fight with you or any house. I just want to live in peace with my family. I knew the night you came out Deon wouldn't rest until we owned you like we own the other powerful witches. I knew you would be trouble for my family. I just didn't know it would be this kind of trouble. I have handled Deon. In good faith, for both of us, put my family to rest so I may bury them where they belong. They didn't deserve to die like this. They definitely don't deserve to live like this."

He looks to have aged while pleading his case, but to also have lost years, making him seem vulnerable and tender hearted. I can't argue with the truth of his words. At least not the truth behind the fact they don't deserve this. The rest is lies and hidden motives to my skeptical mind.

"Asking for peace while using the word 'own' is an interesting strategy," I tell him, bringing voice to my concerns.

He nods, looking more and more like a lost youth than a threating boogey man.

"I'll put them to rest," I'm drumming my fingers on the glass counter as if in thought. "But I'll keep them, for now. Once I know the rest of the witches are safe, that we're safe, I will release them to you to take home."

Isabell whines again when Roman's mouth opens.

"I think you should listen to your cousin," GiGi offers from the side lines.

Roman nods with a face less than agreeable. "For now," he repeats.

"Just until I can trust you and yours." I smile with what I hope looks caring and not mocking. "You haven't exactly proven your family to be of the neighborly type."

"Where will they rest?" he asks with gritted teeth holding back the things he really wants to ask.

I walk towards to the basement door, mentally summoning my furry death squad to follow me down. The wooden stairs complain with our weight, creaking and moaning with hints of their age and limitations.

The basement is exactly what most basements are, cold, dusty, and mostly used for storage for the things we have no idea what to do with on a daily basis. Which is what makes it the perfect place for them to be placed, for now, as I was reminded.

"They will be safe here," I tell Roman, who has only come half the way down.

He is looking around the now tight space with an appearance of neutral interest. I know a part of him wants to rebel against this, to force his hand and see where the cards land. I also know a part of him wants to go back to that night with his father with hopes to somehow prevent all of this from ever happening. I know all of this because, just as he can hear my heart, I can feel the magic which makes him what he is, filled with remorse and trepidation.

"I promise you nothing will happen to them. Once we leave this room, I will seal the door so that no one other than myself, or of my blood, may open it," I say to reassure him, but to also let him know if anything happens to me, GiGi will be able to seek her revenge. Unfortunately, there seems to be no secrets in the paranormal world.

"There is no one left of your blood," Roman says to me, filling his words with a curious pitch.

"I bound her to me when she was little," GiGi remarks from the top of the stairs. "As far as magic is concerned, we are blood and blood we shall be until blood pours no more."

"I don't need the line, Jo. I'm well aware how the spell works," he tells her, never glancing up where she stands.

"I guess that's why you have so many cousins," I hear myself say, and quickly try to recover. "Alright, so let's get this done?"

Before he can remark on my momentary slip of madness, I pull the jade fire around me. I pull it close like a second skin to build its strength and warmth. When the false flames start to devour me, I send it to each of the wolves. Spreading like wildfire around the room, each of them start to glow from the flame's light. I let it cover the wolves, the room, and the air around us until there is room for nothing else in this small space.

I don't want to do what I have to do next. My chest already feels as if the weight of the magic is crushing me, breaking my ribs to return to its source. I have expanded it to search for all traces of itself and now it wants to come home. All of it wants to come home.

"Damnit," I whisper before I inhale and brace for the return.

Like a vacuum, the flames retreat from the room, rushing back to me with a speed that bows my chest inward from the collision. As it retreats, the magic is pulled from the wolves and they fall, one by one, back to the deaths they were granted hours ago. With the magic gone, their bodies return to their human forms. Without the fur to hide the wounds, Roman sees more than he ever wanted to about what happened in that house. He can now see the true horrors the members of his family faced and the horrors to which they lost.

I can barely breath with the magic inside of me. It feels as if it's breaking bones, tearing apart tendons and thicker meats inside of me to make itself a new home. The pain brings tears to my eyes and robs the strength from my legs. Kneeling, panting, and almost crying, I am surrounded by the Ripples I helped to kill, twice now.

"You should go, Roman," GiGi tells him, seeing my distress and unsure exactly what he will do seeing his family in such a way.

"Give me your word, Necromancer," Roman whispers with a voice soft with rage and unsaid threats.

"I hate that title," I say between fighting for air.

He chuckles a sound of false amusement. "We don't get to pick our titles, Harper. Life does that for us. Promise me they will be safe."

"I promise they will be safe," I repeat the words I hope I can keep.

As he climbs the stairs, I hear him say, "I wish we had met under different circumstances, Harper. We might have been friends."

"Friends are just people who are better at hiding their daggers. I like it better this way. This way I won't be shocked when you stab her in the back, wolf," GiGi says with all the salt and vinegar I've come to love her for owning. "Get out of my shop and the next time you barge in here with false threats, and more penis than sense, I may just hand you your balls."

"I don't doubt you'd try, Jo," I hear him tell her from where I am still kneeling amid the dead. "I don't doubt you'd try."

The little bell over the entrance door rings a sound I've never been so happy to hear. The sliding of the dead bolt makes me almost giddy.

I lay my face on the cold stone floor and stare into the empty eyes of the woman nearest to me.

"I'm sorry," I tell her lifeless body. "I'm so sorry."

The last words I hear before I slip under the waves of exhaustion is from the woman I have come to know as my family and savior.

"None of this is your fault, Harper. You have nothing to be sorry for."

But she's wrong. I have many things to be sorry for, but for now, they are my little secret.

29

"S he has to know everything," Regan says from the other room, and I can't remember when she arrived.

In fact, even as I know I have been sitting here, in our little kitchen nook, I can't remember how I got here or how long I have been sitting at the table. The coffee is cold. My ass is numb. Putting the clues together, I'm guessing for some time.

"It would only put her in more danger," GiGi tells whoever is in there, gossiping about me as if I'm not sitting here, numb with cold coffee.

"She can't get in that much more danger!" Regan shouts, totally blowing the attempted cover up of their conversation.

"I mean, I could. It's only what, Thursday? There's still a whole day to end the week on an epic fail," I say to my depressing coffee and the two women sitting in a room they thought was soundproof.

"Glad to hear you're back with the living," Regan tells me through the wall. "Might as well come in."

My body protests the idea. Everything, and everywhere, hurts. It's the type of ache which makes you want to drown your sorrows in a hot bath and under a warm blanket. Neither of these things I imagine I will get to do tonight.

Regan is sitting with her legs tucked up under her in the large recliner. Her jeans are dark and they accent the one-shoulder purple shirt perfectly. Her light purple hair is tossed up in a high ponytail with her many braids accenting the sides. I could never pull off those colors, but she looks vibrant in them.

I'm leaning on the doorway, per my normal when I ask, "So what's this little chit of the chat?"

"What all *do* you know?" Regan asks, squinting her eyes to peer at me, or at least something about me.

"Like my ABC's? The names of the states? What year is it? What are you asking me?" I ask, clutching my cold coffee like a shield in its little cup advertising in a scrolling font, 'Hexy Witch'.

Regan rolls her eyes and I don't have to hear her sigh to know she sighed.

"Hocus pocus shit, Harper. She wants to know what you know about all of this," GiGi answers, still wearing her murder face and gesturing around her.

For a moment, I consider telling her about the house. I could tell her about the wood floor we had to reseal after GiGi over watered one of the hanging plants or maybe about the fourth stair going up which always screams with its wooden angst just to continue the game, but mostly, just to be the impressive pain in the ass I am. I don't want to admit I really know nothing about all this hocus pocus shit, as we have termed it.

"I know the basics," I sullenly admit, taking a sip of cold coffee, which I also won't admit to doing.

"The basics being?" Regan pries, squinting her eyes again.

"Oh, tits and ticks!" GiGi exclaims, slamming her mug down on the side table near her. "She knows what she needs to know!"

"Do I?" I ask, just barely brave enough to look over my cup towards her.

I watch as GiGi moves her jaw back and forth with unsaid words and heavy thoughts.

"Jo," Regan coaxes, "she needs to know. The power she used this afternoon will be felt by many others. I felt it and I'm small time. They will come to see who she is, what she is, and she needs to be ready."

GiGi waves her hands with defeat. "Fine. Tell her. Tell her all of it."

"I feel like I should be sitting for this," I say, making my way further into the room with a bit of hesitation and touch of passive aggressiveness.

"Do you know what it means to be born of blood and death?" Regan asks, jumping right into it and ignoring my attempt to avoid it.

"Isn't everyone born of blood?" I ask her with my deflection of sarcasm.

"That's not the same, but yes, I suppose," Regan is tiling her head and looking to be reading something off the ceiling's paint. "Born of blood and death means your mother died while giving birth to you but was brought back before you were separated from her."

I look to GiGi who has become fascinated by one of the long vines of the plant she's petting. Feeling my stare, she answers, "Your mother's heart gave out during the cesarean, but they were able to restart it before the cord was cut. You were born of blood, as in cut from her body, and from death, since she technically died for a second or two there before being brought back."

"You were connected to both worlds, Harper," Regan says, jumping on the explain train. "That connection carries now. You're not just a necromancer. I know plenty of necromancers, or mediums, or such. You are something more. You don't just talk to the dead or see the dead or even work with them. You can literally command them, control them to do whatever you want. Should you want."

"And why does that make me such a threat?" I ask her, doing my best to not sound interested.

"Because over half of the power houses are the dead. Vampires. Demons. Demons in humans. Which means even Angels since they were never 'alive'. They are animated by magic. Magic you can tap into and control. You could enslave almost all the top houses."

I listen to Regan and I feel as if I'm watching the old cartoon with the teacher of sounds and not words. How can I, unicorn wearing, still jumping into bed so the monster under it doesn't grab my foot, be a threat to powers such as theirs?

"You could walk right now into Da Luna Dela and shut the whole place down since it's run off the dead witches who once lived and worked there," Regan says with a tint of awe.

GiGi, still petting her plant, tells me, "The spa. That's the name of the spa."

"Oh," is all I have to form. I keep sipping the cold coffee like it's just going to randomly be warm with my brain drowning in the words Regan keeps offering. "This collector? Who is she?"

Regan squirms. "No one I know really knows. Every witch knows about her, or should, at least. She's our boogeyman. She's who parents threaten to call when we abuse our powers. I don't know of anyone who has ever met her or even dreamed of her."

"Then why should I be afraid of her if there's no proof of her?" I ask with sincerity.

"Because that's the point. Whoever she collects, just vanishes. They are gone from memory and script. Sometimes you'll find a blank line in a coven's book where a name should have been, but no one can remember the name. Mostly because no one I know can awaken a whole army of dead wolves, or pull the magic from them back into themselves, or can jedi mind fuck an Original demon."

"Why do you call him that?" These are the questions I want answered. These are the facts I need. I'm stumbling pretty well along on the magic part, but the whos, and the whats, that's what I want to know.

"Jedrek, as he now calls himself, fell with Lucifer in the great war. He was right there when it all went down making him one of the firsts, an original. Other demons are promoted from death by deeds done since their death. They can jump meat suits or linger around to make your life hell, but they can be handled even by strong-willed mortals. Originals always have a plan when topside and witches are taught to avoid them at all costs. Jedrek makes sure we are reminded of it. For a while, I was taught, his main job was to keep witches sorted and accounted."

"Why?"

Regan shrugs, "No one knows, and if you ask him, he just says because he was told to. Not shocked to see him now since Johanna caused all this."

"What is it that I need to know?"

GiGi huffs with my question as if insulted. "Everyone thinks you need to take some crash course in your life history and trigger your powers. If I did as they suggested, you would have been walking around with hormones and dead dates. I felt it best to teach you just enough to understand why you feel the way you do but not enough to fully open the doors, per se."

"Now my doors should be wide open?" I lift an eyebrow with my question.

"Your doors need to be cracked, at least," Regan suggests. "You have powers you don't even know about, things you can do which will scare you. If you can't control them, you'll lose control and hurt someone."

"Like my mother did?" I ask, breathing into the room the topic which is banned.

"What did your mother do?" Regan is almost leaning off the couch with curiosity.

"We don't talk about that!" GiGi shouts. "There's no need to talk about any of that!"

"If there's a history of it in the family…" Regan trials her words like a smoke-filled warning before the flames show from a fire.

"Then I could lose control, too? Is what you're suggesting?" I dare her to admit.

"You made an Original rip his own face off because you were tired of his smirk, Harper."

"That's fair." I nod, and out of habit sip another bitter taste of the cursed coffee.

Regan waits, looking from me to the pouting GiGi, thinking one of us will surely speak up soon. I know GiGi won't. She has buried that day so deep, I'm not sure if she even remembers it all. Her denial over what my mother did, and then what I did, is thick. I was wearing blue the day the cops dropped me on her doorstep after having so many other doors slammed upon my arrival. We own very little that is blue. If it is, it's nowhere near the same shade of my arrival.

"She got angry at my dad. Killed them both when she lost control of her anger and magic. Not much to tell," I tell the waiting Regan.

GiGi glances my way, knowing there is much more to tell. Like how my mother killed my father. Or how she killed herself. Or even maybe what I did to both of them when I came home from school and found them. There is, in fact, plenty to tell, but I won't. Some scars are better left unexamined.

"Your energy gets all weird when you lie," Regan tells me with a smile. "But whatever, keep your dirty secrets. We all have them. You need to know all sorts of types will come for you now. Some will come for your help and some will come to use you. You need to be aware of the difference."

"Should I join the coven?" I ask, not prepared for their answer.

"No!" both GiGi and Regan shout at the same time.

"Covens are for witches with no house. They are the odds and the broken who need someone stronger than them to keep them in line for their own good and the good of the community. You are your own house. There is no one more powerful than you," Regan says with arms in full motion of animation.

"You know what covens are good for? Chick flicks and dick jokes. Never been a fan of them. It's one thing when a girl has two or three friends to complain to when a guy hurts her. Imagine twelve or more, with power and anger issues. No thanks," GiGi declares with her normal flourish.

"Don't you technically belong to the Ripples?" I ask, with small hints of shade.

"I belong to their house, yes. It's not something I'm proud of but there aren't a lot of options for us. We can do the coven route where you become almost a clone of each other once linked. You can try it solo, but I'm not good at being alone. My power is energy. I need to be around people. The Ripples offered protection. For witches it's either belong to a house or be abused by all the houses."

"The devil you know," I quote the classic quote and she nods in agreement. "If I'm a house, couldn't I create my own?"

Regan giggles the same way as when Jedrek was missing parts of his face. "Easy there. You're going to be something, but right now you're kinda in limp mode. Everyone knows by now, you and Jo are your house. To mess with one means to mess with both."

"I'd be more afraid of the old lady," I loudly whisper with amusement, but also honesty.

GiGi smiles and blows me a kiss.

"What are you going to do about the last item?" Regan asks me.

I chew my bottom lip, wondering how much I should share in this girl chat we are having. Should I do as Jedrek suggested? Should I risk my own life?

"I'm going to do whatever I have to do," I answer in the same riddle fashion they use so well.

"Save the family? Or save yourself?" GiGi asks with a look of knowing.

I don't lie to GiGi. I can't. She knows my every facial tick and tone of my voice. She knows what my fidgeting means and what my silence screams. I say nothing, sipping my cold coffee as if it were a life vest. If it is, it's a vest for the people on the Titanic. It's not going to save me. Not really. I'm still going to drown under the gaze of her all-knowing eyes, but maybe it will slow it, drag out the death so I can lie to myself about what is about to happen in the morning.

Just a little lie. Just the littlest of lies. What's the harm? What could possibly go wrong? Tonight, I will lie. Tomorrow, I will find the truth when I visit Miranda.

I can hear the music from Bella's room floating down from her opened upstairs window. With the cooling temperatures, everyone's window is open. It makes spying so much easier in the upscale neighborhoods. Not watching the neighbors, Dear. I'm just sitting by the window enjoying the breeze.

With Johanna gone, and the magic returned to the rightful owners, I can feel this house again. I can see the elderly couple who owned it before the Tortes, coming and going as life has one doing. I can hear the many conversations of the land, with the many who have owned it. I can also feel the soft tickling of magic like mine. My magic has perked its head, listening to see what can be heard.

Still unsure of what to say, I knock on the heavy wooden door before someone calls the cops for me standing here so long. The wait seems forever. I fidget with my hair, fluffing the red curls in hopes to not look like a matted mess. I pull on my grey shirt and brush off invisible lint on my black pants. There's so much time, I knock again, thinking maybe the first one wasn't heard, but still nothing.

Bella's music continues to rain down on me with its perky pop vocals. Someone is home. Or should be home.

Closing my eyes, I push the perked magic through the front of the house. I use it as my eyes, sensing and feeling its way around the home. It doesn't go far, before it finds what I was afraid it would find.

If magic had a smell, this house would wreak with it. It's heavy, like a burden and not a casting. There's sadness and something darker, something which still covers my childhood memories. There, under it all, is a touch of madness. I've run out of time.

Testing the front door to find it locked, I do what any uninvited guest does, I scale the tall privacy fence and make my way to the back door, fully expecting to hear sirens at any moment.

The side garage door is unlocked, and with extreme caution, I push the door slowly to expose a garage not nearly as perfect as the house. One car still sits, waiting for the next grocery run or work trip. Shelves are disorganized against the far wall. Everything from sports to holiday boxes are arranged like a game of Jenga. When I don't hear the screaming of a house alarm, I take my first steps.

My magic may be slithering around with no flair or worry, but my mind is listing all the many reasons this is stupid. When the door to the house is also unlocked, it is practically screaming to not do what we both know I'm going to do. It's reminding me how my mouth will cause so many problems for me in jail. Like always, I don't listen. I take the first steps into a very still house.

There's a moment when I debate calling out, announcing myself just in case I have mistaken the husband's degree of firearm proficiency, but the house is silent. Other than the music rolling down the stairs, there is nothing. Not a sound of any life from a television to a microwave joins the female vocals above me. There is no conversation. No sounds of movement. There is just silence and somehow it is suffocatingly loud.

"Bella?" I call up the stairs.

When nothing is returned, not even an adjustment to the volume of the music, I begin my slow climb. These stairs don't complain the way mine do. There's no wooden creaking or moaning as I slowly make my way up to the second floor. The wall beside me is framed with rectangles holding smiles, and for the first time I see Becky. There is no question her and Ben are twins. Every framed moment of their lives they are wearing matching outfits down to even their crooked smiles. I can see how her death could fracture a family.

"Bella?" I call again when reaching the hallway.

Still there is no response. At least not verbally. Clothes have been thrown around the hallway. They lay with their many colors like scattered fall leaves blanketing the ground. Doors are wide open, spilling forth their room's items. The framed art along the wall is tilted as if it's been roughly bumped one too many times.

I shouldn't be here. I should leave now. This isn't my problem. Not really. Bella wanted her sister to be put to rest. If I just wait it out, it will happen all on its own. Yes, Miranda may go insane and kill half her family before she dies herself, but the main problem will be solved, right?

All these thoughts are racing through my mind, fighting to be the first thought, the main thought which will convince me to turn around and leave. They almost do. If it weren't for that soft little noise coming from a room ahead of me. A sudden noise amid all the silence which encourages my death threat filled antics.

The sound came from the same room as the music. Its door is open, showing a room stuck between childhood and adult. The pink walls and many decorations showcase a growing change in taste and design. The queen-sized bed boasts of white sheets and a pink gingham comforter. Teddy bears line the wall the bed rests on, staring at me with black button eyes catching the overhead light when I enter. Other than being filled with disorganization, there is nothing obvious about why such a mess has occurred in a normally very organized home.

"Bella?" I whisper, hoping what I heard was a mistake.

The sound comes again. The same soft sound of something only slightly moving. A sound which leads one to creep around, straining to hear clues of from where it came.

I'm looking for blood, a pattern in the scattered clothes, something to hint at what has happened or what is waiting. There's nothing, and the one brain cell of self-preservation I have, has me stop and call out again with hopes nothing is waiting to jump from a closet to kill me.

"Bella? It's Harper," I add, thinking it will do any good.

I'm shocked when it does.

"Miss Harper?" a small voice under the bed whispers. It's so soft I doubt for a moment I actually heard it, and just imagined it with hopes of an explanation. "Miss Buckland?" the little voice comes again.

I kneel slowly, praying that my knees are strong enough to lift me in a hurry should I have to run from what is calling my name. With my heart feeling lodged in my throat, remembering every horror movie I have ever watched, I lift the edge of the thick comforter to stare into the wide eyes of Bella.

"What are you doing under there?" I ask the visibly scared teen.

"She's lost her mind," Bella whispers.

"Who?" I ask, already knowing the answer.

"Mom!" Becky hisses. "She was tearing apart the house looking for the pink dress for Becky which matches Ben's pantsuit. She kept saying how they had to be perfect. When I told her we gave Becky's clothes away a long time ago, she lost it. She started hitting me," Bella pauses, and I watch as the memory overcomes her before she can push past it to talk again, "and hitting Dad. She kept dragging Ben around like a rag doll despite Dad trying to take Ben from her. I couldn't take it anymore."

"You hid under your bed?" I ask, trying to keep my voice sympathetic.

"She was tearing apart all the closets," Bella says, trying to not sound like a little girl who is in fact hiding under her bed.

"Where did everyone go?"

"Mom said something about having to make everything perfect, and when she wouldn't let Ben go, Dad went with them. I think he was more afraid of what might happen to Ben than Mom."

Knowing what I know, he's most likely correct.

"But she didn't say a place?"

Bella shakes her head. "Maybe I can text Dad? I wasn't sure if they were really gone or if they were coming back. I've been under here waiting to figure out what to do."

"I think you should text your dad. See if he can tell you where they are."

Bella stares at me with eyes overflowing with hope. "And you'll go save them?"

I nod, not willing to put the possible lie to words. I don't even know where they are, or what she may be doing. I can't honestly tell her, out loud, that I will save them. Nor which 'them' I may not be able to save at all.

Bella slides from her hiding spot, watching every little thing for the monster she's imaging to be lurking behind it. Finding her phone on the nightstand amid the many random items, she quickly pushes the buttons with a speed I've only seen teens possess.

We are both holding our breaths, waiting for the screen to light up with a response, a clue, something to give me an idea of what I am facing. With each second feeling like hours, Bella begins to tap the phone's pastel cover as if it will make the words appear faster.

"Maybe he's busy?" I offer seeing her body tight with anxiety.

"Maybe he's dead," Bella says, and the first tear slides down her high arch of a cheek.

Before I could stumble my way through some form of encouragement or sympathy, the little screen lights up and we both exhale for different reasons.

"He says they're at the cemetery. There's an open crypt past Becky's grave. He wants me to go there."

Bella is already shoving her feet into the tennis shoes closest to her upon reading the request. I don't point out they are two different shoes. I do point out how it may be a bad idea to go.

"You stay here. I'll go check it out. See what is going on," I offer, trying to make my voice neutral with my request.

"No way!" Bella shouts, suddenly over the under the bed routine. "He may need me."

"To do what?" I ask with more bite than I meant. "Bella, if your mom has lost her mind, you could get hurt. I will go and you stay here safe in case they return before I make it there."

"I can't just sit here. Can I sit in your car? I won't get out until you tell me it's safe, but at least I'll be there." Bella is pleading with me, and when she doesn't see me moved by her needs, she adds, "I promise, Miss Harper. I won't be in the way, but I can't stay here not knowing."

We both know she's not going to stay in the car and we both know she is not going to stay here, but we both play along like we don't know any of the above.

"Fine. In my car," I sternly tell her. "No hero moves."

"I'll save those for you," she smiles a genuine smile and my stomach drops with it.

"Your mom," I ask remembering something said, "where does she spend most of her time when she's home?"

"In the creepy shed out back," Bella tells me. "She used to lock herself away in her bedroom. Then it was the basement. Now, it's in the backyard. I'll hear her get up in the middle of the night when she thinks everyone is asleep to go out there."

"Show me," I tell her with less of a question and more of a command.

"What about Dad?"

"Few more minutes won't change the world," I tell her, exiting the room.

Actually, a few minutes may change everything, but it's something I'm willing to risk if I can find some answers of which to arm myself with before heading into a new flavor of crazy.

I didn't really need help finding the shed. Like the house, the backyard is landscaped with everything in its place including the stone path to the little wooden mini-replica of what we just left. The lock on the door, for that I do need her help.

"Four. Four. Five. Six," Bella tells me, watching to see if their universal code works here too.

It does and somehow that's less comforting than if it hadn't worked. Seeing as it is the home's address, it speaks volumes for the safety of their little world. What I am about to show Bella will ruin that forever. What the other members of her family have already seen, their illusions have already been shattered.

It always amazes me how the mind can ignore the scent of death. Standing this close to the closed doors, I should have picked up on its delicate fragrance. The many planted flowers' perfume should not have been able to cover it, but they did somehow, resulting in the gut punch of the scent when we open the doors.

"What the hell is that?" Bella asks when the rolling stench almost topples her.

"Your sister," I tell her, without any band-aids or cozy words to help soothe her suffering.

The room is dim, hiding away its shame from the rays of the sun. I can make out the pile of blankets in the far corner. Clothes and toys are scattered around the dirty floor, but it's the irregular dark patterns beside the toys which keep my attention.

As I make my way near them, I fear what their silent message will mean for this family. I worry every fear I have danced with is now a fact, red and bold before me.

"Is that oil?" Bella asks from the safety of the doors.

"Sure," I tell her with a flat voice. "Oil for the body."

"Your jokes are worse than my dad's," she remarks with an attempted scalding. All it's done is remind her of what is at hand. "Can we go now?"

We can. I don't need to know every inch and detail of what has happened behind these wooden walls. I know enough about what hasn't happened. What hasn't happened is a little girl being left to rest in her grave. I know this same little girl had to be fed, and whatever functions of her life, still kept going. She was playing, eating, and sleeping, for some time here. All of it only a few feet away from the family she once called her own.

I once understood the need to keep those who were stolen away from us close. I can't stand here in judgment of what Miranda has done. I can shake my head over what she has done to recreate these moments. She's risked so much for a few days of lies. Lies built around magic and a desire to hold a piece of her once more. That piece may just cost her everything.

Y ou remember what we agreed on?" I ask Bella as we both stare past her sister's grave from the safety of my car.

"I remember," she tells me with a voice shaking with fear.

"You going to actually do it?"

Bella is polite enough to not answer, letting the truth hang in the air between us. She may have promised then, but now as we sit with her family's dirty secret upheaved and displayed before us, she's not so willing to keep to the same offer.

"Just at least don't come running into who knows what unarmed." I slip her the little secret I keep in the glove box. "There's only one number programmed into that phone. When the woman answers, tell her the shit's hit the fan."

"A phone? You're handing me a phone? Why not a gun or something? I have a phone!" Bella shouts with her emotions spilling over from the stress of the day and the stress the day still holds.

"Yeah, but your phone doesn't have GiGi's number in it."

Bella's jaw still hangs open, staring at the phone before she asks, "Will she bring a gun?"

"By all the Gods, I hope not," I honestly tell her, leaving the safety of the car.

She's saying something, but through the metal door and the glass of the windows, and mostly my indifference to know what it is, I don't hear her. I have already let my walls down, allowing my magic to seep through my skin, escaping from the cage in which I keep it locked and hidden deep in denial. It touches every wilting flower, plays with the sagging bows drenched in remorse, and calls to those lost to years of dusty slumber. The dead know I'm here, and even as familiar as I am to them, they don't know this new me or what she now brings. I can feel them waiting, watching with their ancient eyes to see what may unfold this night.

"What'cha doing?"

I almost levitate when I hear Jedrek in my ear with how he startled me. I was so focused on what lies ahead of me, I wasn't watching around me and he took that as the perfect time to announce himself.

"Would you believe me if I answered wondering if I have a spare set of pants in the car?"

"With the noise you just made, yes, yes I would." His face is set in taunting. He's smiling his false mirth which once looked so genuine to me. "Any idea what we are up against?"

"One crazy housewife and the spare members of her family," I offer, still not completely sure what awaits us.

"You remember what we talked about?" he asks me, feeling very familiar to a conversation only a few moments ago. "Do you know what you're going to do?"

Just like Bella, I don't answer him, letting that same uncertainty hang between us as it had her and I.

"You're going to do the mortal thing, aren't you? You're going to do the whole 'what's my life compare to theirs' speech?" He doesn't bother to hide his disgust.

"No," I tell him with a smile equal to his own. "I wasn't going to give a speech at all."

"Mature!" he shouts to my back as I walk away. "Very mature."

I know he would try to talk me out of the road I have started on if I let him. It's his job to plant the seeds of doubts in our minds, to sway and steer us away from the paths we picked in our life. This path, this road, only has one ending for me, and for the family, as far as I'm concerned.

I can hear the quarreling voices coming from the stone building ahead of me. The male voice is softer, almost pleading in its pitches with the shouting female. Her words are a fast frenzy of syllables I can't make out. Their whole conversation is threaded together by the sound of sobbing, a high-pitched cry of fear, and sounds only a child could make. I've run out of time.

My feet carry me faster than my nerves wish they would. I maneuver my way around the standing monuments to enter the large, erected building of one built a long time ago. Kerosene lamps cast a glow in the stone space. Shadows are almost real things, mocking the two adults below them with their broken shapes and dramatic movements. Dust floats through the air, sparkling with a hint of forgotten times, before landing back at rest in darkened corners of the room. The whole space feels crushing and tiny with the emotions and the magic pulsing through it.

"Well, here is the happy little family," Jedrek tells those in front of us, so lost in their moment they hadn't noticed my arrival. "Husband. Wife. Son. Dead daughter. Seems we are almost all here."

"Did you bring Bella?" Miranda asks him, ignoring her husband's confused face.

Jedrek shrugs with his face, making it a guessing game of what, or who, he may have brought. If there's anyone at all.

I ignore them as the two settle into a verbal game. My attention is for the little girl peering around the concrete stand where a coffin is supposed to sit. That same face stared at me as I climbed the wooden steps in her home. I watched her grow and age frame by frame until she couldn't anymore. Those same eyes, once so filled with youthful innocence and joy, are now blank and almost hateful as they watch me.

"Hello, Becky," I call out to the little girl stuck amid the drama around her. "Come here."

She doesn't want to answer me. She doesn't want to come away from the safety of her mother, but she's dead. She's mine to command. One shaky step at a time, she makes her way to where I kneel waiting for her. Each step pulls more of her new self to the surface and discards any resemblance of who she was once. She throws away the cute outer wrapper for the evil animated inside of her answering the last few remaining doubts in my mind.

"You're not Becky, are you?" I ask it, tasting the wild magic from which it comes. "You've never been Becky. You were never any of them, not really. You've always been you, waiting until you could return to your box and then angry when forced out again."

The living magic behind Becky's eyes stares at me with caution. It hisses, wondering where I am going with my ramblings and what those ramblings mean for it.

"What are you talking about?" Miranda asks, panic making her voice a little higher than her normal tone.

"I know how to kill her," I offer as an explanation to the hysteric voice and the hissing trick in front of me.

"What is she talking about?" Miranda screams to anyone who many have a better answer than I gave her.

Jedrek holds up a hand to hush the woman screaming at him. "What are you talking about?"

He isn't asking from a place of pure curiosity. There's a touch of self-serving fear amid his words. Afterall, he too has come to reclaim this lost magic.

"You can't kill my daughter. Please," Chad pleads, "there must be another way? We have her back. I can't let her go, now. We can't lose her again."

"This isn't Becky, but you've known that all this time, haven't you, Ben?" Turning to the little boy who is as far away from his sister as the room allows, I repeat my question. "Haven't you?"

So similar to his twin, but so different, he nods before returning to his crouching fear. He won't look to the man he's depended on to keep him safe his whole life. He doesn't trust the woman who rocked him back to sleep when the nightmares woke him. She's brought the nightmare home and his father has begged for it to stay.

"Are you sure?" Jedrek asks.

"Very." And I am, because beyond them all stands a little girl confused why her body isn't at rest; why she isn't at rest and why her family is so sad. "This is as you said, old magic, original magic. It's a spark of divinity confiscated and corrupted a long time ago. Now it's angry and enjoys the game. It becomes whoever it is asked to become for kicks and giggles while it devours the one who thinks they are in control of it. This is how you've been collecting your souls."

Chad, ever the smart one, jumps to the end of my explanation. "What do you mean devours? What soul?"

"I know this one!" Jedrek shouts. "You see," he pauses extending his hand to Chad, "Jedrek by the way." When Chad doesn't offer an extended hand in return Jedrek begins to speak again, "Rude, but okay. You see, your wife made a deal with a witch who stole a bunch of items which weren't hers to use. Well, your wife here, just happened to pick the biggest whammy of all of them. Where most of the little deals just end in a little quick round of suicide by insanity, your wife picked familicide by madness. The rest of the prizes I could have unlinked, but this one, this one binds itself to the source of energy from the one who made the deal. Once that energy grows weak, that little grinning thing there is in control," he explains pointing to grinning Becky. "No doubt Becky here told Mommy she wanted her whole family to come be with her on the other side because she's lonely and scared, which is why we are all gathered here today."

Miranda stares at her little girl with a look somewhere between insanity and horror. A part of her knew this whole time this wasn't her little girl, but she lied to herself, told herself she was wrong and lived in the happiness that the denial granted her.

"You're wrong," Chad tells us. "Miranda didn't bring us here. Bella did."

I had planned for almost everything. I had rehearsed every avenue, every dead end, and still, I never saw this ahead of me. All this time I was so sure it was Miranda, lost in the grief of a mother, I had never thought to entertain the idea it could have been anyone else.

"She went crazy, shouting about needing the perfect dress for Becky. We told her Becky was gone. She didn't need a dress, but she insisted she wasn't. She told us to come here and we would see for ourselves. We came just to calm her down. I just wanted to get Ben to safety." Miranda's voice is trembling. "Becky was sitting here, hiding where Bella said she would be. When she texted, we told her we were here. She said she was on her way and she could explain everything."

"So, explain," Jedrek says to someone standing behind me.

I don't want to turn around. I don't want to admit, yet again, I was so focused on what was ahead of me I completely forgot to look around me. Reluctantly turning, I see the teenager who I met nights ago after a failed blind date. She, convincing me her family needed help, brought me into their lives knowing everything was true. Her sister did walk again, but it wasn't because of her mom, as she led me to believe. It was because she had signed the deal which trapped them both in this drama.

"Why?" I ask the mute teen.

"I couldn't make her stop," Bella stares at her baby sister. "I just wanted her to stop."

"Yeah, that's great, but I'm going to need some back story here," Jedrek has started his dangerous slow walk of strings towards Bella. "How does a teen working at a knock-off chain restaurant find not only one witch, but two?"

I hold up a hand to stop Jedrek, not willing to force her confession. "Wanted who to stop?"

"Mom," Bella says. "Mom just kept crying all the time. She said she doesn't blame me, but I know she does. I just wanted to try to make it right."

"And Johanna told you she could bring Becky back?" I ask, still holding Jedrek at bay.

"No," Bella tells us. "She did."

"She who?" Jedrek asks, but I've already put it together.

Bella didn't pick this spot for Becky to be discovered. Deon did.

"Deon," I mutter, tired of hearing the name.

"Excuse me, what?" Jedrek asks me, although we both know he heard me perfectly well.

"Where is she?" I ask Bella, because there isn't any more places for me to turn around to be surprised. We are already facing the entrance of the crypt.

"She said she could make it all stop, if you promise to return the magic to her," Bella answers.

"Yeah, that's not what I asked."

"Or she would kill us all if you didn't," Bella continues with a quivering lip.

"What did she promise to make stop?" I ask, stalling. If she won't answer where Deon is, it most likely means she is closer than I would prefer a pissed off she-wolf to be lurking.

Bella is staring at the nightmare watching her. "The whispering in my head," she says weakly, almost with a whisper. "It would all stop. Her voice would stop."

"Where's the box?" Jedrek asks from behind me, still held back by my hand.

Bella pulls the music box from her jacket pocket. It's small, so small one would most likely never look at it twice as something of interest. The silver-colored metal is tarnished, speaking of the many hands which have touched it with hopes all turned to despair. I can see the white runes glowing around its edges. Like a bold warning, hinting of the dangers of what could happen if the box should be played, these runes were placed long ago. Warnings which were ignored, or exploited for a dark goal, also glow with a hidden promise of how to contain what has escaped.

"Tell me you know how to make it all stop?" Bella asks with her broken soul before me.

I do. I can see many ways to make it all stop. My eyes follow the invisible silver cord tied to Bella and the box. It sparkles like a spider web in morning dew, heavy with what it has caught under the light of the moon. Just as fragile, it would be easy to sever, breaking the cord draining her of life and sanity. She would be free. It would all stop. The magic would slither back into its cage, leaving the husk of the child it animates. There would be no more whispers, no more regrets or remorse. It would all stop because Bella would die, ending the transaction of this curse.

"What did you offer for your sister to return?" I ask with hesitation, wondering how much she really knows about what she has done.

A single tear begins to roll down the youth filled face of Bella and I know she knows. She knew exactly what the cost would be. She, like all the rest of them, just never thought it would come due.

"Just make it stop," she almost begs, and for a moment I almost do what she is asking of me.

In a breath of hesitation, touching the silver string binding the three, I almost kill a child. I almost make it all stop. Almost.

"Make it stop," Bella pleads, ready for whatever may be coming as long as it means the voices in her head stop. The nightmares stop. The lies stop.

"What are you going to do?" Jedrek softly asks.

He too can see the thread holding it all together. He too knows how easy it would be to pluck it like a demonic harp string, ending this round of the chorus of a song played again and again. Pluck it and send Bella's soul to the contract. Pluck it and send the magic back to the box, waiting for the next person to wind its silver key to play that damning chorus once again. Pluck it and awaken a witch who lives in the deepest fears of her kind.

"Ms. Buckland," Miranda is softly weeping my name. She doesn't completely understand what is happening, but she's figured out enough to know tonight she may lose more than one daughter. "Harper," she calls again. "Please, save my babies."

"Harper," Jedrek whispers, fearing the road I am willing to walk.

"It's just a spark of divinity," I whisper, mostly to myself.

"Harper!" Jedrek shouts, but he's too late.

I can make it all stop.

The world pauses, frozen in the seconds before I tempt fate. In this span of time, a thousand fears are spread before me and in these same seconds, I grow numb, letting whatever will be, will be.

This ancient magic isn't mine, but it's so similar, so like mine, I can feel its tickle testing me. I can taste its power like molten gold running down my throat, metallic and scorching. I don't pull on the cord dancing before me in the waves of magic I am weaving. I pull on the source. I reach my power deep into the blonde little girl growling at me, finding that pulsing gold buried deep inside of her. With a hope and a prayer to whichever deity is watching, I wrap my own source around it. I entwine it, making it a part of me. This dead magic, this power to animate those long since gone, I blend it, melding my own to every inch of it.

The room is filled with the colors of green and gold, fighting and twirling to escape and yet claim the other. My skin is crawling in its power, ripping and burning with an unseen flame. This invisible fire is burning inside of me, consuming every inch with overwhelming pain. Screaming, I pull my power back, commanding it to keep its golden prey ensnarled in the green wisps. My screams ravage my throat till there is nothing left but raw tissue and hoarse sounds of anguish, but it's mine. That golden fire, the golden lava churning inside of me, eating and melting my deepest parts, is mine.

With blurred vision I watch as Becky slips to the ground. Her body almost floats, feather-like upon the deep breath she exhales before she grows still. Without the magic, her body withers, returning to what it should look like if she were still deep in the earth's womb and not the fake replica of the little girl they lost.

Bella falls to her knees, cradling the sin she created. "I'm so sorry," she whispers to her baby sister with tears falling on her grey skin. "I'm so sorry."

There's a soft song playing in my mind. Like a dark piano, it sings the song of every person who cried those same words into its metal walls. The song is mine now and I will carry their guilt and sorrow for the rest of my life. Bella's is just the latest verse to the long sheet of music.

"What have you done?" Jedrek hisses somewhere near me. "It will destroy you, Harper."

It will. I feel it agree with him with a sinister excitement. It whispers to me of all the ways it plans to kill me while stroking its melancholy keys.

"Let it go, Harper." Jedrek is standing in front of me, holding the empty cage of a box. "You saved the family. Good for you. Now put it back."

But I can't, I want to tell him. I knew the moment it entered me, it would never return to those metal bars and if it does, the cord would be restrung. As long as I hold it inside of me, Bella is safe. It can't harm her. Instead, Bella is now tied to me. The evil witch will never know what happened here because the energy is still the same.

"My littlest witch," Jedrek says, tenderly pushing my red curls behind my ears. He cups my face and kissing my forehead he whispers into my hair, "you're going to be the death of me."

"Maybe," I tell him, letting his warmth calm the broken part of me. "Or it may be the wolves stalking us."

"Tough choice," he tells my curls. "Are you up to playing red riding hood?"

"No," I answer honestly feeling the exhaustion encasing me and the magic rebelling inside of me. "Besides, my grandmother would never let a wolf eat her."

He laughs a deep laugh. I can feel the vibration of it, and it pulls a smile to my lips despite my best efforts to deny it.

"She wants the magic," I whisper to his chest, absorbing these moments of comfort.

"Then let's give her the magic," he says, and I can hear the mischief in his voice. "Just don't forget where you are."

Placing one more kiss on top of my head, he turns to go play with our latest round of danger. He almost skips with his departure, never looking to where the family huddles around each other at our feet. Their sobs don't reach him nor does any of their rolling emotions as they try to grasp what has happened so far tonight.

"Stay in here," I awkwardly say, not really sure how I keep landing in the role of savior when I trip over my own feet coming down the stairs. "Bella, you remember what I gave you?"

Bella pats the same pocket that she pulled the box from. "I'd still rather have a gun."

"Trust me," I tell her. "You don't want her bringing a gun."

Jedrek is whistling when I catch up to him. He stands almost bored amid the many tall crosses and arches placed like flowers in a garden. The dead are lurking on the far corners like spectators to something they don't want to witness but can't look away. The air is alive with their tension and it stirs my magic like a sleeping beast stretching and ready to defend itself.

"Where are they?" I whisper, knowing I may as well have shouted my question.

Jedrek lifts one eyebrow, still whistling the many pitches of his song, he tilts his head to his right with a smile.

I shouldn't have looked. I should have just stood, faking the same level of composure which comes so easily for Jedrek, but I don't. I let human nature pull my eyes to the direction he motioned. Staring into the many sets of glowing eyes watching me, my stomach drops.

They pace, running in and out of the shadows the markers create. Using their sleek bodies, they create images from every dark dream ever had. Their eyes are watching, waiting for some signal to do what they were made to do – kill.

"How many fucking werewolves are in this town?" I hear myself ask, considering the large number we have already encountered.

"As many as I need there to be," Deon's voice taunts from where she has been watching.

There is no torn jeans or discarded shirt for tonight's meeting. She is as she was when I first met her. Wearing a skirt suit so black the darkest of nights would envy it. Her blonde hair and pale skin appear to shine with their contrast. Deon Ripple, in all of her power-hungry glory, didn't come to fight. She came to conquer.

"I thought your brother put you in time out?" Jedrek is kneeling to read the words on the headstone closest to him.

If he is bothered by the sheer numbers around us, he doesn't show it, but I suppose when you have lived through the war of heaven and hell it takes a bit to frighten you. For me, this is a bit. It's all the bits and I have no idea how to remain calm.

The stalking shadows are growing closer, encouraged by the scent of my fear and the voice of their alpha. As if plotting and planning, little barks and yips are exchanged among them, pulling them closer and tighter around us with the scent of my fear exciting them.

"My brother thinks too highly of himself," Deon tells us with a sense of pride. The way she smirks leaves much unsaid, hidden between her words with a meaning of a thousand different possibilities. "You didn't really think I'd just walk away after that last little stunt of yours, did you Jedrek?"

Jedrek shrugs, as if he hadn't really put any thought to it, or to her. "Walk, no. Crawl, maybe. Thinking all fours with your tail tucked tight."

Deon's reply isn't human. It's guttural, raw and deep, from somewhere humans can't pull sounds, but it doesn't need words. It's rage, pure and simple.

"Do you really think it's wise to push buttons right now?" I ask him, watching the many lurking shadows form into shapes and then into the many shades of their pack as they gather around us, no longer keeping to the outskirts.

"You should listen to the witch, Jedrek. Especially since only one of you is immortal." Deon is also now inching forward, her smile secure in her victory.

"I'm guessing I'm not the immortal one?" I ask him, taking steps to try to keep everything moving around us in my sight.

"Guess we are about to find out," Jedrek says between laughs.

Laughs which send shivers down my spine and dread climbing through my skin. Laughs which call the very darkness they had used to hide in closer to us as if it's a living thing. I watch as the edges of this human garden blur before disappearing behind a wall of a moving void. The wolves swallowed by it howl, putting voice to their pain before that voice melts into the abyss creeping forward. Soon their howls and screams flow over one another, blending their many voices together in their shared torment and deaths.

Deon screams a different pitch. Her suffering isn't physical. Hers is mental and she voices it just as loudly before she lunges, erupting in the air into her wolf shape. She's larger than her family with fur a deep red not found in nature and brown eyes glowing an amber shade of hate.

"Oh damn," comes from my throat before I can stop my inner fear from forming words.

"The fur doesn't match the drapes," Jedrek says, titling his head back and forth while staring at the fur-covered death in front of us. "Figured you'd be lighter."

Whatever remark he was going to make next, is stopped by the wolf nearest to me. I had turned my head to stare in confusion at Jedrek and that little motion triggered an avalanche. I felt the wolf move before I knew it was charging towards me. The prey aspect we still hold, clutched deep and only surfacing in the moments we know death is near, whispered the warning, pulling my attention back to the spot I neglected to keep watch.

The grey beast maneuvers around the cement shapes as if it were made of water, flowing and undeterred by anything in its path. The grey eyes never leave me, focused and heading towards me with a speed I can't counter. I brace, waiting to be toppled by pure strength and sharp teeth.

Lifting my arms to absorb some of the impact, I watch in panic and fear as the ground underneath the wolf opens and decayed arms grasp it tightly. The wolf spins, ready to destroy whatever has locked onto its legs. Almost securing its escape, another set of arms erupt, spilling dirt and darker things into the air. This set digs into the fur of the wolf's neck, pulling it to the ground. The arms begin an almost tug of war, each unwilling to release their part of the prize. Bones and joints begin to pop like dry twigs causing the wolf to howl as it's pulled deeper into the dirt and stretched impossibly further apart. I close my eyes when the sounds become wet, sloppy, and telling of more than I need to witness of what is happening. I'm grateful when the howling stops but I know I will never remove the sound of the final tug pulling it in two from my memory. The final moment when the hands and arms win their pound of flesh echoes around us in a way, I didn't think possible. Where the wolf once stood is now nothing but a bloody pool of dirt and shredded meat. The copper scent hangs heavy around us, turning my stomach with the truth it tells with the tall markers near it coated, raining, and dripping blood.

"Wanna do that a few more times?" Jedrek whispers, not attempting to hide his amusement from those watching us.

I want to tell him I have no idea how I did it the first time, much less wanting to witness that over and over again, but my mouth is dry and words aren't forming.

Deon doesn't react the same as I do to seeing one of her own destroyed in such a brutal manner. Her rage has hit its peak, and she rushes towards Jedrek with the same fluid run, full speed and eager to destroy.

I open my mouth to scream at him as he points at something behind me. I never got the chance to glance at the beast who didn't make the same mistake as the last. This one waited, timed the attack when I was focused on another. I didn't have time to summon on instinct any survival tricks. There was nothing but weight and hot breath forcing me to the cold ground, heavy on my back and bone crushing to my ribs.

As I fall, I watch Deon overtake Jedrek. She too wastes no time with his distraction, latching her large muzzle over and over again on his body. The last sight I have of them before a large cement cross blocks my view is of her mouth tearing into his throat and the red meat of his muscles exposed and bleeding.

The wolf on my back isn't as eager as his Alpha. His weight is slowly pushing the air from my body, suffocating me with just his presence securing me to the ground. I can feel his hot breath as he sniffs my hair and nudges it away from the back of my neck. I'm drowning in my panic, unable to even scream with my body fighting, clinging to every small breath I am able to take. I dig my hands into the dirt and I do what I know how to do. I remember where I am. I summon the dead.

In my panic, overtaken by fear, I pull every slumbering body to life around us. I force them from the deep ground, and not having the focus to fully reanimate them, they crawl forth in whatever form they can still hold together. They are corpses, rotting and shambling, with torn clothes and missing pieces, towards the rest of the wolves without any care for their own bodies.

The slaughter is a soundtrack of howls, screams and sounds I never wanted to hear. Sounds of pain and death pierce, not only the night, but my mind, pulling me deeper into my panic. There is no air in my lungs. My head feels as if it wants to explode from the pressure built inside of me. Fighting to find that last breath, my body begins to shake, almost convulse, with the desire to survive.

"Kill her!" I hear Deon shout. "Kill her, now!"

The hot breath wraps around my neck. He licks me, enjoying every last moment of this victory. He shouldn't have. He should have done what he was told. He should have ended me when he had the chance because Bella used the phone. The crazy old woman brought a gun.

The gun shot silences the war zone as the one who was holding me captive falls limp and heavy to the ground beside me. Air rushes into my body. My lungs, having been so empty for so long, almost fight against it causing me to gasp and cough painfully. Dirt fills my mouth and throat. I choke on it, gasping and coughing to crawl where I last saw Jedrek.

He has Deon by the throat. She's shifted back to her human form, nude and doing her best to fight against his strength. There is dried blood where his shirt has been torn. He is covered in the red streaks from their battle, still moist and clinging to his rapidly healing skin.

GiGi kneels by my side. I can hear her comforting tones, but they seem far away, down some long tunnel and I can hardly make out what she is trying to tell me. She's stroking my red hair, pulling it away from my face. The dead flowers at the base of the marker beside me, long forgotten in their ceramic vase, turn from brown and wilted to green and the vibrant shades for which they were once picked. All around me grass pushes through the tumbled dirt. It springs between my fingers, wrapping their green blades around my hands. This is GiGi, earth and healing, flowing her magic through this death covered ground. The grass sooths my panic, filling me with calm and peace. The taste of her magic, cloves and oranges, fills me with comfort, reaching through my thickest panic to exhale and softly cry.

She is home. She is safety. She is here, with a gun, and threats flowing from her verbally gifted mouth.

"Don't you move, wolf," GiGi tells Deon, pointing the old revolver towards her head. "Wouldn't lose a second of sleep over putting this silver into that thick skull of yours."

The same grass which comforted me, now wraps its long shoots around Deon's body. The harder she struggles, the tighter it pulls against her.

"It's over, Deon," Jedrek says, releasing her with a pushing motion to the ground.

"Is it?" she asks, and my heart does that little sinking feeling.

I want to ask what more can she do? But I don't. I don't have to. The screams from the tomb we left provide all the clues we need. She knew she was losing. With my dead army destroying her kin, she reached for the last trophy left in the case. She's determined to claim the victim of her contract, one way or another.

I stumble to my feet, tripping and almost falling back down as I run towards the voices screaming for a little boy's future. Someone in that room has Ben. Their begging propels my weakened body forward. I stumble, fighting to stay upright, fighting to make it to them in time. My dead army shambles forward, fed by my fear as commands.

There's so little space left between me and the tomb. I can almost reach out and touch the stone entrance. My army is near, pulling, crawling, or running, whatever their bodies allow them to, to reach this new threat, but we don't have to. As the screams change from begging to wailing, I know I'm too late. Limping into the stone room, I watch as the wolf drops the disemboweled body of the little boy to the ground. She is drenched in Ben's blood. It drips from her snarling jaws. She wears it like a shade of her coat, thick and matted.

Lost in shock, the army stands motionless, waiting on me to feed it with a goal. "Kill her," I whisper to them and they pour into the room silent and eager to carry out my command.

There's too many for the wolf to fight. The few she manages to destroy only reanimate what parts are capable, causing a never-ending loop of assault. I don't feel remorse this time. I don't look away as they flay her alive, pulling fur and flesh from skin and bones. Her whimpers and howls don't reach that part of me which holds guilt for all that I have done. When she switches back to her human shape, reaching her hand out to me for mercy, I don't even blink as they pull her head from her throat, leaving large arches of blood along the walls and the names engraved upon it.

Having made their target nothing more than raw meat and oozing fluids, they go back to motionless statues, awaiting my next mood swing. With exposed bones and withered faces, shrunken deep with decay, they stare at the walls like silent art critics admiring the shapes that the flowing blood is making upon the walls. They stare, maybe reading the names of those they were resting with before my need awoke them. Either way, whatever they are doing, they are just as much covered in death's display as the walls and the ground underneath them.

Ben's body is twisted at an angle suggesting it was more than just his flesh she ruined. She broke his spine with her strong jaws, tearing into his stomach in the process. When she discarded him, his soft, youthful flesh became torn, spilling forth everything it contained around him. Miranda, lost in her grief, is attempting to put the organs back, stuffing his body with make-believe hopes it will bring him back. She keeps whispering to him, telling him it's all going to be okay, even as his blood cools on her arms.

"Bring him back," Bella says from her corner of the room. "You can bring him back."

Shaking my head, I tell her, "You know I can't."

Her eyes look to the many dead standing in their puddles of death before looking back to me. She's calling my bluff without having to say it.

"Haven't you learned?" Jedrek says from behind me. "The dead are dead."

Hearing him, Miranda lets out a wail. It's pulled from the depths of every mother's fear being forced upon her. The body of her dead daughter still lays where it fell once the old magic was pulled from it. Now, the body of her son lays before her too, but she can't see what I see.

I watch as Becky takes Ben's hand. Ben, once lost in confusion over his death, smiles at his sister, knowing this is really her and not the monster which tormented him. The pair turn to leave this abandoned tomb which has become theirs. Running past me with the laughter only childhood could hold, the two play tag around the many bloody markers and decimated bodies. Neither carry the cause of their deaths upon their tiny bodies. They are at peace, free from their deaths. They are together again, as they will now be forever.

When their shapes become nothing more than floating sparks in the air, I let my tears finally escape. I cry for the two lost souls who are floating to the beyond. I cry for everything I couldn't stop, for everything that didn't need to happen. I cry for a family who has lost so much because of such a little lie told to a grieving teen. A little nudge of hope in her darkest hours exploited and used against her. I cry because in the classic-colored Cadillac, Cass has arrived.

Cass walks amid the battlefield with shock and disgust. His eyes scan the dead humans in their various causes of death and broken bodies of the very dead humans littering the grounds. The car's headlights illuminate the whole scene, letting all of us see it gruesomely displayed.

What I hadn't expected to see is the coven. Like the parade of a funeral, they are leaning on their many black sedans with blank faces and empty eyes. Even the annoying blonde is here, and when I can't help my reaction to seeing her, she smiles a playful smirk knowing fully what I think of her.

"Well shit," Cass says when finally making his way fully towards where we stand. He runs his fingers through his oily hair, before resting his hands on his wide hips shoved into a baby blue suit. "We gotta get this cleaned up," he whispers to Jedrek.

I can't help but drop my jaw in shock.

"Now don't be looking at me like that, Ms. Harper. The cops will be here soon, and we are going to have a hard enough time making this look believable."

"Not that it will matter," Winnik says from where she stands, one high heel pressed to Deon's throat. "The sheriff will believe whatever we tell him."

My head is on a pivot, turning from GiGi, to Cass, to Winnik in her high waisted dress slacks and white buttoned shirt. "This family just lost their child and there are dead people everywhere. How can you two be so crass?"

Winnik chuckles, heartless and cold. "You really are new."

"Look," Cass says, pleading softly since the dead around us have begun to stir again with my outburst, "just put 'em all back and let the witches handle the rest. This isn't our first supernatural rodeo. Your kind gets a little out of hand every month or so."

Jedrek is leaning on the stone archway passively watching me. "Welcome to the shit show," he tells me without any mirth or joy.

Choking on my tears, I will the dead back to their graves. With less speed than before, they walk back to each rectangle plot of earth they call their own. Mindlessly, they collect the lost pieces of themselves they pass, hoarding their missing limbs as the ground swallows their returning forms. The dead wolves, in their human shapes, are pulled under by the tall grasses, carried deep into the earth by green arms of comfort. Like swaddling a newborn, one-by-one the grass and flowers from GiGi's magic pulls them to rest, to be cradled in the earth, by Earth herself.

It's not just my army who returns to their final homes. Becky's body crawls to standing before heading back to where she belongs. The sight of it brings moans from Miranda. With her sanity already stretched thin, she crawls after her daughter. She calls her name, tormented by the facts she has buried in grief's denial.

Jedrek kneels, reaching out to her to hold her while she wails a sound close to that of a banshee. He whispers something into her ear and slowly Miranda fades into slumber. Carefully placing her head on the cement below her, he almost glares over to where Chad is standing, so lost in his own grief he has nothing to offer his wife.

"Moments like this make me wonder why Eve picked Adam," he says with remorse and coloring of curiosity.

"What?" I ask, confused and exhausted.

His mask of mischief is replaced, winking at me, mirth dances with history behind those blue eyes of his.

"Let's get you home," he tells me, kneeling to scoop up the discarded trinket which caused all of this. "Winnik knows what to do."

"Deon?" I ask them, watching the she-wolf glare at us.

"Like I said," he repeats, "Winnik knows what to do."

"I sure do," she tells us before pushing the heel of her shoe through the neck of Deon.

It's a slow kill. Inch by inch she pushes her foot down, enjoying the sounds of Deon choking on her own blood. With the thick grass still holding her down, all Deon can do is convulse, spewing the blood over her face with each gagging cough. When she stills, the night stills with her, like a final exhale from the universe, and just as with the others, the grasses pull her dead body down into the earth.

The grounds are green. Flowers are revived, blooming again in their neglected vases. Not a single grave is disturbed. If I wasn't here for it, and if the murder behind me wasn't still fresh in the air, I would never believe what took place. As many sirens head our way, Jedrek and GiGi both rush to grab me.

"That's our que," GiGi tells me, pushing Jedrek's hands from my arm.

He doesn't argue with her. Not many do when her face is set to stone and her eyes hinting a dare if one would.

I follow GiGi to our parked cars, numb and almost in shock.

"How do we just walk away from this?" I ask her.

"One foot in front of the other," she tells me, rubbing my chilled arm. "There's nothing more we can do here. The coven has been cleaning up our little fights since the beginning of time. Cass will tell the police something tragic has happened to explain Ben, and the witches will cast their spells to play their little mind games. Even Miranda and Chad will never really remember everything which took place. The hospital will blame it on shock, and no one will question it."

I stare at her in disbelief. Leaning on my car, I can't help but ask, "Has it always been this way?"

"Goodness, no!" GiGi laughs. "Normally there are more bodies to bury. Like he said, darling girl, welcome to the shit show. I tried so hard to keep you from all of this, Harper."

"I just want to go home," I tell her, defeated and lost in a current of questions I don't want answers to.

"I wish you could, but you have a basement of dead dogs to deal with."

"When did they turn back to wolves?" I ask, refusing to use her term.

GiGi sighs, feeling the weight of the day as much as I am. "Right before the phone rang. It's why I grabbed the gun."

"But why?"

"The gun or the change?" GiGi asks, starting the engine of her car over my question.

"Both."

"The gun because you're stupid to only trust magic to save your ass and the change because I'm willing to bet their Alphas had a little family feud and called in their bonds for backup."

"So, it's not over?"

"So, it's not over," GiGi agrees, shutting her car door and backing her car out of the gravel side lot.

The part of me covered in frustration wants to scream into the night. The part of me covered in exhaustion wants to sit here in my parked car and cry while the ghost judges me from the back seat. But the part of me which makes me Harper Buckland takes a deep breath, puts the car into reverse, and heads to Great Hexpectations to whatever is waiting for me there.

I can do nothing for the Tortes. I can do nothing for Ben and Becky. Maybe, just maybe, there is something left I can do for Roman and his family waiting to be put to rest. I'm lying to myself. I know this, but isn't that what we have all been doing for days now?

GiGi, with her idea of forty-five really meaning eighty on our town streets, has beaten me to the shop. There are only a few lights on, casting an almost empty feeling to the building. I don't have to be a witch to know something is wrong. My magic doesn't need to whisper to me what my body already knows – GiGi wasn't the first to arrive.

"Any advice?" I ask my ghostly partner.

Myrtle purses her lips, staring into the shop as I am. "Wouldn't," she says before fading to wherever she randomly goes.

"Thanks," I mutter to the empty back seat.

I'm not as worried about GiGi as I was the Tortes. The old woman has more tricks than treats and should someone bring the fight to the shop, her home-base filled with more charms than have names, it's them I worry about. Not just physically, but mentally, as well.

My body screams with each step I climb to the shop's little porch. I'm covered in dirt and things I don't want to think about. My patience is as thin as my mood and my tolerance for the wolf's family battles is nonexistent.

I had left the cemetery amid the abundant red lights with hopes to still being able to salvage some part of today. With the chime of the bell above my head signaling another round ahead, I will be satisfied just to live to see it end. Let someone else be the hero. I've failed enough at it for one day.

Roman stands with his back to me when the comforting scents of the sage candles and the familiar shop smells wrap their arms around me. He's pretending to read the many titles of books stacked deep on the wooden case painted black, like all the wooden accents of the shop. From his posture, and years of working retail, I know he's just trying to find something to do until he's ready to talk. If there was a pop-up porn in there hidden among the many titles, he still wouldn't see it because he's not seeing any of them. He only sees his problems and I have a feeling I'm about to hear about all of them, if I want to or not.

"Hello, Roman," I call out with false surprise. "How shocking to see you here uninvited. Twice."

GiGi keeps her face neutral behind the counter. She's flipping the pages of the black ledger she uses to keep the sums and totals of the day's sales as if it's just another closing. Minus the blood dried to my clothes, the dead werewolves below us, and, oh yes, the dead Alpha I helped kill added to today's list of accomplishments, I suppose it is just another day, indeed.

"I've come to collect what's mine now that we both know Deon is handled."

Roman is only slightly rude with his hidden accusation. I lift one eyebrow before pulling my hair into a mess of a ponytail with the ever-abundant ties I keep hostage. Not sure if I'm preparing for another fight or just tired of its weight, but either way it seems like a good idea while I say nothing to confirm or deny his claim.

"Don't play coy, Harper," he insists with a little less hostility. "If you're here, she isn't. There was no other option for her. She left the mansion either already dead or already the victor."

"What did she want the magic for?" I ask, letting my choice of tense confirm what he's already said.

"Mortella, the vampire queen, is pushing against our territory. Deon was convinced the magic could be used to keep her and her clan away. If they thought we had the power to control the dead, they may not rise against us."

"There's a vampire queen named Mortella? A little cliché." I scoff, suppressing the many other comments spinning around in my mind.

"It's the name she took." Roman shrugs, either too polite to join in my mockery or too scared to be caught in the mockery. "Vampires have strange customs."

"The magic doesn't control the dead, though," I explain, wondering why I am even bothering. "It reanimates the husks, getting all cozy in something left to rot to manipulate the living into doing very bad things. Vampires are already, basically in some way I don't even want to debate tonight, alive. There is nothing the magic can do to them."

Roman softly laughs. "I never said she was the smartest of the family. She was convinced and I knew I couldn't stop her."

"She killed the little boy," GiGi throws into the conversation as if it's just an offhanded trivia fact. "You could have stopped that."

Roman closes his eyes, lowering his head with the news. "I heard. A few of them made it back to the mansion. I also heard what happened to those who didn't."

Our posture must have changed from false relaxed to alert. Roman lifts his hands, signaling for a miscommunication or surrender. Maybe both.

"They were given the chance to stay or go. They knew the risks. We voted no harm would come to either party for revenge or punishment," he tells us, easing down the tension in the room. "It's still never easy to lose family."

"You should put that on a card. I'm sure the Tortes would love to read about the vote and the acceptance of the deaths tonight," Jedrek says from the dark shadows from the back of the shop.

I watch as he pulls away from them, as if they were a part of him, forming his body in the space he now stands. He's fully healed and the trickster I met in the bar with his bright blue eyes and dark hair gleaming under the low lights. Dressed in the same dark shades as the shadows he stepped from, he flops down in the chair he's called his own a few times now with a taunting smile and wink when I feel my own lips smirking in greeting.

"You don't belong here, demon," Roman says, not even turning to acknowledge the new person in the room.

"Why do so many use that term like I should be insulted? I don't greet you with terms like fleabag, stray puppy, or inbred pedigree." Jedrek shrugs with false confusion, emoting more than necessary to achieve his goal of button pushing.

"Spare me the testosterone," GiGi bemoans. "Tell us what they want and let's just settle this."

"What who wants?" I ask blindly, leaping right back into a fire which was always smoldering right under my feet, waiting to fully be brought to life.

Jedrek sighs, a genuine sigh, before skipping my question to answer GiGi's. "What they all want – her."

The silence in the room is heavy with each of us swimming in our own murky pond of thoughts. Naturally, it's me who speaks first, ruining the understood, yet fragile, peace of the room.

"What the fuck does that mean?" I bluntly ask, no sugar coating or sprinkles.

"It means, my littlest witch," Jedrek begins with a face etched in mirth over my outburst, "you are going to have to make a choice."

"And I have a feeling I'm not going to like any of your choices." Crossing my arms, I wait with unease to hear how this little side trip will go.

Roman clears his throat, announcing his entrance into the verbal foray. "They aren't his choices. They are yours and yours alone."

"Oh good, so everyone knows about these choices, but me. Again." I turn to GiGi who has enough sense to look away, suddenly finding something under the glass display case remarkably interesting. "What are these super fun choices?" I ask whoever is brave enough to answer.

Jedrek takes the bait, which doesn't shock me.

Marie F. Crow

"You have to pick a house to align with or you declare yourself your own house and deal with all that," he says with a matter-of-fact tone. "You're a potentially walking time bomb of power, untrained power and, might I add, mood swings."

"If you aligned with a house, you'd have that house's protection," Roman offers softly.

"And that house's enslavement. You would look cute in a dog collar. Rhinestones and black leather, maybe?" Jedrek asks from where he is still lounging in his large chair.

It takes a great deal for Roman to swallow down the comment lodged in his throat, but he says nothing, not letting Jedrek provoke him.

"Every house will come with rules," GiGi offers, still staring at some unseen thing. "Just depends on what you can live with."

"Or we make our own?" I ask her, watching her slowly look in my direction. "He said one option is to declare my own. If I have the power to control the demons, angels, and the vampires, why should I align with them? The wolves we have beaten twice. The coven seems happy to just be background players. They just want to be left alone. How many other houses can there be?"

GiGi scoffs, half laughing and half choking. "A few more, but mostly low key."

Jedrek is watching our debate with a frozen smile. I've come to learn it's his nervous look. He becomes still, unmoving and waiting. It would be almost unnerving if I hadn't already seen his many other sides.

Roman stands unmoved by my facts or uncaring. I have a feeling, he too, just wants to live in peace. It was his sister who constantly found reasons to anger too many. With her, and those who thought like her, gone, I don't predict a lot of trouble from his pack in the future.

"Most won't accept your choice. They will come after you," Jedrek warns.

"Because if they beat me, they own me?" I ask, already knowing the answer.

"Pretty much," he agrees.

"Good thing I have you and Roman then." I smile, watching the two men for the first time glance towards the other. "I'll just have to let the two of you council me and my little mood swings while the coven trains me." I shrug playing up the false pout and very helpless female.

"You're not aligning, but you're declaring?" Jedrek laughs, putting together the plot and all its holes. "You won't concede, you little minx, but you'll listen, giving them what they think they want but really giving them the middle finger. How incredibly feisty."

"Seems like a reasonable truce," Roman says with a smile. "And it strengthens our territory from the other houses."

I don't mean for my face to dismiss Roman's offer for a truce. It just does. I blame it on the lack of caffeine and the many hours already spent dealing with his little family.

"How do we declare for our own?" I ask GiGi, the only one here I completely trust.

"Tell them all to fuck off," GiGi answers with her normal flare. "But he's right. There will be push back and I'm not positive you will be able to trust everyone to back you when that arrives."

I'm sure GiGi also didn't mean for her face to dismiss Roman from the line of support. I blame it on her Italian and the lack of care to coddle people.

I open the basement door with my will, letting it swing wide and open for Roman. It's a neat trick, simple as it is to perform. Sometimes, the simplest trick has the most profound effect.

"Hey guys," I say, "how about you all fuck off?"

Pulling a phone from his back pocket, Roman calls in the muscle he kept waiting in the unmarked box trucks nearby to help retrieve their family members' bodies. I knew they were there, as I'm sure GiGi did too since the revolver with its silver bullets sits hidden under the edge of the black notebook.

Jedrek stands with a stretch, playing off his dismissal as something of his own idea. "I'll be seeing you, littlest witch," he tells me with a soft smile. "If you need to burn off any rage again..." he lets the taunt hang in the air, ducking the book I throw at him with a laugh.

A part of me feels sad as the same shadows he appeared from take him from view. It's a new feeling to me. Something I don't really like or want to dwell on what it could mean. Turning to GiGi, and seeing the glint in her eyes, I know she missed nothing. She pushes me playfully with a smile that annoys me.

"Demon and a witch? Not the most original storyline, but there's worse out there, I'm sure," she tells me with a jest.

I roll my eyes, knowing until I make another epic blundering, this moment will be the running joke of all of our future conversations. Fortunately, epic blunders are my thing.

The men are loading the tall, metal shelving units with shrouded bodies of their family. As they zip the last covering around the racks, hiding what's inside, each nod in my direction before lifting the whole thing in pairs to be brought out the front doors. A sound of appreciation for their brute strength, and their cleverness, escapes from my mouth. Sadly, it just shows the many times such a thing has happened for them to be so prepared.

"Can't have the whole town gossiping, now can we?" Roman asks, watching the last of the units being carried away. He knows fully well the town already does and the Ripples have used that to their advantage, keeping their real secrets hidden away.

'Look," he tries again with his lack luster of a joke falling flatly around him, "I would really like to have you over sometime. No pretense or threats. Just you and me, talking, figuring things out."

"Things?" I ask before GiGi can.

"Our future," he shrugs, finally looking less collected than he has ever before, stumbling verbally before me. "Well not 'ours' but, well..." he stops, giving up on any attempts to save himself.

"Our future for the truce," I add, throwing him a life vest, and here I thought I didn't have any hero left in me.

"Yeah," he agrees pointing towards the open door where his family is waiting. "Guess I'll head out and let you two ladies call it a night."

"Good night," we both call after him, one with snark and one with relief.

"Can we go home?" I ask, leaning my head on GiGi's shoulder. "I'm really over peopling today."

"You don't want to disinfect the basement first?" she asks, and I can't tell if she's teasing or serious.

Sighing, I risk it. "Isn't there a spell or charm or something for that?"

"Yeah, and a mouse with a blue wizard's hat."

"A girl could hope."

"No. A girl can grab a mop."

We spent hours down there, her and I, cleaning and laughing, completely forgetting everything which transpired in the hours before. It was our little world again, small and tight with just our horrible jokes and secrets being shared between the two of us. As it was and as it may never be again. She had tried so hard to keep this pace, this small-town life, of just us two oddballs and our little shop, of failed blind dates and guilt trips for grandkids. She had tried so hard with little lies here and there spread thin, and sometimes thick, to keep my curiosity at bay.

I know there will come a time when I will yearn for that life I gave up. If today was any hint at what may come in the days ahead, I will crave these small moments. I will desire nothing more than to be Harper Buckland, neighborhood witch, town oddity, and granddaughter to one of the most amazing women I have ever met - but that, too, is a lie. Just a little lie.

35

I go to the beach to be alone. I let the soft waves whisper their foam-covered secrets and their comforting words to my mind. The warm sand, even in this early fall weather, coaxes my aches away as it pushes between my toes. I go there to settle my soul, but since meeting him, nothing about my soul is calm. Not even the waves could settle my skipping heart today with my mind continually pulling his name forward. Jedrek, it says in the dark of night before I fall asleep. Jedrek, it calls, and I'm undone every time.

Today is no different. With sand covering my car from my afternoon escape, I give up trying to force it. I drive to the one place which always turns my own problems off and fills me with the problems of the world – the cemetery. There I can drown in the stories of the dead, the stories of those forgotten by their own loved ones and grateful to speak with me, even if it's the same story again and again.

Strolling along the marked and unmarked rectangles of future and current residents, my mind does that annoying thing where it wanders back to the last time I saw Jedrek in the weeks which have passed. I hate it. I hate that I've become this woman. I used to make fun of these types, throwing popcorn at the television before fast-forwarding to something more gore-filled and less gagging. Now, here I am, waiting on the t-shirt and bumper stickers proudly displaying my membership.

I'm deeply lost in my self-loathing. I don't hear Bella when she calls my name. I feel her. Another annoying new thing since this all ended. When I absorbed the magic claiming her life, her life became mine. I can hear her thoughts, feel her emotions, sense when she is near. It was originally used to manipulate, using their own dreams and worst fears against them. Now, it's just annoying. There is nothing quite like trying to take an afternoon nap while she mentally gushes over some high school football player seated ahead of her in class.

"What are you doing out here?" she asks me and I'm happy the mind reading only goes one way.

"Walking," I offer with a shrug. "You?"

Bella motions to her feet where she has placed fresh flowers on the markers of her brother and sister.

"Right," I tell her as an awkward apology.

"You never asked why I did it."

I don't have to ask. I know already, but obviously she is aching to tell someone. I tilt my head, waiting for her to explain what all of us in some time in our life has felt. Most just bury it deep under heavy bottles of amber liquid. Some jot it down in pretty notebooks they buy to hide the sins within. There are some, like Bella, who have to talk about it to truly overcome the nightmares and remorse. I prefer the amber liquid and pretty notebooks.

"It was my fault. I mean," she pauses, listening to the demons in her mind, "Dad says it wasn't, but it was. I should have been paying attention."

I watch, and feel, the emotions rolling over her as she once again relives that day.

"I was supposed to drop Ben off at school on my way in since Becky was staying home sick. They hated being apart. Mom practically had to hold Becky back when Ben and I left. I got him in the car. Got myself in the car. I wasn't even thinking. I texted my friends to let them know I might be late while waiting for the garage door to fully open and then I just backed out. I never saw her, I just heard Mom screaming, but it was too late."

Bella pauses, waiting for the scene to finish playing in her mind.

"Becky ran out the front door when she heard us leaving. She ran right behind the car, holding her little arms out to stop us. I used to watch the home security video over and over after it happened since no one would talk about it. It filmed it all from where it sits. I saw everything."

"You thought if you could bring her back, it would make everything okay again," I tell her, saving her some of the pain of telling me herself.

"It made sense."

"Did it?" I ask with the same honesty which limits my number of friends.

"Deon was here after the funeral. She told me she knew a witch who could bring Becky back, but there would be a cost. Becky would only be alive as long as I am alive, and when I die, Becky would too, but since I'm young, it wouldn't happen for a very long time."

"She didn't mention all the fun side notes?"

Bella shakes her head. "It was fine at first. I would pick Ben up from school and bring him here to see her. They played and were happy."

"So, you brought her home not realizing what that would really mean."

Bella nods, filling in the missing pieces of it all. "She started to hurt Ben and Ben started having nightmares, saying Becky was back and hurting him. Mom, because she became super protective, never let Ben out of her sight thinking he wasn't getting over her loss."

"And the voices?"

"They started about the same time. Once Ben wasn't keeping Becky amused anymore, she started being in my head all day and night, telling me things to do if I wanted my family to live. It's when I found you with that awful man."

"He's not so bad," I tell her, having had to work closer with Cass than I had ever wanted to since having met him. "Just don't let him hug you in the summer."

"Ew?" she asks before starting back into her story. "It was weird. Right after you left, like the next day, the witch and Deon show back up. They were fighting about something while the witch did some kind of spell. Deon wanted everything removed so they couldn't be found out and the witch was super annoyed that Deon was telling her what to do. Becky must have known something was up too because her demands kept getting worse until I finally just agreed to show her to the family. I didn't know what else to do."

"You know it was never Becky, right?"

The magic has been listening to the retelling of its latest glory. I can feel it churning, proud of itself and slightly disappointed it didn't get to kill another family. Luckily, the blood it spilt that night has kept it sated, sleeping and happy to wait for our next little adventure. For now, anyway.

"What else would I call her? It?"

"GiGi and I prefer hocus pocus shit."

Bella blushes hearing the word but smiles mischievously. "Hocus pocus shit?" she repeats, nodding and satisfied with her new answer.

"You know I lost my job at the restaurant," she tells me as we make our way back to our cars.

"How?" I ask, wondering why I keep doing that.

"When the voices were really bad, I may have stabbed a customer complaining about the knife not being clean enough."

"Stabbed, stabbed?" I stop, actually wanting to hear this.

"Just his hand," she shrugs as if her confession is no big deal. "It was weird because Roman, you know the totally hot Ripple brother, paid the guy to back off and the guy just backed off. Even sent a card. Totally strange, right?"

"Right," I agree, nodding my head to hide my smirk. "I think GiGi may be in need of some afternoon and weekend help at the shop."

I have no idea why I said that. The last thing I want is this teen hanging around Great Hexpectations like a Sabrina knock-off. This new me is getting to be very inconvenient.

"Really?" she asks, almost jumping in place and one second from clapping. "I mean my parents won't be exactly thrilled but I will totally be the envy of my friends. They still think all this hocus pocus shit is fake."

I want to say not really, just kidding, and a thousand other ways to let her down, but instead I ask her something which has left me confused. "What do your parents think happened that night? And why do you still remember it all?"

Bella shrugs again and I really want to yell at her to stop it. "We don't really talk about it. I know that man told the cops we were visiting Becky and something attacked Ben. No one even asked about the woman's body. My parents just went along with it. The scary woman just winked at me when I didn't understand. She said something about the link will prevent them from blurring my memory, but it would be in my best interest to not argue. I understood what she meant, so I didn't."

"Seems smart."

"Are they here now?" Bella asks, gently like a child waiting to have their hopes destroyed.

Turning to glance in the direction she is watching, I see Becky and Ben standing where the flowers were left. They are wearing matching outfits, as most likely they always did in life. Their blonde hair shines under the afternoon sun. Becky, I'm sure the more outspoken of the two, lifts her finger to make the hushing motion over her lips before they both run to play amid the many statues, stones, and tombs.

With the sound of their laughter floating behind me, I turn back to Bella and shake my head. "No. I'm sure they are at peace somewhere and happy to be together again," I tell her, as we always tell those who have lost someone, as if we ever really know.

Bella nods, still staring at their graves. "Most would be mad at me, but you weren't. Why?"

It's my turn to sigh, and turning to stare in a different direction of the cemetery, a section I no longer visit, I tell her, "Because I kept my parents animated for two weeks before the cops showed up to investigate the smell and why I wasn't in school. I wasn't ready to be alone, and being a child, I didn't really understand what I had done. That feeling, the knowing I could in theory have them back, always gnaws at me and it's something I've had to battle my whole life. I'm not mad. I understand."

"Ever lose the battle?" she whispers.

"Yup," I tell her, turning to leave her and the memories clawing their way from dark tunnels from which they are stored.

"Meet you at the shop tomorrow," she yells from her side of the car and I can feel her excitement.

"Sure," I shout back, glad she can't feel my annoyance. "Can't wait," I tell her.

It's a lie.

A little lie.

Extras

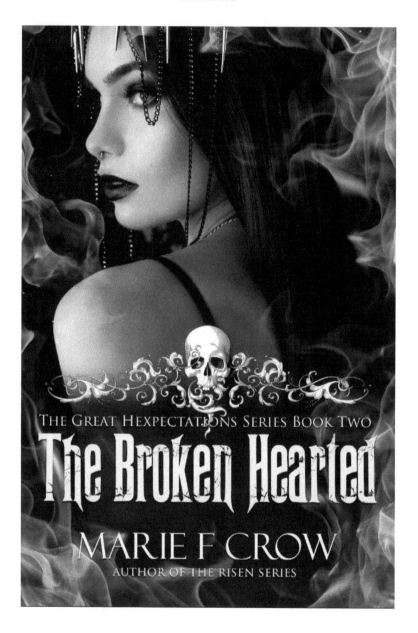

The annoying shop bell chimes again, foretelling the day is never going to end. GiGi had a genius idea to have a store-wide sale to run in time with the whole 'new year, new you' theme. I hate her. At first, I thought I was just angry with her, but after hours of listening to housewives ask how to make their husbands interested in them again, or their children to do better in school, I've come to terms with the fact that I may actually hate her. When she informed me, she was sitting the day out, I confirmed the suspicion. I absolutely hate her.

"You're telling me if I burn this candle, put this here oil on it first, roll it around in these herbs, the jerk's dick won't work anymore?" asks the latest angry wife before me.

"Is that what you really want?"

"Well, I mean, if he's just going to use it to have sex with every student he teaches at the college, might as well not work," she whispers to me with more volume than I think she wanted to use.

"Then technically, yes. Or you could just think about divorce and letting him suffer when each relationship fails and you've moved on," I offer.

"Do you have a candle for that?"

"Yeah," I turn to find my only hope and salvation for the day. "Bella, could you show this lady to the cursing candles?"

Bella, bouncy and perky as ever, waves to the lady and motions for her to follow her safely away from me. "They are right over here."

257

Twisting my neck to stretch out all the things I can't say, I pull the heavy weight of my red curls into a looped-through bun before securing the whole mess on top of my head. I at least had the sense to wear something sensible – jeans and a plain grey t-shirt, knowing how hot the store can get with my temper and the many potential bodies shoved inside it. The black ballerina slippers allow me to easily kick them off when feeling the need. It's not the worst outfit I've put together, but my 'eat me' shirt may have been a better choice.

"Miss?"

I open my eyes to see a glaring migraine standing before me. It's not the leopard print pantsuit or the big hair which is causing the pain. I just know she's going to be a migraine. It's glaringly obvious.

"Yes?" I ask, trying to force some cheer into my flat voice.

"This says made in china."

She's pointing to a white sticker on the bottom of a metal box like it's a whore in church. To Miss Judgey, maybe it is.

"Mmhmm," I answer, waiting to see where this takes us both.

"Well don't you say this place is authentic? Ran by authentic witches?"

"Mmhmm," I answer again, slower, now knowing where we are heading.

"How can you tell people this place is authentic if everything is made in China? Don't you have any shame?" she asks loudly, almost shouting her question through the store.

"How can you tell people your tits are natural with that shape at your age? Don't you have any shame?" I counter, also very loudly and wearing my best smile.

Bella appears as if by her own type of magic, pulling me away from behind the counter to be my replacement. "Sorry. She's just a little testy without coffee. What was your question?"

Bella is making wide eyes at me to go away before turning to calm the now livid, cat wearing woman. Rolling my own, I surrender, happy to escape to the little coffee and tea section GiGi has added. The woman stopped by long enough to drop off cookies and refill the supply of caffeine before slipping away again. She did stash a few Cokes in a cooler beside it for me, but I still hate her.

I half listen to Bella explain the need to sometimes outsource merchandise, but all of the charms and such are locally made as the tiny bubbles of salvation slide down my throat. She uses the perfect explanation any adult would have been able to come up with, but I never said I was a very good adult. I have also never boasted about my patience for stupid.

"Was that really necessary?" Bella asks me with a huge smile while refilling someone's plastic cup.

I shrug, a habit I've picked up on since being so close to Bella almost every day. "Wasn't really a thought-out thing."

"You've been doing that a lot as of late. You and Roman not doing well?"

I cut my eyes at her with a very loud, unspoken warning.

"I'll take that as a no," she answers before rushing away.

Roman and I are supposed to be the new power couple, as head of two houses, making decisions and securing the safety of our territory, as he calls it. He's nice enough, and he tries hard, but that's most of the problem. A relationship shouldn't be this much work. It should just evolve and sort itself out as needed. For Roman and I, our differences and our ghosts are making for sorry bed fellows. And the sex sucks, too.

He's just as polite in bed as he is in life. At first, it was charming, almost romantic. When I suggested something other than missionary, it quickly unraveled. One would think a man who changes into a wolf, and chases prey through a forest a couple nights a week, would enjoy something a little more fun. I think he almost fainted, and not in the good way, when I showed up in nothing but leather and boots. We haven't talked about it and I haven't pushed the topic, either.

"Do you know where the books on -" the woman in front of me pauses, looking around to those nearest to us before whispering, "-sex magic are?"

I laugh before I can cover it quickly with a cough. I hadn't meant to, promise, but the woman in front of me most likely has never bought a battery-operated toy and now she's asking about sex magic books?

"The red bookcase. Second shelf," I point, excusing myself before Bella has to rush and fix another problem.

Janice didn't miss the blunder. She's shaking her head with her black pigtails swaying in judgment.

"Whatever," I whisper, before returning her glare.

Someone who has decided their forever outfit is something from the clearance racks of Hot Topic shouldn't have the nerve to condemn other people. Before I can further share my thoughts about her, with her, she fades away the way they all do leaving the woman who is standing where she was looking at me with confusion over my hate filled glance.

"Sorry," I offer her, motioning to the windows behind her. "Sun made me squint."

She nods, appearing to buy my excuse before returning to her shopping.

"I didn't even know there were this many people in the town," I whisper to Bella as I help wrap and bag the pile of purchased items on the counter.

"Oh, there aren't," she tells me with pride. "I asked Gees if I could run an ad, pushing the sale through social media, and she thought it was a great idea."

"Did she?" I ask, feeling my best smile returning to my face.

"Yup! She said it would be a great chance to see you and I in action together." Bella continues to talk as I feel my anger growing. "I think we are doing great. Well, minus your cranky moments and all, but overall, we are killing it."

"Interesting choice of words," I mutter thinking she wouldn't hear me, and I was wrong.

"What?" she asks, having heard me but not sure what I meant.

And since she asked, I clarify. "Interesting choice of words since I pretty much –"

"– couldn't agree more!" Jedrek's voice cuts me off, stopping not only my latest blunder from happening but also stopping my heart and breath.

In fact, as I stare at the man leaning near the woman shopping the sex magic self, I think the whole world has stopped.

"Oh," he says, leaning over to take the book from the woman's hand before replacing it with another selection. "Try this one. Trust me."

He winks at her before walking away and I'm just waiting to hear the sound of her neck snapping with how far she has turned her head to follow his departure.

"Hello, Bella." Jedrek smiles at the blonde teen flashing her his white teeth and blue eyes. "Seems you've made yourself right at home."

"I do what I can," Bella tells him, either not hearing the sarcasm or skipping over it. When she blushes, I know she didn't hear it. "It's way more fun than serving bread sticks all day."

"Way, right?" Jedrek smiles wider, mocking her teen enthusiasm.

Bella nods enthusiastically, once again missing the sarcasm.

We both watch him walk away to cruise the aisles as if taking note or inventory of his shopping lists.

"Why are you here?" I ask him, trying to not sound optimistic or insulted with his sudden arrival.

"Rude," he returns.

"Can I talk to you upstairs?" I ask him, motioning to the reading loft GiGi had built to hold meetings, and as a way to justify buying more books 'for the customers' she had said.

"Fancy," he says, lifting his eyebrows mockingly.

We don't engage in any more verbal banter as we climb the circular, metal staircase. Not because there isn't plenty to say, but because I don't trust myself to say the things I want to say around so

Marie F. Crow

many people. As it is, they will strain, fighting to hear every syllable traded between he and I.

"It's okay, guys. I'll just hold it down, down here," Bella shouts.

"You're killing it, kid!" Jedrek leans over the railing to tell her, showing her an air high-five for her troubles.

The sound of her laugher floating to where I am standing, waiting for him to stop showboating, does nothing for my temper.

Jedrek shrugs, looking confused as to my mood.

I return the gesture with more hostility. "Why are you here?"

"Maybe I missed my littlest witch?"

I say nothing, waiting for the real reason.

"Maybe because dead people are being found with their chests torn out and a rumor of zombie infestation a few towns over?"

I sigh, "And they want me to fix it?"

"Well, fix is a big word. Investigate fits better."

"Fine. I'll call Roman and have him meet me after we close."

"Yeah, about that, I get to ride shot-gun on this one."

"Why?" I ask, hating the way my heart skips and my stomach starts to flutter. "You've been happy to let Roman and I handle everything since you disappeared."

"Rude, again," he says with a mock pout. "I've been busy. As high on the chain of importance as you are, you're not the top."

"Whatever," I tell him waving away his excuse and an aching feeling in my chest. "Why the change?"

"Because, my littlest witch, werewolves and vampires don't mix."

"You just said zombies."

The smile he now wears is the smile of trouble. It's the smile right before panties are removed, drinks are poured, and bad decisions, in general, are made.

"Who do you think makes zombies?"

Acknowledgements

Special thanks to Beth Lemley for her wise words, advice and spiritual guidance which helped give me courage for this new adventure.

Visit her website:

www.RavensRitualRemedies.com

Facebook:

Raven's Ritual Remedies

About the Author

Marie F Crow weaves her stories around the human element of the horror verses the 'monsters' themselves. She believes that the real horror of life does not come from the expected, but from the unexpected responses of the human nature and what depths of trauma a person must survive in certain situations. She began writing The Risen Series when feeling that the popular genre was slipping too deep into the realm of pure 'slasher' and forgetting what the horror of zombies can mean for a story.

Now, with her children's series launched, Marie hopes to use her favorite 'monster' as a teaching tool to inspire children to understand that not everything that looks scary, is scary. With Abigail and Her Pet Zombie series, Marie hopes to further spread her love for all things "that go bump in the night" with small children showing them that it's okay to be different and to embrace those same differences in those around them.

Marie F. Crow

Social Media Links
Facebook: @MarieFCrow.Author
Instagram: @authormariefcrow
Twitter: @MarieFCrow

Additional Titles by Marie F Crow

The Risen Series
Dawning
Margaret
Remnants
Courage
Defiance

A Risen Series Novel
Genny (Preorder Now)
Lost Doves (Coming Soon)

The Siren Series
Crown of Betrayal
Crown of Remorse (Preorder Now)
Crown of Conquest (Preorder Now)

The Great Hexpectation Series
The Little Lies (Preorder Now)
The Broken Hearted (Coming Soon)
The Whispered Words (Coming Soon)

The Abigail and her Pet Zombie Series
Illustrated Children's Books
Abigail and her Pet Zombie
Zoo Day
Spring
Summer
Halloween
Birthday (Coming Soon)

The Abigail and her Pet Zombie Series

Beginner Chapter Books
Abigail and her Pet Zombie

About the Publisher

Kingston Publishing offers an affordable way for you to turn your dream into a reality. We offer every service you will ever need to take an idea and publish a story. We are here to help authors make it in the industry. We want to provide a positive experience that will keep you coming back to us.

Whether you want a traditional publisher who offers all the amenities a publishing company should or an author who prefers to self-publish, but needs additional help - we are here for you.

Now Accepting Manuscripts!
Please send query letter and manuscript to:
submissions@kingstonpublishing.com
Visit our website at www.kingstonpublishing.com

CPSIA information can be obtained
at www.ICGtesting.com
Printed in the USA
BVHW050204140223
658480BV00013B/37/J

9 781645 332916